"Moving, unapologetically strange, skillfully constructed...
Read this book, whatever your age. You may find it's the
exact shape and size of the hole in your heart."

—*The New York Times*

"You'll find *Still Life*'s exploration of an artist's
inner strength particularly enriching."

—*Teen Vogue*

★ "Lack of original ideas is not something found in work by
A.S. King, who blurs reality, truth, violence, emotion,
creativity, and art in a show of respect for YA readers."

—*The Horn Book*, starred review

★ "Readers won't have to live with abuse
firsthand to recognize the taut, invisible coils of
family dysfunction and the difficulty of gaining
perspective on it, let alone breaking free."

—*BCCB*, starred review

★ "King's ingeniously crafted, deeply engaging *Still Life with
Tornado* will have readers by the collar the whole time."

—*Shelf Awareness*, starred review

"King understands and writes teen anxieties like
no other, resulting in difficult, resonant,
compelling characters and stories."

—*Kirkus Reviews*

"A.S. King is known for crafting deeply sympathetic portraits of
teenagers in crisis, and *Still Life with Tornado* is no exception."

—*BookPage*

WHEN EVERYTHING CHANGED

Ten-year-old Sarah turns to me and says, "Do you remember the big fight in Mexico?"

"Maybe."

"Remember what Bruce told me? In the restaurant?"

"Not really."

"He really hasn't come back yet?" she asks.

We're having this conversation while staring at a suit of armor. I realize that my life feels like this. *Armor for Use in the Tilt.*

Life is a joust. Recently, I've been unhorsed. And yet I don't feel a thing.

"Doesn't call. Doesn't send letters." I hold back on telling her I have his phone number.

"It was my fault," she says.

"I doubt that. I don't think it was my fault."

"You probably blocked it out. It was bad."

"What are you? Some sort of amateur psychologist?"

"I'm ten. I'm not stupid," she says.

Here's what I think. I think we're really smart when we're young. Ten-year-old Sarah is smarter than I am because I'm six years older. Twenty-three-year-old Sarah is dumber than me because I'm sixteen. Someone somewhere was way older and richer and dumber than all of us and paid forty-five million dollars for a bunch of dots. I think this kind of smart isn't something they can measure with tests. I think it's like being psychic or being holy. If I could be anyone for the rest of my life, I would be a little kid.

OTHER BOOKS YOU MAY ENJOY

STILL LIFE *with*
TORNADO

A.S. KING

speak

SPEAK
An imprint of Penguin Random House LLC
375 Hudson Street
New York, New York 10014

First published in the United States of America by Dutton Books,
an imprint of Penguin Random House LLC, 2016
Published by Speak, an imprint of Penguin Random House LLC, 2017

THE LIBRARY OF CONGRESS HAS CATALOGED THE DUTTON BOOKS EDITION AS FOLLOWS:
Names: King, A. S. (Amy Sarig), 1970–, author.
Title: Still life with tornado / by A.S. King.
Description: New York, NY : Dutton Books,
an imprint of Penguin Random House LLC, [2016]
Identifiers: LCCN 2015049462 | ISBN 9781101994887 (hardback)
Subjects: | CYAC: Family secrets—Fiction. | Family violence—Fiction. | BISAC: JUVENILE
FICTION / Family / Marriage & Divorce. | JUVENILE FICTION / Art & Architecture. |
JUVENILE FICTION / Social Issues / Physical & Emotional Abuse (see also Social Issues
/ Sexual Abuse). Classification: LCC PZ7.K5693 St 2016 | DDC [Fic]—dc23 LC record
available at https://lccn.loc.gov/2015049462

Speak ISBN 9781101994900

Printed in the United States of America

10 9 8 7 6 5 4 3 2 1

Design by Kristin Logsdon
Text set in Joanna MT Standard

For Julia

The farther you enter the truth, the deeper it is.—Bankei Yōtaku

Everything you can imagine is real.—Pablo Picasso

The Tornado

Nothing ever really happens.

Or, more accurately, nothing new ever really happens.

My art teacher, Miss Smith, once said that there is no such thing as an original idea. We all think we're having original ideas, but we aren't. "You're stuck on repeat. I'm stuck on repeat. We're all stuck on repeat." That's what she said. Then she flipped her hair back over her shoulder like what she said didn't mean anything and told us to spend the rest of class sorting through all the old broken shit she gets people to donate so we can make art. She held up half of a vinyl record. "Every single thing we think is original is like this. Just pieces of something else."

Two weeks ago Carmen said she had an original idea, and then she drew a tornado, but tornadoes aren't original. Tornadoes are so old that the sky made them before we were even here. Carmen said that the sketch was not of a tornado, but everything it contained. All I saw was flying, churning dust. She said there was a car in there. She said a family pet was in there. A wagon wheel. Broken pieces of a house. A quart of milk. Photo albums. A box of stale corn flakes.

All I could see was the funnel and that's all anyone else could see and Carmen said that we weren't looking hard enough. She said art wasn't supposed to be literal. But that doesn't erase the fact that the drawing was of a tornado and that's it.

Our next assignment was to sketch a still life. Miss Smith put out three bowls of fruit and told us we could arrange the fruit in any way we wanted. I picked one pear and I stared at it and stared at my drawing pad and I didn't sketch anything.

I acted calm, like I was just daydreaming, but I was paralyzed. Carmen looked at me and I shrugged like I didn't care. I couldn't move my hand. I felt numb. I felt like crying. I felt both of those things. Not always in art class, either.

When I handed in a blank paper at the end of class, I said, "I've lost the will to participate."

Miss Smith thought I meant art class. But I meant that I'd lost the will to participate in anything. I wanted to be the paper. I wanted to be whiter than white. Blanker than blank.

The next day Miss Smith said that I should do blind drawings of my hand. Blind drawings are when you draw something without looking at the paper. I drew twelve of them. But then I wondered how many people have done blind drawings of their hands and I figured it must be the most unoriginal thing in the world.

She said, "But it's your hand. No one else can draw that."

I told her that nothing ever really happens.

"Nothing ever really happens," I said.

She said, "That's probably true." She didn't even look up from the papers she was shuffling. Her bared shoulders were already tan and it wasn't even halfway through April. I stood there staring at her shoulders, thinking about how nothing ever really happens. Lots of stuff has happened to Miss Smith. I knew that.

My hands shook because I couldn't draw the pear. She looked up and I know she saw me shaking. She could have said anything to me then. Something nice. Something encouraging. Instead, she repeated herself.

She said, "That's probably true."

So I stopped going to school.

It's true about the letters they'll send when you stop going to school. After a week or so they come after you and make you meet with the principal. But that's happened before, just like tornadoes, so it didn't impress me. My parents escorted me into the school building and they apologized a hundred times for my behavior but I didn't apologize even once.

I couldn't think of one reaction to the meeting with the principal that was original. Apologizing, crying, yelling, spitting, punching, silence—none of those things are original. I tried to levitate. I tried to spontaneously combust like a defective firework.

Now *that* would be original.

I'm at the bus shelter two blocks from school and it's raining and I'm pressed back as far as I can be into the shelter and I'm not doing or thinking anything original. I am on my way to City Hall to change my name. Still not original, but at least I won't be Sarah anymore.

Dad was perky this morning. He said, "I wish you'd do something constructive with these days. You could paint or sculpt or something. At least you'd be productive." He didn't hear the spaces between those words. He didn't hear the rests between the notes. "But I know you're going to school today because we have a deal, right?"

Deals. That's what life with Dad is—a series of deals. He thought I was going to school on the bus and I did go on the bus, but I didn't get to school. I got off one stop early to catch another bus, like I've done for the last eight school days. I could be shooting heroin or dabbing or smoking meth. I could be flirting with boys after school like normal girls do. I could be pregnant. Of course, none of those things are original, but they would be *constructive* and *productive*, which is what Dad seems to want. Right now, I'm going to City Hall.

I still don't know what name I'll choose. I have twenty minutes until I have to decide. I catch my distorted reflection in the windows of the passing cars, and I think about how people elope to City Hall and get married without telling anyone. I'm doing that, but I'm doing it by myself. I will elope with the new me. I will come out with a new name but I'll still have the same face and everyone will call me Sarah but I'll really be whoever I decide to be. I will confuse the Social Security Administration. My number will now match the wrong name. I will not tell my parents what my new name is. I won't even tell myself.

A woman walks up and sits down next to me in the bus shelter. She says hello and I say hello and that's not original at all. When I look at her, I see that she is me. I am sitting next to myself. Except she looks older than me, and she has this look on her face like she just got a puppy—part in-love and part tired-from-paper-training. More in-love, though. She says, "You were right about the blind hand drawings. Who hasn't done that, right?"

I don't usually have hallucinations.

I say, "Are you a hallucination?"

She says no.

I say, "Are you—me?"

"Yes. I'm you," she says. "In seven years."

"I'm twenty-three?" I ask.

"I'm twenty-three. You're just sixteen."

"Why do you look so happy?"

"I stopped caring about things being original."

When the bus comes she gets on it with me, and to prove she's really real she stops and slots a token into the machine. There are two Sarahs on this bus. We are going to City Hall.

"We're eloping," she says.

I'm conflicted. Is this what eloping with the new me looks like? Riding to City Hall on a bus with myself? How will I ever fool the

5

Social Security Administration if there's a witness? Even if the witness is me? I try to concentrate on names I like. Wild names. Names that surprise people. I can't come up with any names. I just keep looking at twenty-three-year-old Sarah and my brain is stuck on one name. *Sarah. Sarah. Sarah.* I can't get away from myself.

I'm stuck on a bus with Sarah who is twenty-three. She has a snazzy haircut and highlights. My hair is still long and stringy like it always has been. It doesn't stop people from staring at us like we're identical twins. She's comedy and I'm tragedy. Even that thought isn't original.

She says, "You're not really going to change your name, are you?"

I say, "You tell me."

She smiles again and I want to tell her stop smiling so much. We have an ordinary smile and it annoys me.

She says, "I'm still Sarah."

"I'm still going to City Hall," I say.

"Fine with me."

"I don't want you to come with me."

She smirks. "You can't even change your name yet. You're only sixteen."

"I'm practicing," I say.

She rolls her eyes. "I guess."

When the bus nears the next stop, I repeat myself. "I don't want you to come with me."

"Suit yourself," she says.

She gets off at the next stop, and as the bus pulls away, I watch her walk up 12th Street and see she still has our favorite umbrella.

Maybe I'm snapping. Maybe I've already snapped and I'm coming back to real life. Maybe this is some sort of existential crisis. I couldn't tell you right now whether my life has meaning or value. I don't even know if I'm really living. Either way, I'm going to City Hall. Either way, I'm changing my name.

As the bus goes east, we pass through the University of the Arts campus. This is where I say I want to go to college. Except I'm skipping school, so I probably won't get to go to college. Or maybe I will. I'm not sure. Going to college doesn't seem original. Not going to college doesn't seem original unless I plan to do something original instead of just not going to college.

I thought being an artist would be the right thing to do. Since I was little, everybody told me I was good at it. Every year on my birthday, Dad gave me something a real artist should have—a wooden artist's model, a set of oil paints, a palette, an easel, a pottery wheel. When I was nine, he woke me up every summer morning saying, "Time to make the art!" And I made art. Sometimes I made great art and I knew it because people's expressions change when they look at great art. When I was ten, after we went to Mexico, he stopped waking me up that way, but I still made the art. Right up until Miss Smith and the pear. It wasn't the pear's fault. It was building for months because sixteen is when people stop saying great things about a kid's drawings and start asking questions like "Where do you want to go to college?"

I just don't think college is where artists go. I think they go to Spain or Macedonia or something.

By the time I get to City Hall, I figure the idea to change my name isn't original anymore. The idea is now two hours old. I don't even go to the sixth floor to get the paperwork so I can practice how I'll do it when I turn eighteen.

I decide my name is Umbrella, but I won't tell anyone else. Not even the Social Security Administration. Changing one's name without actually changing one's name has been done before, but I doubt anyone else on Earth ever opted to call themselves Umbrella.

I take the next bus that comes around. The rain has stopped, which makes my new name ironic. I am useless now in every possible way. I am a sixteen-year-old truant. I am Umbrella on a day with no rain. I am as blank as a piece of white paper in a world with no pencils. While this may sound dramatic and silly, it's comforting to me so I don't care how it sounds. The whole world thinks sixteen-year-old girls are dramatic and silly anyway. But really we're not. Not even when we change our names to Umbrella.

Everything I see from the bus window is the same. The streets, the sidewalks, the people are all the same. Homeless people sit on corners. Businesspeople walk with purpose. Tourists look at maps, trying to find the Liberty Bell or Betsy Ross's house. Half the people are looking at or talking into their phones. Other people are holding their devices as if they could ring any second—like soldiers in wartime—guns always at the ready. But nothing ever really happens.

It starts to drizzle again and I think back to Miss Smith's art class two weeks ago. I couldn't draw the pear. I couldn't draw my hand one more time. If someone asked me to draw anything right now, I wouldn't be able to do it. My hands do not work. Not in that way. Mom tells stories about patients in the ER who need amputations. Arm/hand/multiple-finger amputations. People who drive with their arms out car windows. Unlucky motorcyclists. Lawn mowers. Snowblowers. At least I still have hands. I have nothing to complain about.

I can't draw a pear, though. Or anything else.

My hands ran out of art.

I am simply Umbrella. I am the layer between the light rain and a human walking down Spruce Street talking into her phone, maybe finding out her cat just threw up on the new Berber carpet. I am the barrier between the bullshit that falls from the sky and the humans who do not want bullshit on their pantsuits. In eight days of riding around, that's what I've discovered. It's raining bullshit. Probably all the time.

Twenty-three-year-old Sarah gets on the bus again. She sits next to me and smiles, just like last time. But now, there's something condescending in her smile. Unsympathetic. It says I am silly and dramatic. We don't say a thing to each other and when we get off at the stop near home, the rain has started again and she opens her umbrella and walks north. I walk south and let the rain hit me until I'm soaked.

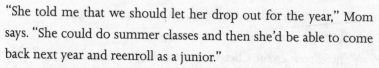

"She told me that we should let her drop out for the year," Mom says. "She could do summer classes and then she'd be able to come back next year and reenroll as a junior."

"No," Dad says. "She's sixteen. She's talented. What about her future?"

"That doesn't seem to matter to her," Mom says.

"You said you'd back me up on this. We made a parental deal. She can't drop out of high school."

"It's that or expulsion. Expulsion would stay on her record."

"I should have called. You're a shitty communicator," Dad says.

I sit soaked and cross-legged on the hall carpet at the top of the stairs and I zone out. This is the most unoriginal conversation I ever heard. Two parents discuss their truant daughter and within five sentences, one of them is blaming the other for something that isn't even relevant.

And yet, this conversation is a novelty. They are rarely awake or at home at the same time. Today, Dad was only home before seven to meet with some guy about inspecting the roof for damage. There was hail last week, and Dad is in insurance. He's a fanatic about maintaining façade and building-envelope integrity. He knows all about *code* and how our kitchen bathroom does not meet *code* because it's too small. I do not meet code because I'm not going to school. Mom doesn't meet code either because they made *a parental deal* and she's not keeping up her side of the bargain.

As I listen to them bicker about who should have called the principal and who's busy keeping a roof over my head, I notice they call each other by their real names. They never do this in front of me. In front of me they call themselves Mom and Dad, and frankly, it's annoying. But when they argue, they call each other Helen and Chet.

Example: "Why do I have to do all the important stuff, Chet?"

"That's the problem with you, Helen. You never give me credit for all I do around here."

"Shove your credit, Chet. I save lives every night and I never expect shit for it, but you take out the garbage and you need a gold star."

We eat dinner together. It's a quiet dinner and I shove food into my face as if I'm starving, because I am starving. I didn't eat lunch today. I don't think I even ate breakfast.

Dad says, "I heard you didn't keep our deal."

Mom turns to me and says, "The school called."

Dad says, "Just *one day*, Sarah. For me?"

Mom mumbles something under her breath and I don't hear it. Dad does. He gives her a look I know all too well. It's like someone scraped his face off and replaced it with a guy who hates us all. Her, me, even himself.

I imagine I will go to school tomorrow.

Last week, on the third day of bus riding, I decided to transfer every time I saw the same bus shelter advertisement twice. It seemed like an original game. Eventually, I ended up in a neighborhood I'd never been in, in front of a boarded-up high school. It was an old building with graffiti-covered columns at the front entrance and the name of some dead educator carved in stone over the doors. I decided this would be my new school.

A guy in skinny jeans, curated high-tops, and chunky, hip glasses was standing on the sidewalk across the street staring into a camera on a tripod. He kept pulling his face away from the eyepiece and looking around. I could tell he was nervous. It wasn't the nicest part of town. I decided he had to be an art student. They infest this town like hipster cockroaches. Every one of them thinks they're original.

This guy looked like he was into ruin porn—breaking into abandoned buildings, climbing bare girders, and taking pictures of collapsed ceilings and piles of rubble. This was a thing now. Ruin porn. But this guy hadn't even broken into the building; he was just taking pictures of the outside. First, from the tripod and then he walked around and tilted his camera in different directions and did close-ups of the usual things: graffiti, rust, broken windows. I knew if I looked hard enough I could find his page on The Social and look through his online portfolio. Maybe he went to the University of the Arts. Maybe he could sell me heroin. I didn't look him up, though. Totally unoriginal. Plus, I don't actually want to do heroin. I want to go to Spain or Macedonia. And I have more guts than to just see a thing from the outside.

When I wake up to my alarm, I smooth out my clothing and I don't even change my underwear. I hear Mom getting in from her night's work and I hear her collapse into her bed and turn on the sound machine that she needs to sleep all day. White noise. It sounds like someone left the TV on static.

I get my favorite umbrella and put it in my backpack even though there is no rain predicted for the day. Dad is in the kitchen making me breakfast, but I walk straight out the door and up to the vendor who makes the best egg, cheese, and ham breakfast sandwiches, and when he asks "Salt, pepper, oregano?" I say yes to all three even though I don't like oregano. Then I sit on the curb and slowly eat every bite.

I'm late to my new school, because I don't exactly remember the buses I took to get here before. There are no ruin porn photographers this time.

The minute I step into the building, I pretend this is my old school on any normal day. I open my umbrella. Superstition abounds. Students act as if I've brought a curse upon the building, but that's only because they don't know that there is already a curse upon the building. The curse is: Nobody focuses on the now.

In first-period English, the teacher asks me to close my umbrella and I comply. She says, "It's nice to see you again, Sarah." I smile. It feels like I have a disease.

By lunch, I'm ready to leave and take the bus to anywhere, but I decide to stay. I sit in the cafeteria at a table of the other sophomore art club geeks. Carmen is here and she's talking about tornadoes. Henry is sketching his milk carton à la Warhol. Vivian eats Tastykake Butterscotch Krimpets one after the other and washes them down with bottomless black coffee. None of them know that my name is now Umbrella. The senior and junior art club geeks sit at a different table now.

Three weeks ago, our art club suffered a fissure.

The art club seniors would say the fissure was my fault, but it wasn't.

I should have bought two sandwiches for breakfast. I'm hungry, but the ceiling seems to have collapsed on the empty vending machines.

I skip gym class the next period and stand in the locker room shower stall. I imagine curtains where there should be curtains, but there are no curtains because my new school isn't a school anymore. There is graffiti on the inside of the shower stall. *The absence of violence is not love.* I think about it for a minute but I don't understand.

I close my eyes and listen.

"I hear [popular girl] is getting a nose job."

"She should."

"And I hear she's thinking of getting a boob job while she's at it."

"What I wouldn't give for rich parents."

"I think I'm going to fail my English test."

"I can help you study."

"I'm so bad at tests."

"Did you hear that Jen broke up with [popular boy]?"

"It means you can go after him now, you know."

"Shit, we're late."

"Can I borrow a pair of socks?"

"Here."

"Thanks."

Here is proof that nothing ever really happens. The proof is everywhere. I just have to stand in one place and listen.

"Brrrrring!" I yell into a room full of empty toilet stalls. *"Brrring!"* My voice echoes down the row of spray-painted half-size lockers with random pried-off doors. In one of the torn-apart lockers is a diorama—a prison cell made of sturdy twigs with a papier-mâché sphere inside of it. The sphere is painted red. The twigs are painted silver. On the floor of the diorama are the words WE WERE HERE in black Sharpie marker.

Next period is art. I imagine the art club sophomores walking toward the art room and I join them but nobody says hello or anything.

Halfway down the hall, someone hands Vivian a note. It's from her wannabe boyfriend. She reads it to us: "I was disappointed to find your name in the boys' locker room bathroom stall. It was on a list titled GIRLS WHO DO ANAL. I always thought you were better than that."

I say, "How original."

Carmen says, "Henry, go scratch that out."

Henry says, "I don't go to the locker room. They all call me a fag."

Vivian asks, "How do you change for gym?"

Henry says, "I skip gym."

Carmen says, "I'll go with you. We'll get a lav pass and do it next period."

Vivian says, "It's probably not even there. This guy is such an asshole."

"So why do you want to go out with him?" I ask.

She doesn't answer. I decide she would say: "I'm attracted to assholes, I guess."

I don't expect to get nervous walking into the art room. I know I can do whatever I want. I can leave when I want. I can say what I want. But when I kick over the pyramid of Pabst Blue Ribbon tallboys (not original) arranged in front of the art room door, I'm nervous. The seniors trickle in and take their places at the back table and pull out their new projects. I haven't been in school for nearly two weeks, so I have no project. I just want to get my stuff and get out. This is very easy to do when everyone in the room is ignoring me because none of us is here. Or I'm here, but they aren't. Or they're there, and I'm not. I have so much to learn at my new school. I sit on a three-legged desk and close my eyes again.

Miss Smith, who should be taking attendance, is at the back of the room with the seniors and the rat shit chattering about art college and what her four years at Tyler were like. All I hear is "And the parties!" Miss Smith is an asshole. I wish one of Carmen's tornadoes would suck her up. It would make things convenient for me, considering what I know about Miss Smith.

Vivian and Henry get their projects and supplies and go to work, and the seniors make an effort to say hello to them. One of them tells Vivian that she likes her T-shirt. Another one walks over to Henry and gives him a random hug.

Carmen is friends with everyone. It's just her nature. She says, "What up?" and the seniors all wave. I'm standing right here. For the first time in weeks. Not one person says "Nice to see you back!" or "Hey, look! It's Sarah!" or anything like that. Everyone gets to work sifting through the broken glass by the windows, looking for the perfect piece. The glass never seems to cut their skin even though they're picking it up by the fistful. I turn and leave the room.

Not even Carmen says good-bye.

I stop a few feet from the door and stand in the hallway and listen.

First, silence.

Miss Smith says, "Well that was awkward, wasn't it?"

Answers follow:

"I don't know why she even came back."

"She's so weird!"

"Drama!"

"Can't make it as an artist if you don't have thick skin."

Laughter.

That's when I start walking. I go to my locker to empty what's left inside. *Thick skin? I have thick skin. They have no idea.*

Someone is sleeping in front of the locker I decide is mine. I see his pink rain boots first. His head is resting on a balled-up coat and his face is covered by a filthy cap. He has one arm slung through a backpack strap. The other arm cuddles a can of spray paint.

I decide he's welcome to whatever's in the locker.

Anyway, it's not about thick skin. It's about one of them being a liar. Or all of them being liars—even Miss Smith.

It's a long story.

When I get out of the building, I open my umbrella and walk home rather than taking the bus. It's not raining. No one seems to care that my umbrella is open. Philadelphia is full of all kinds of crazy people. Maybe I'm one of them now. Yesterday I had a conversation with myself in seven years. This might make me crazy. Yesterday I changed my name to Umbrella.

When I get home, there's a message blinking on the house phone's answering machine and I listen to it. It's the daily Sarah-isn't-in-school-today message. I delete it and walk up the steps toward my room. I don't have any homework because homework isn't original and I'm not going back to real school tomorrow. Or ever.

At the top of the stairs there is a decorative mirror on the wall and a trio of pictures of my parents and me. I am not an only child. My brother is nine years older and lives out west and he doesn't contact us anymore. He wrote me a private message on The Social about a month ago with just his phone number. Then I deleted my profile because what's the point of having a profile if nobody wants to talk to you?

The last I heard about Bruce was that his church people are his family now. Mom and Dad never baptized us, so Bruce got himself baptized. Apparently he got naked in a river or a lake or something. Dad said that that's why he doesn't contact us. Dad said Bruce thinks he's better than we are because he found God.

This was a while ago, so I don't really know if any of it is true.

This was Dad, so I don't know if he's the right person to believe when it comes to Bruce.

I think that's why Bruce sent me his phone number. Maybe he wants to set the record straight. Maybe he wants to convert me. Maybe he has cancer and will die soon. Maybe he got married and had a baby. If I don't call him, then nothing will happen.

Mom gets home from the grocery store and after unloading bags in the kitchen, she walks up the stairs and sees me standing here and asks me if I'm okay.

"I'm fine."

"You went to school?"

"Yes."

"Was it good?"

"Nothing ever really happens," I say.

"Okay," she answers and then walks toward the bathroom.

When she comes out of the bathroom, I'm still standing here and listening to the world. It's pretty quiet. Traffic outside is picking up, but no one is honking their horn and no car alarms are going off. The neighbors on both sides of us work until five and their kids won't be screaming up the block until six or so.

Mom comes out of the bathroom.

"Are you on drugs?" I imagine she asks.

I get asked this question a lot. For the record, no. I am not on drugs.

I say, "I'm thinking about taking a trip somewhere."

"School, Sarah."

"Maybe just a weekend thing."

"I don't think so."

"Maybe I could go out and see Bruce."

She looks concerned. We don't talk about Bruce. I don't see what's so scary about him.

***

When Dad gets home, I'm still standing at the top of the steps in the dark.

Since I don't say anything to him, he's the first one to speak. "Holy shit, Jesus Christ, what the fuck are you doing up here in the fucking dark? Christ! You scared the shit out of me!" That's what he says.

I'm at the bus stop again. This isn't the same bus stop as the other day. Philadelphia has a lot of bus stops.

I was thinking last night about our trip to Mexico when I was ten. It's the last time I saw Bruce. I don't remember some things from that trip. I remember the fish. I remember the food. I remember the flight home—me and Dad in two seats up front so Dad had extra legroom, Bruce and Mom in two seats a few rows back even though Bruce needed leg room, too. Maybe the answer to why Bruce left us is still there in the airplane. Maybe if I find ten-year-old Sarah the way twenty-three-year-old Sarah found me, I can ask her.

She's on the bus, sitting in the long backseat, so I sit next to her when I get on.

I say to her, "Did you know that there's no such thing as an original idea?"

She says, "Okay."

I say, "I want to have original ideas."

She says, "We have original ideas all the time. Whoever told you that is full of shit."

I used to have quite a swearing habit. I tell her that one day she won't swear as much. She laughs like I'm not real. Which is ridiculous because she's the one who can't be real. I am the dominant Sarah. I am sixteen.

I say, "Do you remember the trip to Mexico?"

She holds out her arms and shows me her tan and the speckled evidence of peeling skin on her shoulders. "It was a month ago."

"Do you remember how you drew things in the sand and the water washed them away?" I ask.

"Yes."

"That's what original ideas look like."

She stares at me for a while and frowns. I think she's going to say something about Mexico or the sand washing away the things she drew. Instead she says, "Why don't you wash your hair?"

I say, "Don't be mean."

"I just don't want us to have shitty hair," she says.

I say, "Do you remember Bruce?" It's a stupid question, so I rephrase it. "I don't mean do you remember him, but I mean do you remember if he was nice or not? Did he ever feel like a brother?"

"He's a great brother. He takes me out for ice cream at Ben & Jerry's when Dad works late," she answers. Ben & Jerry's closed years ago. "Hold on," she says. "Did he die or something?"

"He didn't die," I say.

She looks sad. "Did he come back yet?"

"No," I say. "It's been six years."

"Do you remember that thing he said to me in Mexico?"

I don't remember what Bruce said in Mexico. I suddenly feel stupid. Like maybe I'm going crazy beyond sitting next to myself on a bus. Ten-year-old Sarah has freckles and her face is browned. She seems happy enough to be riding the bus with me even though the bus smells like farts. I don't want to ruin her day. I don't even know if her day is real. I don't even know if my day is real. I say, "Can you tell me what Bruce said so I know I remember it right?"

"He said 'You can always come stay with me, no matter where I am' and he was crying," she says.

"I remember him crying," I say. "But I don't know why he was crying."

"I do," ten-year-old Sarah says.

People on the bus think ten-year-old Sarah and I are sisters. They smile as if I'm taking her somewhere educational or something. They are happy with us. They don't think we're skipping school. They don't visit other ideas. They just think about themselves, mostly.

I get off the bus at the art museum and she follows me.

All inclusive. These aren't words that a ten-year-old understands. What a ten-year-old understands is: This was not the New Jersey seashore. The water was a different color—any color, but in this case, it was turquoise. There were colorful fish in the water, not pink plastic tampon applicators or cigarette butts. Mom and Dad let me eat all the tortilla chips I wanted, even for breakfast. I lived on perfectly uniform triangles of corn for the whole week. Mom and Dad drank fruity drinks all day and were generally in a good mood.

For Mom, it was easy to be in a good mood while all-inclusive in Mexico. She was a night nurse. Twelve-hour shifts in the emergency room from seven to seven. The only thing that bothered her was the sun because she considered herself a bona fide vampire. She had great stories from her vampire shift. Things *happen* in the emergency room in the middle of the night.

Her stories used to be funny. Now nothing she brought home was original—not even a patient with a jar of Concord grape jelly shoved up her rectum. Done before. You just wouldn't believe what some people put in their rectums. You wouldn't believe what people swallow either. Car parts. Electronics. Nails. Cement. You name it and someone has swallowed it or put it somewhere that landed them in the ER.

Dad was only in a good mood because of the piña coladas. He didn't even read on the beach. He just sat there on one of the white lounge chairs—one of a hundred in a perfectly straight line parallel to the sea. Every chair had a towel. A blue towel. Every four chairs had a thatched umbrella hut, some had a round table nailed to the tree stump that held up the umbrella part; some didn't. Almost all of the resort-goers stayed on their beach loungers. Very few went into the water. So Dad wasn't an anomaly or anything. He was just a player in the sterile, geometric beach scene he called *Our Family Mexico Getaway.*

Bruce was a mix of emotions. It depended on the day. Mom and Dad ignored him mostly. They gave him his own room key. If Bruce wanted to stay in the room, Mom and Dad let him. If he wanted to take a walk on the beach late at night, they said, "Be safe." Bruce was nineteen. He could take care of himself.

I swam a lot, covered in millimeters of waterproof sunscreen. Mom and Dad stayed under a thatched umbrella and gave the bar waiter bigger tips every time he came back, which kept him coming. I was only allowed in the water up to my chest and that was fine because I could lean back and float there. I floated a lot.

I remember floating, closing my eyes against the baking Mexican sun and talking to the sea god. I was ten. I didn't have a name for the sea god. It was just the sea god. I remember asking the sea god to help me draw better pictures. I remember promising the sea god that if he let me draw better pictures, then I would really do something in the world. I'd be famous. Like Picasso or Rembrandt. I didn't know about women artists back then because in school you only learn about the men. If I knew better, I might have hoped to be Georgia O'Keeffe or Aleksandra Ekster.

I didn't notice the fish until the second day. The first school surrounded me and if I stood as still as I could among the calm waves, they inched closer to me and brushed by my hands and I said, "Hello, fish," and I imagined they said, "Hello, Sarah," but fish don't talk so that's probably not what happened, but I wanted them to say hello, so I decided that's what they were saying. I was the only one in the water. They were my fish.

Over the week, I saw twenty more schools of fish. Sometimes it was the same family as the first—a white angelfish sort of breed. After that it was little blue fish, some fatter yellow fish. Over by the rock jetty, there were bigger gray fish. Each time I saw new fish I did the same thing. I said, "Hello, fish," and I decided they said, "Hello, Sarah." Mom and Dad got drunker, but it was okay because the empties never accumulated. They always seemed to be drinking from that same first, perfect glass.

We went to a buffet restaurant at the hotel for dinner a lot. A few times Mom and Dad went to another restaurant at the resort, but Bruce and I ate buffet every night in Mexico. When we did all eat together, Mom, Dad, and I ate Mexican food but Bruce got pasta and a Caesar salad. Every night, that's what Bruce ate.

I told them each night what I'd seen in the water and they seemed delighted that I was having a good time. Dad told me that when we got home, we'd look up the fish and find out what kind they were. On the second night Mom said that she was so proud of me for being independent and going out into the water by myself. "We waited years to go on a real vacation—until you were old enough to take care of yourself," she said.

This was a compliment and I took it as one, but the comment made Bruce click his teeth and shake his head. The week went downhill from there.

On the last night, Bruce said, after my telling them about saying hello to my fish friends and about them saying hello back, "They aren't your friends. All the people here see them."

Mom and Dad told Bruce to shut up. I said, "Yeah. Shut up, Bruce."

Bruce said, "Fish don't like humans, Sarah. Not even you."

"I think they like me," I said.

"You're delusional," he said.

"She's ten," my mother said. "Can't you just pretend to have a good time?"

"Why pretend? Aren't we doing enough pretending as it is?"

That was when Dad's piña colada good mood wore off. Last dinner in Mexico.

"Jesus Christ, son. We brought you here. We paid for the whole week. Why are you such a pain in the ass?"

Bruce got up from the table and went back to the room.

I had my last Mexican dessert—a three-cream cake that was so good it made me cry as I ate it. Dad couldn't drink enough to get his good mood back. Mom said that she'd had a great vacation and thanked Dad ten times for it. They held hands right there on top of the table.

That was the night Bruce said what he said.

He said, "You can always come stay with me, no matter where I am."

Ten-year-old Sarah has been here five times already. I remember her loving the suits of armor and the big Picasso—*Three Musicians*. Ten-year-old Sarah wanted to be an artist. Mom and Dad encouraged this. Now sixteen-year-old Sarah can't understand why they'd encourage something so impossible.

I ask her, "You want to go in?"

She rolls her eyes like I've asked a stupid question and walks up the famous *Rocky* steps without talking to me. From behind, I can see me in her. The skinny matchstick legs. The no-hips build that makes it impossible for me to buy jeans that fit. When she gets to the top of the steps she waits for me. She says, "One day we're going to be in this museum. One day, we're going to be famous."

I want to tell her to stop saying *we*. I want to tell her that presently *we* can't even draw a single pear or *our* own fucking hand.

We go to the front desk and even though I still wonder if I'm hallucinating, I know ten-year-old Sarah is really here because the lady behind the counter asks how old ten-year-old Sarah is, and when ten-year-old Sarah says "ten," the lady gives her a wristband for free. I have to pay fourteen bucks for being sixteen.

We don't say anything as we walk to the Picasso. We both know where it is by now. When we get there, we both stand and stare as we have done every time before. Dad says art is a way of standing still and finding the quiet inside yourself. That's what I do. Ten-year-old Sarah does it, too, like a trained dog, but I can see her little hands twitching to touch it. I see her look around for the security guard. I remember being her and thinking *just one touch* as if touching the same thing Picasso touched would give her the talent to become him. It was always some sort of scam—begging the sea god, touching the Picasso—a desire for genius the way the desire for money makes people buy lottery tickets.

Ten-year-old Sarah says, "Picasso had original ideas."

I say, "Maybe."

She says, "Not maybe. This is original. No one did it before him."

"I guess."

As we wander around the area, there are similar paintings. Braque, Gris, all of Picasso's contemporaries. I see the style in those, too. It was a movement. Picasso wasn't the only cubist. (Nobody was the only anything-ist.)

"I mean, somebody *had* to be the first cubist, right?" she asks.

"Somebody did. Yes. But maybe it wasn't Picasso."

She shrugs. "You're a fucking downer."

"I'm a realist."

She shrugs again and crosses her arms in front of her chest.

"Just think about it. How do we know that Picasso wasn't walking down the street one day and saw some guy drawing this on a piece of wood? How do we know that he invented this without other people's ideas? We don't. We don't know anything."

"I don't know about art history much," ten-year-old Sarah says.

"Nothing new ever really happens," I say.

"You really are a downer."

"Realist." I refuse to explain to her that you can't trust history books anyway because history books were usually written by people who wanted to sound like they knew something.

29

We wander away from the cubists. Ten-year-old Sarah doesn't stay with me or talk about any of the paintings. She keeps her arms crossed like she's fed up with me. She's a little like twenty-three-year-old Sarah. Aloof—like she's better. At the end of the long hall—the one that leads to the contemporary section—is a Lichtenstein. I've never seen this one in person before so it must be on loan or something. Frankly, I don't think reproductions of old comic strips are all that original, but this one has something to it. It's the look on the subject's face. Ten-year-old Sarah stops in front of it and squints at the dots. She backs up three big steps—animated little-kid steps—and squints again. I walk over to the right and read the description.

Roy Lichtenstein, American, Born 1923.
Sleeping Girl, 1964, oil and Magna on canvas.

Ten-year-old Sarah stands square to the canvas with her arms loosely at her sides. Unlike her crossed arms in the cubism room, she is letting Lichtenstein into her. She is *feeling* the sleeping girl. I stand next to her the same way. Legs slightly apart, arms by my sides, breathing, like some sort of art museum Tai Chi. I try to let the sleeping girl into me, too. I look at her furrowed brow while she sleeps and I feel pain inside of her sleep. I feel like something is unfinished in her life. I feel she is unhappy.

I look over after a quiet minute and see that ten-year-old Sarah is crying. This was Mom's art museum habit. Every time we went and did what Dad told us to do—stood still and found the quiet—Mom would find one painting that would make her cry quietly. It was a sacred act. Tears would fall slowly while she stared at a piece and then we'd move on and look at other paintings. Dad never cried, but I think he wanted to.

I look back at the sleeping girl. I see the beauty of all the dots and the simplicity of the colors and I want to cry but all I feel is numb. Ten-year-old Sarah takes a step forward so she is nearly nose to nose with Lichtenstein's girl and the security guard slowly makes her way toward us. I stop trying to cry and look up and smile. We both tell ten-year-old Sarah to step back from the painting. She steps back.

The security guard says, "Forty-five million dollars."

"For this?" ten-year-old Sarah asks.

"Yep."

"It's just dots," she answers. I don't say anything.

"Lichtenstein's dots," the security guard says. "Forty-five million dollars."

I think about that. Forty-five million dollars. That's like a lottery ticket.

Ten-year-old Sarah wipes her eyes dry with her fists and shakes her head. "Even I can paint a bunch of dots."

The security guard says, "You're not the first person who's said that, for sure."

I'm not sure what she means, but I like that she said it. It is just dots. And forty-five million dollars could have bought a lot of people food somewhere or bought women's shelters or orphan's homes. What's so great about buying a bunch of dots?

I want to visit the Twombly room, but ten-year-old Sarah says she hates the Twombly room. "It's all scribbling," she says. I try to disagree, but I know where she's headed, and I follow her. We go to the armor collection. The Philadelphia Museum of Art has the coolest armor. There is no need to think about originality in there. Armor isn't original. Even some animals have armor—they're born with it.

Ten-year-old-Sarah is happy now. No crossed arms, no tears, no trying to tell me how much of a downer I am. We're by the Saxon suit of armor called *Armor for Use in the Tilt* with the weird spike coming out the front of the breastplate. This is my favorite piece of armor since before I was ten-year-old Sarah. I didn't understand it at first. I looked it up on the Internet when we got home and learned what tilt meant. It's a term for jousting—the armor was used during jousts—games where two horsemen would race toward each other with lances and try to knock the other one off his horse. The spike on the breastplate is there to adjust the shield on the jouster's weak side. We stand and stare at the armor for a few minutes. I read the description as I have a hundred times before. *Geography: Made in Saxony, Germany, Europe. Date: c. 1575. Medium: Steel; leather (replaced); textiles.*

Ten-year-old Sarah turns to me and says, "Do you remember the big fight in Mexico?"

"Maybe."

"Remember what Bruce told me? In the restaurant?"

"Not really."

"He really hasn't come back yet?" she asks.

We're having this conversation while staring at a suit of armor. I realize that my life feels like this. *Armor for Use in the Tilt.*

Life is a joust. Recently, I've been unhorsed. And yet I don't feel a thing.

"Doesn't call. Doesn't send letters." I hold back on telling her I have his phone number.

"It was my fault," she says.

"I doubt that. I don't think it was my fault."

"You probably blocked it out. It was bad."

"What are you? Some sort of amateur psychologist?"

"I'm ten. I'm not stupid," she says.

Here's what I think. I think we're really smart when we're young. Ten-year-old Sarah is smarter than I am because I'm six years older. Twenty-three-year-old Sarah is dumber than me because I'm sixteen. Someone somewhere was way older and richer and dumber than all of us and paid forty-five million dollars for a bunch of dots. I think this kind of smart isn't something they can measure with tests. I think it's like being psychic or being holy. If I could be anyone for the rest of my life, I would be a little kid.

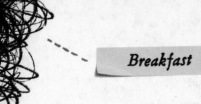

When I get home from the art museum, Mom is awake and eating breakfast. It's four o'clock in the afternoon.

"You're going to get expelled," she says.

"Okay," I say. Expulsion is a buzz when she says it. My heart races and I taste adrenaline. I used to feel that way when I drew something cool. Excited for the next stroke of the pencil and simultaneously terrified that the next stroke could ruin what I'd already done.

"Did something happen?" she asks. "At school?"

"Nothing ever really happens."

"You can't go to college if you don't have a diploma."

"Picasso didn't have a diploma."

"Good for him," she says. "You can't drop out of high school at sixteen."

She looks tired. She always looks tired. Being an ER vampire-shift nurse does this to a person. Some days she looks more than tired. That usually means something gruesome happened.

"Did you have a hard night?"

"Accident on the expressway," she says. "It was ugly."

"Did anyone die?"

"Yes."

"I'm sorry," I say.

"Don't ever drive like an asshole, Sarah. Ninety percent of accidents are because someone was being an asshole."

"I promise I won't drive like an asshole."

"Good."

We're Center City people. We don't even have a car.

Mom goes to pour another cup of coffee. I stand there trying to remember the ten-year-old me who watched her do this four or five nights a week. Always over the weekend. I try to figure out why she chose weekends when it was the only time I was home all day.

"Do you remember when I was ten?"

She stirs in three sugars. "I remember some things."

"Remember Mexico?"

She stops stirring her coffee and stares at the countertop and lets the question float above us for a second too long. "You got such a sunburn on the last day," she says.

"I forgot to put lotion on," I say.

She sits back down. "I always felt bad for that. I should have made sure you were covered up."

"It healed," I say, thinking of my thick skin.

"Still."

"That's when we lost Bruce," I say.

"We didn't lose Bruce."

"I mean, that's when he left. After that."

"Was it?" she asks. I want to call her out on playing stupid. How does a mother forget the last time she saw her own son? Maybe he's an amputated ghost limb that still itches—but it's not like a person forgets the day they lost the limb. "Why the sudden fascination with Bruce?"

"Dunno," I say. I'm good at playing stupid, too.

"He's fine," she says. She takes a slurp of her coffee and puts the cup down too loudly.

"He doesn't call."

"He doesn't need to call. He's a grown man."

"But he's still my brother," I say. "He doesn't even call on my birthday."

"We can't do anything about it," she says, and she does that thing with her eyelids where they flutter in condescension. Adults: quick to flutter their eyelids, slow to *do anything about it*.

"I want to call him."

"Good luck finding his number," she says.

"You seem mad," I say.

She sighs. "I don't want to wake up to another message from the school. I don't want you to be expelled. There's only three and a half weeks left."

She's talking about school. I'm talking about bigger things. Lost brothers that itch even though they've been gone for six years. "I'm sorry."

"Can't you just go back to school and make up the work?" she asks.

"I can't."

"You're sixteen," she says. "You were doing so well. Something happened and you won't tell me."

"Nothing happened."

This is when I realize how much I lie. Real artists don't lie this much.

HELEN'S NOT BULLSHITTING

The most common cause of amputation isn't trauma—IEDs in wars or car wrecks—despite what you'd think from movies or other bullshit. It's diabetes, *peripheral arterial disease*—the vascular shit—that lands feet in medical waste bags on the pathologist's desk with a little slip attached. We don't amputate in the ER, but I've seen enough ruined, ulcerated feet to know what'll happen when we send some poor old grandmother who can't afford her insulin upstairs for a surgical consultation. They usually arrive three weeks late from the nursing homes because the patient-to-nurse ratio at those places is appalling. Like 30:1 sometimes. I get them in double diapers, unwashed, bedsores that drill right into bone. When I was in my thirties I wrote into my will that I didn't ever want to go to a nursing home. I had two kids. One of them could take care of me somehow, I figured. Except now it was just Sarah.

We named Sarah after her father's grandmother. Chet's grandmother was a good woman and was always kind to me, which is more than I can say about his mother.

Gram Sarah was ninety-seven years old when she died. Had all her limbs and never had to go to a nursing home because she was sharp right up to the end—in her own old tiny brick trinity row house in Old City, with neighbors who'd look in on her. She outlived her two kids and her husband and pretty much everyone she ever knew. Except us.

When she died, I was there and Chet couldn't make it fast enough from work.

She said, "Where's Chet?"

"He's coming. He left work a few minutes ago."

"Boy was never on time for shit," she whispered.

"He still oversleeps," I said, and we both laughed slow, like old Southern women in movies laugh. I knew she was dying, though. I've seen people die a thousand times. She knew she was dying, too.

She coughed. "I thought you two were splitting up."

"Where'd you hear that?" I asked.

"Same place I heard you haven't slept in the same bed for a year," she said.

I said, "We work different shifts."

Her chest rattled. "Bullshitting a woman on her deathbed is not you, Helen."

I felt bad talking about this. The woman was dying.

"Let's not talk about sad things now."

We sat in quiet for a minute and she wasn't in any pain. I think that's fair. After ninety-seven years on the planet, I think it's fair to die with no pain. I held her hand because I knew she was at the end. Her breathing was mixed with the snoring sound of death. The rattle. Her eyes were closed and she still had a small grin on her mouth because Gram Sarah was destined to die with that grin.

She opened her eyes and whispered, "Don't die unhappy."

I leaned close to her ear and said, "I won't."

"You could die tomorrow."

"I know."

"Chet wasn't ever anything compared to you." She took in two short, difficult breaths. "Boy never had dedication to shit." And then she died.

She didn't know I was pregnant. I didn't want to tell her I was pregnant because it would make the whole conversation even more depressing.

Chet arrived ten minutes later and the nurses let us have extra time in the room so he could force some tears and seem sad. The charge nurse on duty that day was Julie and she's a dipshit and she came in and rubbed Chet's back and I rolled my eyes and excused myself to the bathroom.

Did I daydream that charge nurse Julie and Chet had crazy hot sex right there, on top of dead Gram Sarah? I did. Those days I wished he'd fall in love with anyone—one of his younger coworkers, random waitresses at bars, my neighbor, another man, I didn't care—and finally just get the hell out of my house.

But there was Sarah, on the way. And Bruce.

We agreed to stay together for the kids.

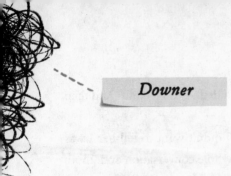

Downer

All I want to know is why Bruce said that. *You can always come stay with me, no matter where I am.*

Mom and Dad are normal-enough parents. They're not cruel or anything. They took us to Mexico. I remember something happened but I forget what it was. I know it was bad. I know Dad was yelling. I know Bruce was yelling. I know Mom was yelling. I know I was crying. I know that sliding doors to the balcony are not soundproof.

But I don't know why Bruce said that. I don't know why he had to go that far—to Oregon or to *You can always come stay with me, no matter where I am.*

It wasn't that long ago. I shouldn't have forgotten it. It's more complicated than that. I'm lying to myself but I don't know why. On the mantel there's a ceramic owl. I made it in the first grade and it's my favorite thing I ever made even though I've made far better things. Dad wouldn't stop praising me for the owl when I brought it home. It was when it all started—this talk about my talent and my prospects and my dad's fascination with taking us to the art museum a few times a year. He said he liked art, but really he'd just researched it the same way he researches depreciation and deterioration of building structures. He learned the language of art but could only draw stick figures.

I look at the owl and wonder what part of it is part of the lie. I ask it, "Hey, owl, are you lying, too?" The owl can't answer back, but if he did, I bet he'd say, "Hoo. Hoo." That's what owls say. It doesn't need an explanation. But what Bruce said needs explanation.

I say I'm going out and Mom says to be careful and I walk up to Rittenhouse Square, go visit the big frog statue, and then sit on a park bench, listening to the conversations walk by.

Not one thing anyone says is original.

I wish I could talk to twenty-three-year-old Sarah again. Ten-year-old Sarah doesn't understand my struggle. She hasn't come to this yet. She hasn't come to the place where my present means nothing but my future is all everyone talks about.

Twenty-three-year-old Sarah sits down next to me. She's wearing a pair of shoes that look uncomfortable. You could never get me to wear those shoes.

"How's things?" she asks.

"I don't know. Good I guess."

"How's school?"

"I'm still skipping."

"Bummer."

"Not really. It wasn't the place where I was going to make my masterpiece or anything."

"Not everyone can be famous," she says.

"That's not even the problem," I say.

She says, "You're just going through a phase."

"I'm not going through a phase," I say.

"Okay, *Umbrella*," she says, and smirks.

When she looks like she'll walk away, I ask, "Why are you so sarcastic?"

"Because you're a downer," she says.

This is the third time today I've heard this. I consider that maybe I really am a downer.

"I want to ask you a question," I say.

"You should call Bruce," she says, and then gets up and walks north in her stupid shoes and doesn't look back.

I sit for ten minutes. I think about how I'm a downer. I think about how I'm not a downer but something is happening here, even though I don't know what it is. I think about calling Bruce, but I don't even take my phone out of my pocket. Instead, I watch a homeless man draw on the sidewalk next to the fountain in Rittenhouse Square. I don't go over to see what he's drawing or even find a bench closer to him. I just watch him from over on the other side of the park.

I wonder if he's ever been to Mexico. I wonder if he's ever talked to his twenty-three-year-old self. I wonder if he has a brother who never calls anymore.

Twenty-three-year-old Sarah is sarcastic because she doesn't take me seriously. I'm a sixteen-year-old girl. *Silly and dramatic.* Pretty much nobody on Earth takes me seriously. And yet, on the inside I know there is something wrong enough that someone should be taking it seriously. Maybe it starts with me. Maybe I have to take it seriously first.

The homeless artist man sleeps in the doorway to a building that's boarded up about four blocks from my house. I've seen him around since before I was ten-year-old Sarah. He never asks for money. Most homeless people here sit on upturned milk crates and say "Spare a quarter?" or something like that. Some of them have signs. HOMELESS VETERAN, ANYTHING WILL HELP—GOD BLESS, I NEED FOOD, HELP A BROTHER OUT?

Some of them are high or drunk. Some are white and some are black, some are women and some are men, and some are foreign and have accents. This man—the one who sleeps in the alcove of the boarded-up building four blocks from our house—is white, has a scruffy beard, and is probably crazy.

This guy makes headpieces out of tinfoil. I find it ironic that he shows up here and now. I've been trying not to think about headpieces since the art club fiasco. Anyway, he's always wearing a different one. He's always doing something new. Right now, he's drawing on the walkway around the fountain and not even the bike cop who hangs out here some days is asking him to leave. He's scribbling and blending with his fingers in some sort of rhythm like there's music playing. Maybe there's music playing in his head. Every so often he screams out. *Hell yeah! Fuck no! What are you even trying to do, son? You ain't worth shit!* He doesn't say these things to anyone specific. They're like the lyrics to his music. The music in his head. Sometimes he stands up and puts his arms in the air like he just hit a home run.

Sometimes he jumps hard on a piece of sidewalk chalk and grinds it into the concrete. Jumps over and over again, bringing his knees all the way up to his chest. His art is a temper tantrum.

He's an acceptable neighborhood oddity. A walking mural. Graffiti that no one ever scrubbed clean. One of those cats you feed but never touch. He's always in a few layers of clothing, even when it's summertime. He wears bags over whatever shoes he has. It probably keeps the rain out.

He always has art supplies. Philadelphia is an art city. Students leave supplies for him as he sleeps. They are art supply fairies.

He makes art anywhere, anytime, all day. The plywood boards on the windows of the building where he sleeps in the alcove are never the same. Each day he paints over them, just a little. The sidewalk in front of where he sleeps is always colorful. If he can't find the right color for a piece, he digs through Dumpsters to find something that will give him the right color. Chicken bones, old pizza, the rubber from the sole of a shoe. Sometimes he burns wood and makes half-assed charcoal.

He never writes words. He rarely paints forms that people would recognize. Just abstracts. Sometimes when he draws on the sidewalk and blends the colors with his fingers, there is blood.

He is on a mission. A real mission.

I want a mission.

Not someone else's mission, either. I want my own mission. Something I think up myself. Something I actually want to do. Something that makes me jump up and down.

The Social is all I cared about for the last two years. High school lives on The Social. I got an account the minute I was in eighth grade so

I would be ready. Carmen and I posted our art projects and the pictures we took from when we'd walk around the city. For three weeks, we were each other's only connections on The Social. Then we connected with black-coffee Vivian, even though she posted passive-aggressive comments all the time. And Vivian knew Leslie, who is Vicky-the-grand-prizewinner's best friend, so we ended up connecting with her, too. And then Vicky connected with us. Slowly, the art club was born.

A few months ago, I saw a study in my Social timeline about how The Social makes people depressed. I asked myself, *Am I depressed?*

I am not depressed.

I'm fine.

The Social showed me I was fine every time I logged on. Everyone else groaning about their colds, their grades, their parents, their stomach flu: *I'm so tired! Insomnia, why do you curse me so!* Vivian and her subtext: *You know who you are, you plebeian assholes!* Vicky-the-grand-prizewinner: *No two snowflakes are alike. Nature is the only original idea.*

On The Social, there is no such thing as an original idea. Not even about original ideas.

On The Social, it's raining bullshit.

By the time I got to high school I got this rush of adrenaline every time I posted and then I'd erase the post before anyone could see it. Carmen asked me one time, "How come you always erase your posts, man?" I said, "I don't know." She said, "That thing you said the other day was really funny." Even back then, before I knew it rained bullshit, before the art club fissure, before the pear, I couldn't tell if I was funny or not. Even back then, I knew I was sitting too still to be an artist and I doubted the whole trick. That's what I saw. A trick. Every time I logged on I felt duped into having to be a snowflake.

The homeless man is different.

He jumps up and down. He is a snowflake.

And people must know it because he is never kicked out of Rittenhouse Square for drawing with sidewalk chalk. No one ever makes him move from his alcove while he sleeps. People care for him. He gets money because he doesn't ask for it. He gets art supplies because he never asks for them.

He has never logged on to The Social. You can tell just by looking at him.

He is everything I want to be.

He is Spain. He is Macedonia.

It's sunny this morning, so I don't want to take the bus and I don't want to go anywhere special, so I walk down Pine Street.

It's a weekend, so this doesn't count as another absence, but last time I checked I only need three more to be expelled. I didn't tell Mom and Dad I was going out, so they might be worried or they might never notice I'm gone. Mom will be sleeping off her night shift and Dad will be doing whatever he has to do at home on tiptoes. Not like it matters because living in a row house on a weekend is always noisier than weekdays. On one side, we have quiet neighbors who rarely come out of the house. On the other side, there are three families with nine hundred kids total. But Mom can sleep through anything.

The whole block between 16th and 15th is set up with a student art sale. I don't know what they teach in these art schools, but the prices are always too high. Carmen can draw better than these guys, even if she does draw a lot of tornadoes.

I take a left so I can escape the art sale and walk up 15th Street. That's where I see the homeless man in his tinfoil headpiece. He's got his back to the street and is drawing on the blank, windowless side of the corner grocery store. He's just started—a few lines and a few shapes from a chunk of burnt-wood charcoal. I cross to the other side of the street and find a stoop to sit on and I watch him.

From over here, he looks like a monster. Like Boo Radley or something. Children would run from him. Parents would point and say *Stay away from that man.* I can't imagine how many coats and blankets he has piled onto his back, but it looks like ten or more. Layered. It's almost seventy degrees out here and I can't figure why he doesn't take the coats off. I've seen him dressed the same way in mid-August.

He adds color to one shape and for a minute it looks like a pear. He uses a dark green and a pale yellow and uses his finger to blend them. He screams out, "What the FUCK is your problem? Don't fuck with me, man. Make it real!" He runs in place and looks at the sketch. Then he concentrates on the left side of the wall where he uses sharp, bold strokes to make some sort of horizon line. Miss Smith taught us about horizon lines. Horizon lines separate the background from the foreground. Even though there is no recognizable form in this drawing, I can see a foreground and background the minute he draws that line.

I look out to the street and the cars that go by and the people walking with their groceries or their kids and I see the world's horizon line separating foreground from background.

Ten-year-old Sarah is in the background. All my future Sarahs are behind me as I view the scene. They aren't in the picture yet.

I am the horizon line.

When I look back to the wall, he has started to scrawl some sort of blurry still life in the foreground. This is the second time in five minutes he's reminded me of the pear. I couldn't draw the pear. I don't know why I'm sitting here torturing myself over it by watching him. He's an artist. I'm Umbrella. We have nothing in common.

When people walk by him they aren't paying attention to what he is, what he's doing, or what he's making. They don't even look at him.

I was like that.

I must have walked by his building with the painted plywood windows a hundred times.

"His name is Earl," ten-year-old Sarah says.

"You don't know his name," I say.

She sits on the stoop next to me. "Yes I do. I asked him in the park last summer, remember? When he was painting the box?"

I try to remember when I was nine and asked the homeless man what his name was but I don't remember.

She says, "It was the day you bought water ice and tried watermelon because Dad always said watermelon was good but you hated it and he wouldn't let you buy another one."

"I remember that," I say. I still hate watermelon water ice. Dad said I was good at art, too, and now art hates me.

"Well, you walked through the park on the way home and that guy was painting an old box. You asked his name."

I shake my head. "Earl, huh?"

"Earl."

"Dad ate the rest of the watermelon ice," I say.

"Yeah. Remember the fight?"

"No."

"Did you start smoking weed or something? How can you not remember stuff anymore. You're, what? Sixteen?"

"I don't smoke weed." Smoking weed is unoriginal. And Carmen smokes enough for both of us.

"Well his name is Earl and Mom and Dad had a huge fight that night," she says.

"Over him eating my watermelon ice?"

"How do I know? They never stopped," she says.

A woman stands in front of us and we look up at her. She says, "Would you girls mind moving so I can get into my house please?"

This is not an hallucination.

49

HELEN'S CHARADES

Last night I had a hallucinating pregnant teenager come into the ER. She was convinced she was going to—in this order—have the baby, die, come back as a bird, and then shit on me. That's what she said. "When I come back as a bird, I'm going to shit all over your ugly face."

She wouldn't tell us what drugs she took. (They never do.) She wasn't even close to having the baby. Or dying. Or coming back to shit on my head. She was younger than Sarah. Just turned fourteen. She had a stuffed animal with her—a furry horse that used to be white but looked like it had taken a mud bath. When one of the techs tried to take it from her she fought him hard and then kneed him in the groin. We had to put her in restraints. That's never fun. Not with a drunk regular or a psych case or, in this case, a pregnant teenager. If she hadn't been pregnant or hallucinating, we could have done chemical restraints, but this time we had to go with old-style straps. Rules are rules. If you hit my staff, you go in restraints until you make a deal that you'll behave. If only those rules applied in the outside world.

Bruce told me once when he was in high school that if Chet and I didn't stop arguing that Sarah would be one of these damaged girls who gets pregnant at thirteen or gets addicted to heroin or something. I blew him off at the time, but he put it in my head and I couldn't stop thinking about my own parents and Chet's father and how fighting adults were normal for us both.

Not like Chet ever put a knife to my throat or abandoned me like his father did.

But we wrecked Bruce. I didn't want to wreck Sarah, too.

I called a truce. Chet shrugged. It's what he does best. Shrugging. Even when he's not shrugging, I see him shrugging. It's like a mirage for me now. He's got to have the most-toned trapezius of any man in Philadelphia. And I have the most-toned middle finger, which is saying a lot for Philly.

Every time he shrugs I just flip him off. A lifelong game of charades. Chet is always a person who doesn't know what to do and I am always a person who is flipping off people who don't know what to do.

I flip Chet off all the time and he doesn't know it. Under the table, through walls, in my pocket, behind the curtain next to the couch. I grew up in a house where cursing wasn't allowed and I wonder what my parents would think of me now, flipping Chet off all the time. I think they'd be fine with it.

My parents adopted me when they were quite old. Probably too old to be adopting a baby, but they loved me. They fought a lot as I got older because they'd just retired and were sick of seeing each other all the time. They weren't mean.

Sometimes I think of my father's stories about working on the big skyscrapers in Philadelphia—walking the iron girders fifty stories high and welding joists and climbing scaffolding—and I can't figure out how I married a man who works in a cubicle all day processing paperwork and making deals. On one hand, it's less dangerous and brings in more money. On the other hand, it causes a lifetime of shrugging.

Which has caused me a lifetime of flipping him off.

When we were still sleeping in the same bed back before Sarah was born, I used to sleep with one hand pointed at the back of his head, finger up. A truce is one thing. But I can't live a lie.

Except I *am* living a lie.

It's complicated.

Alleged Earl leaves the drawing on the grocery store wall unfinished. I get up and ten-year-old Sarah walks back up 15th Street. She says, "See you later!" She has her hair in braided pigtails. It was my favorite look. Maybe my mission should be to bring braided pigtails back into fashion. Maybe I can paint some pop art dots of braided pigtails and one day it will sell for forty-five million dollars. Not original, but at least it will be mine.

Alleged Earl puts his box of art supplies under his arm and it's devoured by his coats and blankets. He shuffles when he walks. He's not that old—maybe in his forties—so I wonder what's wrong with him that he walks this slowly. I think about the stories Mom brings home about ulcerated feet and stuff like that. It makes me want to help him carry something, but then he yells out, "I don't have to do what you tell me!" and I just walk a few yards behind him and stay in his shadow.

With Alleged Earl as my pace car, it might take me a half hour to round the corner and walk one block of Spruce Street. I wonder where he's headed next. I wonder if he's hungry, because I am.

It takes a whole minute to shuffle past the pizza place. It feels like an hour. My stomach growls. I want to ask him why he left the drawing unfinished. I imagine that I ask him and I decide his answer is *Because I wanted to. Because I can do what I want. Because who cares if I finish it? Because none of your business, girl, go back home to your parents.* Of course, I don't ask and he doesn't say any of these things. He just shuffles and occasionally stops to adjust his tinfoil headpiece or his box of art supplies.

When I see the people in the pizza place sitting at tables and eating, I picture Alleged Earl and me in there one day. Middle-class girl takes homeless man to pizza place = not at all original. I decide he'll say no if I ask him. I can see the viral video on The Social already. *She wanted to buy him a slice for lunch, but what he said will make you cry.*

I decide he must know I'm following him, but he doesn't seem bothered by it so I keep with him all the way to 17th Street where he starts to walk south. Past South Street, 17th isn't safe. Once I see that's where he's going, I split off at Lombard Street and walk toward home. In my head I say good-bye and I decide he says *Good-bye, Sarah.* I decide he says *See you tomorrow.* It feels like the fish in Mexico. Fast friends. Someone to talk to. Except really it's not.

I think about ten-year-old Sarah and how she said that last thing she said about my parents on the stoop. *They never stopped.*

I try to remember them fighting. They bicker over little things sometimes, like who should have called the principal, but I don't remember fighting. I barely ever see them in the same place at the same time. I'm sixteen and have some sort of parents-fighting amnesia. Bruce said it in Mexico—*You can always come stay with me, no matter where I am.* Now ten-year-old Sarah said they fought all the time.

They can't be lying.

Maybe I'm just pretending like I did with the fish in Mexico or with Alleged Earl today. Maybe I pretend my parents say "I love you" to each other when they pass each other between work shifts. Maybe I pretend that my family is normal when I know it's not normal to have a runaway brother. Maybe my whole life I've been living inside of an imaginary painting. I can't figure out how I feel about this. But I know I feel uncomfortable. All the time.

I observe Mom and Dad during the two hours they have together. I observe them while standing in random places—the thing I do. I stand behind the door to the kitchen while they talk about dinner.

"I'm making fettuccine Alfredo," Mom says.

"As long as there's garlic bread," Dad says.

"You make the garlic bread," she says.

"Okay," he answers.

Then silence until Mom plugs her phone into her headphones and plays heavy metal and I hear the thumping bass-drum triples of Lars Ulrich a room away. And if you think night ER-trauma nurses who listen to Metallica are original, you're wrong. A lot of her co-workers are metalheads, too. She says metal makes them feel more at home when they're away from the chaos of car accidents, crude drunks, and strokes.

Dad hates metal. He makes the garlic bread. I hear the oven door open. I hear the oven door close. I hear him set the timer. He says, "That'll be ready in twenty minutes."

She says nothing because she can't hear him through her headphones. If she does hear him, she probably just nods. I can't see them. I can only hear them.

I move to the upstairs hallway and listen to Dad talking on the phone in his room. He has a room. Mom has a room. I never thought of this as unusual.

I can't hear much. I hear him say "I'm sorry" twice. I hear him say "Good-bye." I don't move when I hear his doorknob turn. I don't care if he sees me. I congratulate myself for being original compared to most eavesdroppers.

"Oh. I didn't see you there," he says.

"Me neither," I say.

I want to ask him who he was saying sorry to, but I don't.

Fifteen minutes later, I'm cracking black pepper onto a steaming plate of Alfredo and crunching a piece of garlic bread. I wait for dinner conversation between them, but there is none. Between bites, they only talk to me.

"Where'd you go today?" Dad asks.

"Just walked around town," I say.

"You should have told me where you were going," he says.

"I had my phone. You could have called," I said.

Dad nods and shrugs.

Mom puts her hand under the table for a second and I think she's wiping it on her napkin, but her napkin is on the table next to her plate.

"I saw the museum ticket on your dresser," Mom says. "So you're skipping school to look at art?"

"You were in my room?"

"Delivering laundry. Can't afford drones. Yet," she says.

"What are you going to do about school?" Dad asks.

"I'm going to get expelled," I say.

"Great life plan," Dad says.

I shrug and nod.

Mom looks at me a little too long and then takes a deep breath.

Before she can say anything, I say, "I think I'll just drop out this week if that's okay with you."

"It's not okay with me," Dad says.

Mom chews on her garlic bread.

"You can't go to college if you don't have a diploma," Dad says.

Mom says, "Picasso didn't have a diploma."

Dad shrugs. Mom puts her hand under the table. I just eat my food because no matter what they say, I'm not going to school.

I stand in the study while they do dishes.

Mom says, "Did you unload the dishwasher?"

Dad says, "No."

Mom says, "What did you do all day?"

Dad says nothing. I picture him shrugging.

Mom turns off the water and says, "I have to get ready for work."

When she walks through the study, she does it backward with her hands aimed at Dad in her sweatshirt pockets until she sees me. Then she turns around and walks normally through the living room and goes upstairs to take a shower and get ready for work.

I don't think they love each other. I don't think they even like each other. I can't figure out what to think about this, but I feel instantly lonely.

Since I deleted my profile on The Social, I don't have anything except real life. And this is my real life. Anyway, by the time I deleted my profile everyone I'd connected with disconnected from me. Vicky-the-grand-prizewinner posted some crazy stuff about how she was *accused* and how she was *innocent* and how anyone who knew what she was talking about should block *the accuser*.

I didn't accuse anyone of anything.

I just asked the same questions anyone else would have asked.

Vicky-the-grand-prizewinner is lucky I didn't ask more questions about other things. Because there were other things.

It's a long story.

MEXICO—*Day One: Vomitorium*

Day One, when we arrived at the resort and checked in, a man was supposed to take us to our room but instead he took us to a desk claiming that he had to "show us around the resort map." Mom and I had to pee, but we sat in the chairs in front of the desk because we were told to. Dad kept his eyes on our luggage, which was stacked on a cart and sitting next to twenty other carts. The lobby was wide and open. There were cushioned benches, ceiling fans, a bar, a baby grand piano, the sounds of foreign birds. Paradise.

Bruce was still okay then. He was excited to come on vacation with us. He'd just finished his first year of college. He said he really needed the break.

The man behind the desk, Alejandro, talked so fast none of us could keep up. He wasn't talking about the map or the resort. He was talking about the opportunity we had as a family to *increase our vacation potential*. It wasn't a *time-share*, he said. It was a *vacation club*. After listening to him for ten minutes, we had a raffle ticket and breakfast appointment at ten the next morning for—we weren't sure. But we could finally go to our room and pee.

I let Mom go first because she said something about her pelvic floor. I had no idea what a pelvic floor was and, come to think of it, I still don't know. But I'm thinking it's something you get later on.

When it was finally my time to pee, I went into the bathroom and saw it had a bidet. It was my first bidet and I didn't know what it was for. While I peed, I stared at the bidet and tried to figure out what it was. I decided that it was a special toilet where one throws up. It was clean. It had that nozzle thing. It didn't have any water in it to splash back. And it was right next to the toilet. I'd heard about Montezuma's Revenge and Mom had warned us not to drink the water in Mexico. She'd packed every type of medication there was for vomiting, nausea, and diarrhea. I decided that this thing next to the toilet was a vomitorium. I'd heard the word. Had no idea what it meant. Now I had a face to put with the name.

I turned on the water in the bidet as I sat on the toilet, peeing the pee of a hundred little girls who'd just deplaned in Cancún after accepting every beverage offered by the flight attendant, and I tried to move the nozzle around and I went too far and the water started to spray onto the bathroom floor and even though I turned the water off right then, the floor was pretty soaked. When I was done peeing, I took the hand towel from the bathroom and cleaned the floor and I threw the towel under the sink basin so everyone would know it was dirty.

I didn't think it would be a big problem.

I was a kid and I'd never seen a vomitorium before.

A half hour later while Mom was putting sunscreen on me and Bruce was already in his swimming trunks and flip-flops, Dad came out of the bathroom holding the dirty towel.

"Who used this towel?" he asked.

Bruce said he didn't know. Mom said it wasn't her.

I said, "I used it to clean up some water I spilled on the floor."

"How'd you do that?" he asked.

"I just . . . did."

He was far too angry for our first day in Mexico. Maybe he knew we'd just been had by Alejandro.

Mom said, "Chet, don't make a big deal."

Dad said, "We're not even here an hour and they can't be mature."

Bruce said, "I'm mature."

I said, "I was just checking out the vomitorium."

Day One: over. Day One: vacation potential, a dirty towel, and a vomitorium.

HELEN'S PENDING CONTEMPT

A vomitorium has nothing to do with vomit. If you've been to a baseball game, then you've probably been in a vomitorium. The word comes from the Latin vomō, which means to "spew forth." And as a baseball fan, once the game is over, you spew forth through the vomitorium to get back to the parking lot.

Some dumbshit got the meaning wrong once, and for all time, we think it's about some gastrointestinal bug that made Caesar hurl in a vomitorium. The irony is fine, but it still doesn't mean that people go there to vomit.

I hate when people think they know a thing they never even thought about. I have to deal with this every single night in the ER. People hit the Internet for medical advice and suddenly they're diagnosticians. Last night it was a guy convinced he had gallstones but had indigestion, another one with assumed throat cancer who really just had postnasal drip, and a woman who was convinced she had a tapeworm. She actually did have a tapeworm. Did you know they poke their heads out of the anus at night? True story. If you want to be in medicine, remember—you might one day see a tapeworm wave at you.

I don't know what Chet sees in his cubicle during the day, but it's nothing compared to what I see. Whatever he sees, he's always taken it out on the kids. Poor Chet. That's what he should call his memoir. Poor Chet. Except his memoir wouldn't be all that long. All he does is go to work, shrug, and eat vendor hot dogs on the way home because I refuse to buy hot dogs. Nitrites. Avoid ingesting them. Trust me.

***

You probably think I'm being hard on Chet. I am. Life is hard. Marriage is hard. Parenthood is hard and if you add all three up, it's harder. Chet's still acting like he's at home with his mother. He treats me the way his mother treated me when she was still alive. Mean. Like it's my problem that he doesn't do things right.

I'll own my problem. My problem is that Chet doesn't do things right and it makes more work for me. When the kids were little and I went to work seven-to-seven, Chet called his time with them "babysitting." I'd come home at seven thirty in the morning, and the dinner dishes would still be in the sink, the house was a mess, and the kids would be late for school, homework undone. That's not even babysitting.

Remember this. If you plan to get married and have kids, find someone who will never say they are "babysitting" their own kids. They'll expect trophies for just being there and by the time the kids grow up and leave the house, you'll have nothing but contempt for all of them.

The time in Mexico when he yelled at Sarah because she'd played with the bidet and cleaned up her mess, I took Bruce and Sarah out to the beach. Bruce didn't say much. I told Sarah I was proud of her for cleaning up the mess with the towel.

"It shows real independence that you cleaned up after yourself," I said.

All she could see was that her daddy was mad at her.

Vodka Cranberry

On Sunday morning Mom comes home from her seven-to-seven shift and makes herself dinner-for-breakfast. She has a vodka and cranberry, a rare steak, a baked potato, and carrots, and she blasts Rage Against the Machine in her headphones while she cooks. She sings every word out loud, though, especially the "Fuck you" parts.

Dad stays in bed even though he can't be sleeping through this. I pour myself a bowl of cereal. Mom takes off her headphones, turns off the music, and gestures to me to join her for dinner-breakfast.

"It was a good night," she says. "Nearly cleared the whole ER before I left. That never happens."

I crunch on my cereal.

"Three days off," she says.

"Awesome," I say.

She taps me on the shoulder. It snaps me out of an early-morning stare-at-my-cereal daze. She's smiling at me with her head cocked to one side. Rage Against the Machine always makes her this sort of aggressive-happy. She says, "You want to do something fun?"

I want to say *What happened to you?* because Mom has never asked me to do something fun since I turned thirteen, but I just say, "Depends."

"You're dropping out of high school at sixteen. It's not like you have anything to do, right?"

I can hear my cereal go soggy as I look at her with my confused face.

"Well?"

"You're okay with me leaving school?" I say.

"I'm okay with anything," she says. "I just want to have fun."

"This is new."

She looks at me with her confused face. Then she takes a bite of steak. "So you don't want to have fun with your mom. I get it," she says. "What do you plan to do, then?"

"I'm sixteen. I can get a job or something."

Her Rage Against the Machine happiness disappears. Her concerned-mother face arrives. She says, "You need to go to summer school and get your diploma. Then art school. You shouldn't mess up your plan." I feel like I've just witnessed a magic trick. Magician's assistant goes into the sword-trick box in one costume, comes out, unscathed, in another. With a dove or a rabbit or something.

"I don't know," I say. "I don't think I want to do that anymore."

Confused face again. "You have real talent. I mean, *real talent*. Why give up on it?"

"I just don't see myself ever being an artist. And what kind of dream is art, anyway? It's so subjective and stupid." All around me on the kitchen walls, I see imaginary Lichtenstein dots.

"When did you figure this out?"

"About a week before I stopped going to school."

"No wonder, then."

"Yeah."

She fixes herself a second vodka cranberry. She'll be sleepy in about fifteen minutes.

"I didn't want to freak you out before. I just want us to have fun on my days off," she says. "I miss fun."

"Okay."

"You sure nothing else happened?" she asks. "I mean, at school? With a boy or . . . or a girl or anything?"

"I'm sure," I say. "Nothing happened with a boy . . . or a girl."

I never told her anything about the art show. The opening was on a Friday night and she was at work. My project was so secret I hadn't even shown it to her or Dad. The plan was to take them to the art show the next day—it ran from Friday night to Sunday afternoon—and present it like you present a prize cow at a farm show or something. I thought they'd be so proud. But, of course, by the time that Saturday rolled around, there was nothing to present. My cow had disappeared.

It's a long story.

I wash my cereal bowl and put it in the drying rack. Mom goes back to her dinner and vodka. She doesn't mention anything else about fun. She doesn't ask me anything more about what happened. She just chews her steak twenty times and swallows. Do you know how many people come to the ER after swallowing unchewed steak? You wouldn't believe how many problems it causes. You've been warned.

I find Alleged Earl at eight thirty curled in his alcove with his back to the world. I sit on the sidewalk with my back against the wall and my knees to my chest and I wait. After an hour, I think Alleged Earl might be dead. I can't see him breathing under all his coats and blankets. He doesn't move in any way. I wonder if he dreams.

I didn't shower before I left. I have a bandanna on my head, two sloppily braided pigtails in my hair, and I'm wearing an old sweatshirt and jeans. As people walk by, they don't see me most of the time, but when they do see me, they look away. I think they must think I'm homeless, too. This is funny to me at first, but then I think seriously about it.

This could be me. I'm about to drop out of high school for no real reason except that high school isn't original and while dropping out also isn't original, it's not like I'm a normal case. Good grades. Art club. Even Mom says I have talent and Mom doesn't bullshit.

I feel stupid for saying that stuff to her today about getting a job. Who hires a sixteen-year-old high school dropout?

Alleged Earl stirs. He rolls onto his back and coughs. The coughs are wet, and he spits into the side of the alcove. He sits up slowly and looks like he's in pain. He sleeps on concrete. It can't be comfortable. He digs into his blankets and coats and comes out with a small bag of Doritos, opens it with a tug, and eats the chips in fistfuls. Little bits of Doritos fall into his massive beard and to me they're like Lichtenstein dots. Alleged Earl would know what to do with those dots. I wouldn't. He backs up against the boarded-up door and lets his legs stick out like a little kid would do—in the letter V. I look at how he's sitting and how I'm sitting. I flop my legs out in front of me even though if anyone walked by, they could trip over me. Maybe that's the point.

When Alleged Earl slowly makes his way to his feet, he shuffles across Spruce Street and puts the empty Doritos bag in the trash and starts shuffling east.

I follow him.

I follow him all the way to 12th where he takes a right and sits down in a bus shelter. I don't know why I never imagined Alleged Earl on the bus, but we make assumptions when we have a bed to sleep in, I guess.

I check my pocket and I have my SEPTA bus pass in my wallet. Also in my wallet are my school ID, seventeen dollars, a copy of my health insurance card, and behind the billfold area, there is a slip of paper with Bruce's phone number on it.

This is more than Alleged Earl has. Alleged Earl doesn't even have an address. When the bus comes, I step onto it and sit across from him. He sees me now, but he looks like he's looking past me and I smile and say, "Hi."

Alleged Earl shifts in his seat and looks right. The bus stops twice, but he doesn't get off and neither do I. I decide that wherever he goes today, I go. Even if it's dangerous.

The bus turns and makes its way up Lombard. At Broad Street, three people get on and I stare at Alleged Earl and try to get an idea of what he looks like, what color his eyes are, or what his skin looks like under all the hair and dirt, but he's still hidden under all those coats and he's got a hood up over his head and pulled right over toward his nose. He isn't wearing a tinfoil crown today. He looks like he's in his own sort of armor. Maybe he's in his own sort of joust. His lance is an oil crayon or a piece of sidewalk chalk. His opponent is everyone who doesn't believe in art. Which could be me now. I'm no longer sure if I believe in art.

Ten-year-old Sarah sits next to me.

She says, "Didn't expect to see you up so early on a Sunday."

"I'm dropping out of school," I say.

She thinks. "So doesn't that mean that you *shouldn't* be up this early on a Sunday?"

"Every day is Sunday," I say.

"Oh," she says. "Why are we dropping out of school?"

"Don't say *we*."

"I think I have a right to know what you're doing with my future," she says. "Or at least why you're doing it."

"Have you met twenty-three-year-old Sarah?"

"Have you?" she asks.

"We turn out okay," I answer.

"You following Earl again today?"

Alleged Earl should be able to hear this. He doesn't take notice. I consider that maybe Alleged Earl is deaf. Who knows? I don't. All I know is a bunch of ideas I made up in my head—like ten-year-old Sarah did with the fish in Mexico. We all do it. I bet thousands of passersby have decided why Alleged Earl ended up where he is the way ten-year-old Sarah used to decide what those fish said to her.

Alleged Earl gets off at 16th and Lombard. I follow him. Ten-year-old Sarah follows me. We just went in a big circle, really.

"We're a block from home," ten-year-old Sarah says.

"I know."

"He's walking us home," she says.

"I see that," I say.

As we walk by our house, ten-year-old Sarah crosses the street and heads for the front door.

"What are you doing?" I ask.

"I have to pee."

"You can't just walk in there and pee."

"It's my house," she says.

"It's—" I have no idea how to finish this sentence. I'm talking to a ghost or a hallucination. I don't know what I'm talking to. Alleged Earl can't go too fast; we won't lose him if we stop to pee.

So I cross the street and walk in the door ahead of her just in case.

"You know what you are? You're a loser, Chet. You're just a loser."

"Then you married a loser. How's that my fault?"

Ten-year-old Sarah closes the downstairs bathroom door behind her. I can hear her peeing. Hallucinations don't pee.

"I've always been a loser."

"Well then, why don't you try *not* being a loser?"

"You won't give me the chance."

"Jesus Christ! So now I have to give you a chance to not be a loser? I just worked a twelve-hour overnight. I need to fucking sleep. Figure it out yourself."

When ten-year-old Sarah comes out of the bathroom, I go in. Our downstairs bathroom at the end of the kitchen is smaller than an airplane bathroom. Now that I'm tall, I can't close the door and sit on the toilet at the same time. So I watch as ten-year-old Sarah wanders around the kitchen.

She says, "They changed this. It looks nice."

"I don't know why we're doing this anymore!" Dad screams upstairs. He says something else that ends in the word *divorce*.

I say, "Yeah. A pipe burst and the old kitchen got ruined."

I finish and flush and when I come out of the kitchen area, I find her looking at the old painting behind the piano no one ever plays.

"Still my favorite," I say. It's colorful and abstract. When I painted it, I said it was flowers, but really I didn't know what it was when the paint was going on the canvas. That was when Dad taught me about the muse. *The muse is a made-up person who gives you the images in your head when you paint* was how he put it. I don't know where my muse is now. Every time I look at any old paintings, that's what I wonder. I wonder *Where the hell is my muse?*

"I did it in second grade," she says. "Mom bought me canvas and acrylics. She painted one, too."

"Just get out of my room and let me sleep, will you?" Mom yells.

Dad comes down the stairs and we're still standing in the study looking at our painting of abstract flowers. He storms past us and into the kitchen. He opens the back door and then stops.

"Sarah?"

"Yeah?"

"I thought you were out."

"I was. I just had to pee."

I hear him walking back toward the study and I try to hide ten-year-old Sarah behind me, but she won't stay hidden.

He looks at us—both of us—from the doorway between the kitchen and the study and he says, "I didn't know you had a friend over."

Oh

Ten-year-old Sarah smiles at Dad and I say, "We're going back out now. Home by dinner."

He says, "I've seen you before," to ten-year-old Sarah.

"Yep," she answers. "I live a block that way." She points east.

Dad blinks a few times and says, "Oh."

We can still see the anger on his face from the fight he just had with Mom. There's a line that curves like a *c* above his nose. When we went to Mexico and he got a dark tan, that line stayed white because even when he lies in the sun, he's angry.

Ten-year-old Sarah walks to the front door first and I follow her. Dad stands in the doorway to the kitchen watching us. I can feel it.

I follow Sarah east even though I know Alleged Earl has gone west. I suddenly don't care about Alleged Earl. I care about my parents getting divorced. Or I care about how they call each other names. Or I care about what Bruce said to me in Mexico. I feel this burr in my chest, right behind the top of my sternum. It's where my tears live. They never come out. Maybe my muse is there, too. Stuck on a burr in my sternum.

We keep walking, me following ten-year-old Sarah, and we end up on Broad Street. It's Sunday and it's pretty empty. The banks are closed. The theaters are closed until later today when the matinees will open and people will drive in from out of town and try to find the cheapest parking.

I see Carmen taking pictures half a block up Broad Street. She's never been afraid to lie flat on the sidewalk to get the right angle for a shot and, when I see her at first, she's sitting, brushing the dirt off her T-shirt and looking through images on her camera. Part of me doesn't want to talk to her but part of me knows she's Carmen—the only one who stayed my friend after the art club fissure. We walk up to meet her and she says, "We miss you in school."

She looks at ten-year-old Sarah and smiles the same strange smile Dad had. I've known Carmen since I was in first grade. She knew ten-year-old Sarah when she was ten.

"Nobody was even talking to me when I left," I say.

"Well, I miss you."

"I miss you, too," I say.

"They say you got expelled."

"I didn't."

"They say you got caught with drugs."

This makes ten-year-old Sarah laugh. She laughs so well. I don't laugh like that.

"I don't do drugs and you know it," I say to Carmen.

"Yeah. I told people it was a lie."

Ten-year-old Sarah asks, "So why aren't you going to school, anyway?"

I look at Carmen looking at ten-year-old Sarah and see she's blinking and trying to figure us out.

"I drew four more tornadoes," Carmen says. "Big. On pieces of recycled wood. We're doing acrylics on canvas for the next month."

Ten-year-old Sarah says, "That sounds so fun."

"Yeah," I say, but I don't really mean it. Carmen can paint all the tornadoes she wants. I'm not painting anything. *Muse, burr, sternum.*

"I know you," Carmen says to ten-year-old Sarah.

"I live down the street," ten-year-old Sarah says. "That way." She points south.

"So . . . are you ever coming back?" Carmen asks me.

"I don't think so," I say. "Things are kinda messed up right now."

"Miss Smith thinks it was something she said," Carmen says. "I've been helping her after school. She says she thinks she's the reason you're not coming to school."

Carmen was born to be the art teacher's pet. There is nothing original about being the art teacher's pet. I only hope Carmen steers clear of Miss Smith's lipstick. I don't think Carmen is her type anyway.

Either way, Miss Smith is kinda right about it being her fault. But telling Carmen this wouldn't be original because Carmen already knows, only she can't talk about it. So I say, "Nah. It wasn't Miss Smith." I look at the sidewalk and a piece of gum that's been ground into it. "We'll see you around," I say. Ten-year-old Sarah has been walking around a signpost for the last minute and she's making me dizzy.

"I hope things get better," Carmen says.

"Have fun painting your tornadoes," I say.

I walk up Broad Street, and ten-year-old Sarah follows me until I realize that she brought us here and I have no idea where she wanted to go.

"We lost Alleged Earl," I say.

"He'll be near City Hall," she says. "It's Sunday."

"You're ten. You never followed him when you were ten," I say.

"You don't remember things all that well, do you?"

"I remember lots of things."

"You don't remember asking his name. You don't remember that he goes to City Hall on Sundays. You don't even think we did this before."

"So this isn't original?" I ask.

74

"Nothing is original. We know this already."

Ten-year-old Sarah walks under City Hall into the underpass. I'm about to ask her if she knows that Philadelphia City Hall is the tallest municipal building in America, but then I remember she's me and she knows because I know and I've known for years.

She says, "Did you know that City Hall is the tallest municipal building in America?"

"Yep," I say.

"Did you know that this is where Dad proposed to Mom?" she says. "And then they went upstairs and got the license?"

I search my brain archives. I seem to have forgotten this, too. I say, "Not very romantic if you ask me."

Alleged Earl isn't at City Hall. Ten-year-old Sarah says, "He must have changed his routine." She walks west toward the art museum, and I walk back down Broad. "See you tomorrow," she says. "Maybe you can tell me why we dropped out of high school."

"Stop saying *we*."

MEXICO—*Day Two: Selfish Bastards*

I was mortified that Mom wore a bikini. She never wore a bikini on the New Jersey seashore, but in Mexico, nearly everyone wears a bikini. As I watched the drunk adults—most of them younger than Mom and Dad—swagger around in their bikinis, I felt like Mexico was all about sex.

Sex and drinking.

I was ten, and this was obvious. So looking at Mom in her bikini, ordering drinks from Martín the beach bar waiter, just grossed me out.

The other people at our resort were animals. They left their empty beer cans on the sand. They talked in that loud, drunken way all day and night long. One time I saw a couple making out so hard that it was nearly sex right there on the water's edge. There was a kids' club place—glorified babysitters—but there were only a handful of younger kids in there. The thatched hut sat next to the spa-massage tent between the pool and the beach, and the little kids could look out at the animal-people doing their animal-things while they made crafts or played bingo.

Every thatched beach umbrella had a hand-lettered wooden sign nailed to its trunk. The sign said:

RESERVING BEACH SEATS AND UMBRELLAS IS STRICTLY PROHIBITED. DO NOT LEAVE PERSONAL BELONGINGS OR TOWELS ON BEACH CHAIRS. CHECK LOST & FOUND IF YOUR ITEMS HAVE BEEN REMOVED.

This sign was also posted on the wall behind the beach chairs. It was posted at the towel exchange hut, and it was even posted in our hotel rooms. And yet every single morning on vacation, 85 percent of the beach chairs had random towels and personal items on them and there were no people in sight. If you were late to the beach, you didn't get an umbrella until you waited long enough to figure out which chairs were really being used and which were inappropriately being reserved while the people who reserved them went to breakfast. Sometimes people would just walk around the beach chair area, scoping. Sometimes they would make the towel attendant come to the beach and remove things from the chairs so they didn't have to do it themselves. It drove people crazy. This was resort behavior. No rules—even when there were rules.

Our family followed rules. It was in our nature. Dad was in insurance. Mom was a nurse. We never reserved beach chairs. Day Two was the first time we realized that everyone else did.

Day Two started with a two-hour-long "vacation club" time-share presentation. I'd explain it to you but it was so boring there's no point. The only things that came out of it were resort credits for all of us—Bruce and I got a kayaking adventure and Mom and Dad got a romantic dinner on the beach—and my fascination with people who can do math upside down on paper. I still try it sometimes. My best numbers are zeroes and ones.

By the time we got to the beach, it was eleven o'clock and all the chairs were taken—some legitimately, some not—but it was hard to tell which were which. Dad walked around three times until he found one chair under a thatched umbrella with a dry towel slung over it in the way that chair-reservers do it. Dad removed the towel from the chair, and Mom said, "We'll have to share until we can find more chairs." Dad went off to find a beach attendant to get us another chair. Mom took the extra towel and spread it on the sand, sat down, and looked out to sea.

I said I wanted to get in the water so she covered me in sunscreen and looked at her watch and said, "You can only stay out there an hour."

I ran into the surf and then stopped at ankle deep and walked slowly instead.

The water wasn't what I thought it would be. Mom and Dad told me it would be crystal clear and turquoise. But seaweed had come in from the Atlantic. That's what the Amstar vacation-guide guy said later. He said, "Nothing we can do about it. Storms do this." The water past the huge globs of seaweed still looked dirty because the seaweed had been tumbled there on its way to the shore, and if I looked at it long enough, it looked like watery diarrhea. No chance of seeing fish. No chance of seeing my feet or even my own hands underwater. Once I saw what it looked like, I didn't want to get into the water at all, really, but I did. In my head I imagined what it was supposed to look like. Clean, blue-green, with white angelfish. Just like the website picture Mom showed me. I didn't last the hour. I managed to avoid waves and clusters of seaweed for about fifteen minutes and that was it.

By the time I got back to the towel, Dad was agitated because the beach attendant wouldn't give him another chair. Dad kept pointing to two chairs a few feet from us and saying, "They just throw a magazine or a rock on the chair and then leave for the day. Selfish bastards." *Selfish bastards.* He said that every time he saw a reserved chair. Rule followers don't know what to do with selfish bastards.

Mom went into nurse mode. She solved the problem. She said it was time for Bruce and me to use our adventure credits and the three of us went over to the kayak shack while Dad stewed over all the selfish bastards.

The kayak adventure wasn't all that exciting. Not exciting enough to call it an adventure. They made Bruce and me wear life jackets, and it was maybe a hundred degrees out there. It was midday and I wore a thin, long-sleeved dive shirt and a wide sun hat because no amount of sunscreen would keep me safe at noon in the Caribbean sun. I put it on anyway of course, but I put the shirt on over it.

I had never kayaked before so that part of it was adventurous. Bruce taught me how to paddle and we got out past the string of buoys and the sea was rougher than it should have been. We battled just to get from one end of the resort's water boundary and back to the other. Salt water got up my nose and I almost started to cry because it stung so much. Bruce said if we paddled out between sandbars, we would find a calm place to just sit in the kayak and talk so I paddled with him to get there.

Once we could rest and bob in the kayak for a while, Bruce asked me if I thought Mom and Dad would be mad if he dropped out of college. Just like that. First thing he said. "Do you think Mom and Dad would be mad if I dropped out of college?"

I said, "Does it matter if they get mad?"

"Yeah."

"Why? You're, like, almost twenty."

"You know what it's like when they're mad at you," he said. "Doesn't change just because I'm older."

"I think you should do what you want to do," I said.

He didn't answer. He just sat there and looked into the water. "God, this water is disgusting."

"I know."

"And the pool is filled with drunks."

"Yeah."

"That's a shitty vacation right there," Bruce said. "Bet Dad picked the cheapest place to go and never even looked at any reviews."

"I don't think he plans on swimming."

"Wanna head back?"

"Is our hour up already?" I asked. I looked up at the sun as if it were a clock.

"I just want to wash all this crap off me." He had bits of brown seaweed stuck to his arms. I looked down. So did I.

We started paddling back over the breaking waves, and the ride back was a bit smoother than the ride out.

"Why do you want to leave college?" I asked.

He stopped paddling, which made the boat go in a circle until I stopped, too. "It just seems pointless," he said.

"I thought you wanted to be a psychologist," I said.

He laughed a little. "I think I need to *see* a psychologist, not be one."

We paddled to shore and gave our life jackets back and walked to the outdoor showers and rinsed off. Bruce said he had seaweed in his swim trunks and told me to tell Mom and Dad that he went to the room to shower. I went back under the thatched umbrella and told them. Mom said, "Aren't you going to swim, honey?"

I wanted to tell her that the water was a toilet bowl but I thought it would be rude with Dad sitting right there. So I said, "Sure," and went back into the water. I closed my eyes. I imagined the fish and I said hello. They said hello back.

That night at the buffet, I imagined I liked seafood tacos and runny refried beans. Bruce ate his lasagna and Caesar salad. I told them about the fish as if they were real. I ate three desserts and we stopped to take pictures of a two-foot-long iguana on our walk back to the room. We all fell asleep the minute we hit our beds.

Day Two: over. Day Two: kayak adventure, swimming in a toilet, selfish bastards.

Mom wakes up at four in the afternoon on Sunday. That's a good day's rest for her. I hear her go into the shower while Dad is in the living room half dusting the entertainment center. He just goes over the tops of things with a feather duster and forgets the filthy TV screen all together.

I walk into the kitchen, but I stand in the doorway and watch him vacuum. He runs it in every direction and misses most of the dirt. He's not even watching TV. There's nothing to distract him from the sliver of tissue right in front of him on the carpet but before he can vacuum it, he turns the vacuum cleaner off and puts it back into the closet. Then he sits in the chair by the door and picks up a *Time* magazine and leafs through it.

I stare at the tissue sliver. If I can see it from here, he should be able to see it from there. It's white and the carpet is dark blue. No one could be that lazy without knowing it. He picks his nose while he reads *Time*, and he wipes a booger on the armrest of the chair. I wait for him to have his finger up there again to walk in.

"Hi," I say.

He removes his finger from his nose and doesn't know what to do with the booger this time. He wipes it on his sweatpants.

"Anything good in *Time*?"

"Not really," he says. "Did you clean your room today?"

"I cleaned it yesterday. Today is Sunday."

"Oh," he says. "Right."

"What are we having for dinner?"

"Probably breakfast," he says.

"I'll make waffles," I say. "Mom loves waffles."

"Sure," he says.

I know Dad hates waffles. I don't care. Before I go to the kitchen to make batter, I draw three triangles on the TV screen's dust. The small one represents me. The medium one represents waffles. The biggest one represents how much I don't care that Dad hates waffles. Then I pick up the sliver of tissue on the carpet, wet it with my spit, and stick it right in the middle of the smallest triangle.

I make corn waffles and I put on a pot of coffee for when Mom comes down. She sings in the shower. Today she's singing a Nirvana song called "School." I love that song. I played it for Carmen once but she said it's too angry. And she's the one who paints tornadoes. Seriously. What's angrier than a tornado?

Dad.

Dad at breakfast-for-dinner is angrier than a tornado.

He's a shrugging machine as he makes himself a fried egg and toast while Mom and I eat corn waffles at the table.

"Dad told me you were out with a friend today," Mom says.

"Yeah. Neighbor girl I see a lot."

"Is she nice?"

"Totally nice."

"She's a bit young for you," Dad says.

"It's like a little sister thing," I say.

Mom nods. "Tomorrow is Monday." I have no idea why I need a human calendar until she adds, "Do you think you could make it back to school?"

"I don't think so," I say.

"It's a high school diploma," Dad says. "It's not rocket science. You need it to get a job. You need it to get to college."

Mom nods.

I say, "I'll think about it."

"Good," they say in unison. And then they look annoyed that they said something in unison. Then they fake smile at each other, but I'm starting to understand that smiling is really just another way of baring one's teeth.

HELEN'S SONG

I get fakers all the time in the ER. Last week a college girl said she swallowed staples. We rushed her to X-ray, and there wasn't a staple to be found. She cried and screamed and kicked and said she was sure she swallowed staples. "A whole roll of them!" she said.

Staples don't even come in rolls.

She begged me for painkillers. She said she was dying. She said she was going to sue the hospital for not taking care of her. And she wasn't even a psych case. She was just bored, I think. She walked out of the place just fine an hour and a half later.

There's a song I sing sometimes. It's a terrible song. I feel bad for singing it but I also know the truth will set me free. I call the song "You're a Dumb Prick and I Hate You."

It never has the same words except for the chorus, which goes like this: *You're a dumb prick and I hate you.*

I've been singing this song since about two years after I married Chet. I never sing it to any other people. Just Chet. I dedicate the song to Chet as if it were the radio days when we were young and you could call a number over and over and when someone finally answered at the radio station, you could request a song and the DJ would read out who the song was dedicated to and who it was requested by. Sometimes before I sing the song, I say, "Dedicated to Chet from Helen."

Do I hate Chet? I might. I think I do. I look mean when I say it here. I look mean and awful and you're reading this thinking *I'm glad* she's not my wife or I will never be like that to my husband. You have no idea.

Chet isn't here. Chet was never here. I married him when I didn't fully understand how he would disappear because he only knew the men he saw around him. Abusive father. The sportscasters on the TV. The annoying weatherman on CBS. The guys he works with who watch porn all weekend.

He says, "At least I don't hit you."

He says, "At least I'm not jerking off to porn."

He says, "I wish I could show you how much I love you."

I wish he could, too. If the weatherman just shrugged all the time, would anyone know what the weather was going to be? Would he say, "I wish I could tell you what the weather could be," and still manage to keep his job?

Chet's happy like this. As happy as he can get, I guess.

He's a natural-born faker.

And I have no time for fakers.

I have the song. I sing it loud in my head and, when I have the house to myself and I see the peanut shells Chet dropped on the floor during the baseball game he watched on TV the night before, I sing it as loud as I can.

It's like swallowing staples.

It's like every single day, I'm swallowing staples. And yet I can't figure out if I really hate him, but I'm pretty sure I do.

Kids Love Tacos

I stand in the hall outside of Mom's room. Dad is in there.

MOM: We should invite that friend of Sarah's over for dinner.

DAD: Okay.

MOM: Maybe on Tuesday. I'll be back on my sleep schedule by then and I'll make curry.

DAD: Too hot. She may hate it.

MOM: Tacos, then. Kids love tacos.

DAD: *(silence)*

MOM: I don't think you pushing Sarah to go back to school is helping.

DAD: She's rebelling. She needs boundaries.

MOM: She's never had a problem before. Maybe she just needs someone to talk to.

DAD: You're better at talking.

MOM: *(silence)*

Dad goes back to his room. I stand in my bedroom by my open window. It's Sunday late afternoon in the city. Not much traffic. No one talking. No dogs barking. No kids playing next door. Nothing to hear.

I stand at the front door and say good-bye to Mom at six thirty as she heads out in her scrubs. Mom is strictly a solid-color scrubs kind of nurse. She says all those flowers and prints are for the day nurses.

"Think about school tomorrow," she says to me.

"I will," I say, but I'm lying.

"And we're going to have your friend over for dinner!" she says. "I can't wait to meet her."

I don't know what to say to that, so I just nod.

"Why don't you pull out your sketchbook tonight and draw me a comic or something?" she says. "Something about you and me having fun."

I want to tell her that she now sounds like the mother of a six-year-old, but I know she's trying, so I say, "I'll try," even though I never drew a comic in my life.

When she gives me a hug, she whispers, "Maybe this week you can take me to the museum or something. We can go out to lunch. Fun, right?"

"Okay," I say.

As she turns to leave, she misses my eyes filling up with tears, and I'm glad because I don't know why it's happening. I think it's because she has to say things like this now—about having fun.

My skipping school is throwing off her plans, but she rolls with it because she's a solid-color-scrubs kind of nurse. She's going into the ER tonight and she doesn't know what to expect. She has mastered the art of the unexpected.

Sometimes it's college students who have a cold. Sometimes it's an unexplained seizure or some Jane Doe who's all slashed up. Sometimes it's little kids who broke a leg or broke a collarbone or got shot by accident by one of their cousins. Mom has put her hands in a man's chest and pumped his heart back to life. Mom has had to strap down drunk people who spit at her. Mom doesn't really care about plans because Mom sees people's plans change all the time at three o'clock in the morning.

Your Mother and Me

Dad is sitting on the couch watching a baseball game on the TV. My triangles are still drawn on the screen. The sliver of tissue I stuck to the smallest triangle is still there. It blocks right field if the camera is behind the batter. Dad doesn't seem to care. I wonder how many tissue slivers I'd have to stick on the TV before he'd care. I decide the number is probably five.

I sit down on the couch and draw a blank comic on a stray piece of paper. It's five panels long. I decide to draw whatever comes to me in each panel. No thinking first, no planning. I just rough sketch right there on the couch next to Dad.

The first panel is a tornado.

The second panel is my family—all of us—Bruce included.

The third panel is the tornado hitting my family.

The fourth panel is just a tornado again, but like in Carmen's tornadoes I can see many things in the tornado. Miss Smith, my art teacher, is in there. Alleged Earl is in there. Oregon is in there. Two lawyers and a judge are in there.

The fifth panel is me and Mom at three o'clock in the morning. The clock is in the foreground. Mom and me are tiny in the background and we are changing plans.

I have no idea what this comic means. I don't plan on showing it to Mom, that's for sure.

A commercial comes on. It's one of those louder-than-life commercials, as if boosting the volume would make us buy the thing they're selling.

Dad talks over the commercial rather than muting it.

He says, "You're making a big mistake."

He says, "You're too smart to make such a bad decision."

He says, "I really think you should listen to your mother and I."

I say, "Me."

He says, "What?"

I say, "Your mother and *me*."

He says, "Don't be a smart-ass."

"I only got to be a smart-ass because you're a smart-ass."

"Touché, my creative little clone."

Dad and his creativity. *Time to make the art!* He must be so disappointed after all those trips to the museums and all those summer art classes and all those birthday gifts. I am, too. I'm disappointed. I just drew a comic, so why can't I draw a pear? My hand? A vase of spring flowers?

I mute the commercial. I say, "Do you ever wonder about Bruce?"

Dad says, "No."

I say, "That's kinda cold, isn't it?"

Dad says, never taking his eye off the screen, "Bruce decided to leave our family. There isn't much I can do about it."

I say, "You could call."

"Don't have his number."

"You could find it."

The game comes back on TV, and Dad puts the sound back on and talks loudly. "He doesn't want to hear from us. He made that quite clear."

"Don't you miss him?"

"No."

"Well, I miss him. He's my brother."

" . . ."

The guy on the TV hits a single and Dad gets all excited and says, "Yes! What a hit!"

I look around the living room. Everything is normal here. There are framed pictures of me as a little kid on the mantel. My ceramic owl lives there, too. We have art on the walls—some prints of classics and a few oils Dad bought at student art sales over the years. A lot of still lifes.

I think about still lifes. Until I met ten-year-old Sarah, that's what I had. A still life. The more I pay attention, the more I see I was wrong.

I look back at my comic and pencil a thick title at the top.

STILL LIFE WITH TORNADO.

It's Monday and Alleged Earl is curled in the alcove like he is every morning. I didn't even get on the bus. I just ate breakfast, waited for Dad to leave, and walked here.

As I sit on the sidewalk near Alleged Earl, I think about school and what happened. Sometimes the whole thing just washes over me like a river gone over its banks. No matter what I do, I can't stop thinking about it.

I had an original idea once.

Sculpture class, third quarter, sophomore year. Final project, two and a half months ago.

First, Miss Smith gave us materials: a few spools of wire; a big box of colorful Plexiglas; a bucket of broken-up tiles in case anyone wanted to do a 3-D mosaic; clay. We were all still friends then. Vicky-the-grand-prizewinner was extra nice to me because she knew what I'd seen. She'd sent me a private message on The Social the day it happened. It said, *Let's keep that between us, okay?*

Everyone in art club chose the Plexiglas because we'd never worked with Plexiglas before. Miss Smith explained that she had special epoxy to bond pieces to other pieces. We took a day to sketch ideas and to figure out which colors we wanted to work with, which pieces. On the second day while some people still riffled through the box for the right piece, I cut my three pieces— primary colors—with the little band saw we had in the art room that no one ever used. I cut out shapes. Triangles and squares and rectangles. The saw spat plastic dust as I worked and it smelled awful, but there was something cathartic about cutting up a big thing into little things. Miss Smith ignored my doing this. She didn't even tell me to put on safety goggles, which is probably against the law. Miss Smith didn't care about laws. I knew that.

In the end, I had a pile of small random shapes in red, yellow, and blue. I planned on mounting the shapes on a larger piece of neutral-colored Plexiglas. I thought the idea was boring. The rest of the class was drawing on their Plexiglas and most of the art club was lining up behind me at the band saw to cut their pieces into curvier shapes than mine. I could see the curves drawn in Sharpie on their Plexiglas. It was always a competition, the art club. If I did something, they would do something-plus-one.

I took my pieces of Plexiglas home and showed them to Mom and complained that I thought my project was boring. She asked if I'd ever tried bending it and she showed me how to bend Plexiglas over the heat of the electric stove. She gave me a pair of silicone oven gloves to wear but I found them restricting so I took them off once she left the kitchen. I spent an hour bending the shapes I'd cut out—my squares were now wavy, my rectangles were cylinders, my triangles a mix of both. I burned my fingertips a little, nothing awful, and I turned on the exhaust fan so the whole house didn't smell like burning plastic even though the house already smelled like burning plastic before I turned it on. When I was done bending, I laid my new pieces out on the countertop and they were less boring and I felt happy enough with the Plexiglas project.

When I got back to class the next day, the band saw was already on and Vicky-the-grand-prizewinner was cutting curves into her flat

Plexiglas. Miss Smith stood behind her, smiling. Vicky-the-grand-prizewinner was wearing safety goggles.

I pulled out my flat piece of neutral-colored Plexiglas and then, one by one, I started to pull out my bent, curved shapes. Vivian asked, "How did you do that?" and I explained how I did it, which was probably a mistake. By the end of the day, Miss Smith produced an electric hot plate that she stored on the shelves behind her desk. By the end of the week, all the art clubbers had bent Plexiglas projects, too. They said they planned on painting theirs. Carmen twisted a tornado out of a large triangle and planned on drawing the things within. My project still seemed boring to me. There's only so much an artist can do with Plexiglas. I had a week before the final project was due.

So I changed my project. This time, I didn't tell anybody what I was doing. I started to weave a basket out of thin wire. I had stainless steel wire, brass wire, and copper wire. My fingers were still a bit scarred from the Plexiglas bending, so when the wires bit into my fingers until I bled, I barely felt it. I went into the zone when I wove. It was far more interesting than working with plastic. The faster I wove, the more I went into the zone. The more I was in the zone, the more I wanted to make something other than a basket. I sat staring at what I'd done so far. I stopped weaving. I opened my sketchbook and started drawing. I knew what this project could become. I knew it could be great. And when Carmen said, "Are you weaving a basket?" I lied to her. I said, "Yes."

But I wasn't really weaving a basket. I was weaving a headpiece. I wove a curved rectangle about five by eight inches and wove in complicated designs and threaded in decorations like beads and other flotsam. Everyone was so busy bending Plexiglas and decorating it with pop art dots, Miss Smith didn't even notice I'd changed mediums. I did most of the final touches at home so no one would steal my idea.

When I was done weaving, instead of clipping off the extra wires that acted as warp spokes, I turned them to the sky and made them into shapes and curlicues and other things and spread them out so it looked like you were wearing the sun on your head. I spent the final weekend sewing a lining into the headpiece. Stitch by stitch, I knew this was the coolest thing I'd ever made. My hands were a mess—fingers red with old burns and pricks and a few tiny blood blisters from pinching myself with wire snippers. As I sewed the black felt and padded it out with stuffing, I felt tired—like an artist should feel after pouring her soul into a piece. I felt quiet, at peace, and not like the chattering art club every day in class. I polished the wire when I was done, and I put it in a box to take to school for the day we would unveil our final projects.

All the other students still just had their curvy Plexiglas projects. Carmen's tornado was the best of the lot. She even cut some thin strips of Plexiglas and bent them to represent wind.

They got As.

I got an A+.

Miss Smith was wowed. She said she wanted my headpiece in the annual art show. She said, "This is really awesome, Sarah! This could win!" I remember feeling humble because artists should be humble. I looked at my hands. I picked at the scabs on my fingers.

I could see the art club seniors getting all worked up over it—feeling sorry for themselves and feeling like their projects were better—but mine was original.

Either way, the headpiece never made it to the art show.

That was how they showed me my place.

I wonder how the world showed Alleged Earl his place was in the alcove. I don't think anybody should have to sleep on the street. I don't think anybody should have to dig in the trash for food. It seems wrong in every possible situation. If he's poor, someone should help him. If he's mentally ill, someone should help him. What kind of place do we live in where so many people have to live on the street?

Doesn't make any sense except that people have to show other people their place. And Alleged Earl's place is in the alcove. And my place is not-in-school.

We both have original headpieces, but he makes a new one every other day and I only made one, which was stolen.

It's a long story.

"Skipping school again?" ten-year-old Sarah asks.

I didn't even see her coming because I was so busy looking at Alleged Earl.

"I guess," I say.

"Let's go for a walk," she says.

I get up off the concrete and walk with her.

"Something happened at school," she says. "That's why you won't go back."

"Nah. I just don't feel like it."

"Something happened. Stop clamming up."

"I'm not clamming up," I say.

"It's nothing to be embarrassed about," ten-year-old Sarah says. "Whatever it is, I'm sure it's happened before."

I think about this. She's right. I'm sure a disappearing art project has happened before. It is not at all original. Maybe had something happened to me that *was* original I'd feel better about it.

"I'm not embarrassed."

"Do you remember Julia?" she asks.

"I know a few Julias in school."

"No. The one from the restaurant. The little girl."

I remember Julia. I don't think I'll ever forget Julia. "Yes," I say.

I was six. We were at our favorite Mexican restaurant for *Día de los Muertos*. We ordered dinner and, like always, right after we ordered Mom took me and Bruce to the bathroom. Bruce complained because he was fifteen and didn't think he should be told to go to the bathroom anymore. Mom and I went into the ladies' room and found only one stall open. The other stall had a roughly written OUT OF ORDER sign.

Mom said, "Just come in here with me and we'll take turns." We went into the stall and I got to pee first. While I was peeing, the ladies' room door opened and a woman came in and started yelling at her kid. She was so mean, my pee stopped. She said, "Come here." The kid made a little moan. "You can't act like that at a restaurant!" *Slap.* "I told you to be good tonight!" *Slap.* "You need to behave, Julia!" *Slap.* At the third slap the little girl wailed. And when she did, I noticed she was really little. I was six and I didn't wail like that. The woman said, "Are you ready to go back out? Stop crying! Are you ready?" The girl quieted down and huffed a few times. She finally said yes, and that was when Mom and I knew that the kid didn't even really talk yet. She was probably, like, two years old.

Mom was frozen, a lump of toilet paper in one hand that she was handing to me, and her other hand on the door. By the time the ladies' room door slammed shut, only about fifteen to twenty seconds had passed. I was able to finish peeing, but everything in the bathroom was different.

The fluorescent lights were flickering. I hadn't noticed that before. I could hear one of the taps had been left running. Mom sat down to pee and even though we had a rule of turning our backs when we shared stalls, she said, "Look at me."

Since she was sitting on a toilet, her eyes were at the same level as mine. She was crying a little. Tears were on her cheeks. Her face looked old. It looked tired. It looked scared. She just stared at me for what felt like a whole minute with this face. With those tears. I didn't know what to say.

"I will never hit you, Sarah. Okay?"

"Okay."

"I will never ever hurt you."

"Okay," I said again. Then we hugged.

She motioned for me to turn back around after the hug. She finished peeing and flushed the toilet.

As we washed our hands, she took a bunch of deep breaths. She wiped her eyes with her used paper towel and she helped me dry my hands. At the time, I didn't see what the big deal was. It was sad the little girl got spanked or whatever, but I never thought of anyone hitting me before, so I don't know why Mom was so weird about it.

When we got back to the table, Mom looked around the restaurant for the woman and her daughter. I scooted into the booth next to Bruce and said, "Some lady just hit her baby in the bathroom and it made Mom cry."

Mom looked down at her fork.

Bruce looked down at his place mat.

Dad looked at me like he was angry that I brought this scene back to the dinner table.

Then dinner came and I ate enchiladas. That's the Julia story.

I look back at ten-year-old Sarah. "Yeah. I think about her sometimes. She'd be just a little older than you now."

She says, "Anyway, you shouldn't be embarrassed about whatever happened in school."

"I'm not embarrassed."

I am. I'm totally embarrassed even though I didn't do anything wrong.

"Bruce was embarrassed, too. In Mexico. When it happened. You know."

"I don't know what Bruce would be embarrassed about."

"Like Julia. Don't you remember playing tooth fairy?" ten-year-old Sarah asks.

I stop walking.

I remember playing tooth fairy. To a nineteen-year-old boy. My brother.

I remember slipping my tiny hand under his pillow in our hotel room.

I remember leaving two dimes, three shells, and a note.

The note said, "I love you."

The note said, "I'm sorry."

It wasn't me who'd done anything wrong, but I was still sorry. Just like the art club. Just like everything in my life. Things happen that aren't my fault and I say I'm sorry.

"I don't want to talk about Mexico anymore," I say.

MEXICO—*Day Three: Mango Tango*

Bruce and I decided that after our kayaking adventure the day before, we wanted to do something indoors for the morning so Mom and Dad headed out to the beach and we went to play Ping-Pong, and we all agreed to meet up for lunch at one. Bruce beat me every other game. I was ten. He was nineteen. There was a clear advantage, but he let me win half the time because that way I'd want to keep playing.

We stayed out of the sun, out of the grungy water, and away from Mom and Dad, who kept talking about the resort like it was some sort of heaven even though the day before it was all about selfish bastards. The difference: Dad reserved chairs under an umbrella at six in the morning with two magazines and a rock. He said, "When in Rome." I didn't know what that meant.

We met for lunch and Dad was clearly drunk. Mom said after lunch we had to come down to the beach and have some fun. "We didn't come all this way for you not to swim in the Caribbean!"

So after lunch Bruce and I went for a swim, me in my one-piece bathing suit and him in his oversize surfer trunks, which looked even bigger on his lanky frame. There were no other kids on the beach. They were all in the crystal clear pool surrounded by drunk adults in bikinis. We trudged through the seaweed toilet water, and I didn't mind it as much as I did the day before. I even took a few blobs of it and put it on my head. Bruce followed. We crowned ourselves prince and princess of the seaweed. I felt tiny fish brush past my legs but I still couldn't see anything. I tried not to look down. I floated awhile in the water and asked the sea god to please get rid of the seaweed. I asked him to make the people at the resort stop being selfish bastards. I asked him to make me a famous artist.

Bruce and I played a game of catch where the water came up to my chest and it came up to his waist. I always tried to throw the little Nerf ball hard and high so he'd have to jump for it. Each time he jumped, his trunks ended up a little lower on his hips.

I thought this was funny, but Bruce didn't, so he stopped playing catch.

Under the thatched umbrella, I asked Bruce why he got so mad at me for throwing the ball high.

"I don't want my junk out for everyone to see," he said.

"Junk?"

"You know—my penis?"

Mom disallowed weird names for body parts. I knew what a uvula was by the time I was four. And a patella. And a sternum. And a penis. I didn't know what Bruce was learning at college, but junk was a step backward if you ask me.

Bruce ordered himself a beer. He was nineteen and in Mexico you can drink beer at nineteen. When the beer came, he drank it like he was drinking Windex.

"Why'd you order that if you don't like it?"

"I don't know," he said.

When Martín the bar waiter came back around, Bruce ordered a Mango Tango—the drink of the day. When it came, he drank it down like it was lemonade. He let me try a sip and it was good. But he wouldn't let me have more than a sip. I went out to where the tide was coming in and I drew a few pictures in the sand with my finger. First, it was a fish. The water washed it away. Then, I drew my feet. The water washed it away. Then, I drew a pelican. It was a really great pelican and I wanted Mom or Dad to see it but they were still under the umbrella drinking Mango Tangos and the water came and washed the pelican away.

None of this is original, but when I was ten-year-old Sarah, I didn't care about things being original. I just wanted to have fun on the beach and with my brother. I'd missed Bruce during his first year in college. Even though he was nine years older than I was, we were a good match. We both knew the right name for body parts (even if he'd stopped using them). We both still cleaned our rooms on Saturday mornings like we'd been trained to. We both still made grilled peanut butter and jelly sandwiches the same way and, even though he was so much bigger than I was, we had the same walk, the same logic, and the same curiosity about things.

The one thing that was different was how we saw Mom and Dad.

He told me, in Mexico—on night three when we went to the buffet restaurant together while Mom and Dad had a reservation at the hibachi at the Japanese place in the resort—"I think Mom and Dad are finally getting a divorce."

I said, "They are not."

I remember looking at him like he was breaking my heart. And I remember him looking at me like he knew he'd just broken my heart.

He said, "I thought you knew."

"They're normal."

"So? Normal people get divorced all the time," he said.

"They don't even fight."

"They fight all the time," he said. "And they don't even sleep in the same bed."

"This is bullshit," I said.

"I'm sorry."

"They're not getting a divorce," I said.

"They're only together because of us," he said. "That's the only reason they're not divorced yet. Because of you. They're waiting until you go to college."

"Bullshit," I said, stuffing tortilla chips into my mouth.

Bruce didn't say much after that.

There was a magic show that night in the theater and we all went. It was the cheesiest thing I ever saw. The hostess of the preshow spoke in Spanish and occasionally translated so the audience knew what she was saying. The music was loud and the preshow was just this woman in her high heels and crazy outfit asking members of the audience to play a game. After the game, the magician came on in a puff of smoke and fancy multicolored lighting. His jacket had wide sleeves and he kept straightening his shirt collar, over and over again.

I was ten and I knew each tug at his collar was another trick he was setting up. Each tug resulted in a dove. See this empty hat? Look! A dove! Tug. See this empty box? Look! A dove! Tug. See this ball of scarves I just pulled out of my arm? See how there's nothing here but colorful scarves? See how I crumble them all in a ball? Tug. Look! A dove! Between doves, there were the usual tricks and the usual sequin-adorned female assistants. Audience participation resulted in a surprised woman from Kansas holding an empty box and then suddenly holding a duck. Then, the sword tricks. How many times can you put a woman in a box and slide swords through the box and then reveal the woman as unharmed and still call yourself a magician? The doves were cool, though. And the duck. The duck was cool.

Dad and Mom ordered drink after drink. Dad complained they were watered down. Mom said, "Just order two next time." They acted surprised at every dove. They applauded when they were supposed to. They seemed like good parents. They didn't seem like they were getting a divorce.

I didn't know why Bruce was bullshitting me about that. But every time I thought about it, I got this feeling like a burr right at the top of my sternum.

On the walk back to our rooms, Bruce, Mom, and Dad whispered. I walked ahead trying to find wild animals on the path. They said there was a howler monkey that lived here, but I'd never seen it. Only heard it. It's a horrible sound—less like a howl and more like a roar.

Once I got my pajamas on and brushed my teeth and got into bed, Bruce finally talked to me again.

"I'm taking you somewhere tomorrow," Bruce said. "It's a surprise."

"Where?"

"Just rest up. You'll need your sleep."

I daydreamed that he was taking me scuba diving or snorkeling—or to a beach where I could see my feet in the water the way Mom had explained the Caribbean to me before we left Philadelphia. I fell asleep dreaming of seeing real fish in real Caribbean water that didn't look like a sewer.

Day Three: over. Day Three: junk, magic, and bullshit.

When Alleged Earl gets up and out of his alcove, he stretches and leaves his art supply box in the corner. He walks west and I follow him. He walks north and I follow him. On the corner of 18th and Market he stops and points at the sky and yells, "You're all going to die one day, you know! You're all wasting your time!" I note he is pointing in the direction of the skyscraper where Dad works.

Some guy walks by and says, "Oh, shut up." Alleged Earl says, "I'd kill you with a ripe peach and two green apples." The guy says, as he waits to cross the street, "You'd kill me with how bad you smell. Take pride in yourself, man. Get some fucking help." Before Alleged Earl has time to answer, the guy crosses the street and Earl takes an imaginary ripe peach and two imaginary green apples and throws them at the guy's back. He mutters, "Asshole," and continues west on Market.

His pace is faster than usual. Still slow, but not snail-slow. It makes me wonder why Alleged Earl walks so slowly every other day. Sometimes I don't even think he's really crazy. When he threw that imaginary fruit at the guy a minute before, he didn't really seem crazy-crazy. More like eccentric or bored with how everyone else acts. We have this in common. I couldn't be more bored with how everyone else acts.

Eventually, we cross the bridge and I see he's going to the train station. I can't imagine what business he has there, but I follow Alleged Earl to the train station.

Philadelphia's 30th Street Station has Corinthian columns. It has a portico. Architecture like this doesn't seem to belong here in the middle of the ugly tracks and graffiti on the concrete barriers between the tracks and the world. Homeless people don't belong here, either, so 30th Street Station is off-limits to Alleged Earl unless he has a ticket and he doesn't appear to have a ticket. He just looks inside and looks up and then smells the air as if there's something different in it here, over the bridge from Center City.

University City is not our turf. He is a homeless artist man. I am a high school near-dropout. He shuffles south to Chestnut Street and I walk at the same rhythm about twenty feet behind him. I wonder if he thinks I'm some crazy girl who has no purpose in life. I wonder if he's right. He stops on the corner of 32nd and Chestnut and pulls a piece of sidewalk chalk out of his coat pocket. He sits down on the sidewalk—right in the middle, blocking people's way to work or way to class—and he draws a chicken in one line without looking at the concrete canvas. It's like a blind chicken drawing except that there is no real chicken. He's drawing the chicken from memory in bright blue chalk. It's abstract, but I can tell it's a chicken so it's not abstract. He finishes with a rooster's comb on top. He makes it look like a headdress—as if the chicken's head is pouring out of itself. He takes a piece of cloth—an old T-shirt or a towel or something—out of another pocket and he spits at the chicken drawing and rubs his spit into the headdress and the feet, which look gnarly and rigid. He spits until his spit runs out and then he gets up and dances on the chicken. Moves his feet back and forth like the jitterbug. Waltzes around the chicken. He says, "Not today!" and continues up Chestnut. I stop and take a picture of the chicken drawing with my phone. I see brown-red in spots—the spots where he spat. I wonder if Alleged Earl is spitting blood. I wonder when he last saw a dentist or a doctor.

We get to 37th Street. He walks into a building marked INTERNATIONAL HOUSE. I stay outside because I don't know what International House is and don't want to be kicked out of a place I don't know about.

I go to the Wawa across the street and buy a bottle of water. I can't imagine how hot I'd be if I was covered in a bunch of blankets and coats. I buy a second bottle of water for Alleged Earl because maybe he'll need it. I sit in the shade under the awning of the Wawa and drink my water. Five minutes later, the manager comes out and says, "Move your business elsewhere."

Who talks like that? *Move your business elsewhere.*

Then I see Alleged Earl and a young man come out of International House together. The young man looks sharp. That's something Mom would say. *Sharp.* He's dressed just right in preppy University City student clothes. His hair is light brown and he's shaved and he's got the right haircut. He's smiling and Alleged Earl is talking to him and only now do I realize that Alleged Earl can laugh or even be nice. He's never said a word to people who give him money. Not a *thank you* or a *much obliged.* He throws imaginary fruit and spits. But here he is, smiling. Throwing his head back in laughter. He puts his blanket-wrapped arm around the young man and they walk back toward Center City. I didn't know anyone could be close to Earl— or that he'd ever let anyone in. Now that I see him walking and laughing and being close with this preppy guy, we have even less in common than we did a minute ago. Or, I'm more of a fraud than I thought I was. Or something.

They walk into a small café and I follow them. I buy a blueberry muffin and sit down at a table on the opposite side of the café. The muffin is dry so I open the bottle of water I bought for Alleged Earl.

I'm halfway into my muffin when I see the young man approaching. I expect to feel some sort of emotion—fear, excitement, anything—but I don't feel anything because I decide he must be walking toward someone else until he says, "Can I sit down?"

"Sure. I guess."

"My dad says you've been following him around."

"He's your dad?" I ask.

He nods.

Here is the son of an original idea. I have no idea what to say to him.

"He doesn't want my help, if that's what you're about to say."

"I wasn't going to say that."

"He wants you to stop following him."

"He's an original idea," I say. "I really admire him."

He doesn't smile. "Stop following him."

"I don't know," I say, which makes him pause. It makes me pause, too, because I want to talk to Alleged Earl. It's all I've wanted to do for days but I never do it and he's sitting in a café with me and his son is talking to me and he can answer so many of my questions right here and right now and—

I get up and leave the café. Maybe that's the most original thing I can do. Girl finally gets a chance to meet her idol but just gets up and walks away. Seems original enough. I try to think, as I walk back over the bridge to Center City, what next original thing I'm going to do.

I wish I could levitate.

I wish I could be Spain or Macedonia.

I wish I had a piece of sidewalk chalk in my pocket so I could draw a chicken on the corner of 17th and Spruce.

I catch a bus. I catch another bus.

I walk into my new school and I go to my seventh-period class, which I'm failing because I haven't been here in two weeks. As I sit in a broken three-legged chair and listen to my teacher talk about American politics, I can't help but see how unoriginal she is. She's taught the class for at least ten years. She needlepoints while we fill in worksheets or tests. Behind her is graffiti in six-foot-high multi-colored letters. HEED. That's what it says. HEED. A cockroach skitters across the dusty floor and into a pile of broken plasterboard.

When the teacher gives us a pop quiz on the week's work, I realize that I could be back in the café talking to Alleged Earl. I could be finding out if his name is really Earl. I could be discovering what college his son goes to. I could be hearing stories about art or form or color or what makes an original idea.

I take the quiz paper and I write this on it:

I have to stop following Alleged Earl. He's original, but following him isn't original. Tomorrow I will try something new. I don't know what yet. I hate this class. I'm going to get up and leave now.

I fold the paper and put it in my pocket. The teacher says, "Oh, hey, Sarah. I . . ."

That's all I hear. I'm down the hall before anyone can stop me. More graffiti. More piles of rotting plasterboard. The stairwell door windows are smashed into a million tiny pieces of safety glass, no longer safe. They glow green and blue and look like gems. I scoop up a handful of them and put them in my pocket. I don't notice that my hand is bleeding until I'm outside. On the street, some kids yell something at me but I don't hear them. I just see their mouths moving and their hands pointing. They're laughing at me.

I wish I had my umbrella. There is so much bullshit.

HELEN TAKES SHIT SHE DOESN'T DESERVE

Three times a month I have to go to meetings. Floor meetings, ER meetings, and charge nurse meetings. Because most people don't work the night shift, these meetings are scheduled at the stupidest times. Usually ten in the morning. So I work a seven-to-seven and then have to stay awake another three hours before the meeting starts and then I have to sit there while the day nurses in Snoopy scrubs eat doughnuts and talk about their kids and shit. Sometimes I put my head on the table and slowly bang it. Sometimes I say, "Has anyone else here been up since four yesterday afternoon?" Sometimes I fall asleep. Sometimes I just walk out.

Luckily, I'm liked. I do my job. My boss has asked me why I behave like this in meetings and I tell her that maybe next time the meeting should be scheduled for three a.m. I mean, at least once a month, that would make it fair.

She always says, "Three in the morning? I *sleep* at night!"

I've been doing this for too long not to know that nobody appreciates the night shift. Unless you personally have some shit go down at night, people could care less about the fact that some of us have to do this.

Chet and I have monthly meetings. We schedule them. We tried marriage counseling once. He lasted three appointments. Two and a half, really. He walked out in the middle of appointment number three because the therapist said he had anger issues, had to face those anger issues, and had to stop giving me shit I didn't deserve.

His solution to "shyster therapy" was monthly meetings.

We never solve anything at the monthly meetings. Every conversation with him is like talking to a person with no short-term memory. He forgets that ten seconds before, he was sorry. He forgets that ten seconds before *that*, he admitted to being wrong about something.

He makes excuses, manipulates, gaslights, and we end up yelling at each other every single time. In fact, I have no idea why I even show up anymore. If I can walk out at work, why not walk out of these? Usually, when the meeting ends, I feel completely alone in the world and I comfort myself with that fact that at least I have Sarah.

But this month, since Sarah left school, I realized that every single day that goes by with me playing my part in the deal and Chet playing his part in the deal is a step toward Sarah taking shit she doesn't deserve.

People pleasers make the best victims.

I see it all the time at work.

Tulum. Ancient Mayan ruins an hour away from our resort.

Mom gave Bruce the family camera and told him to be careful
with it. She gave him two hundred dollars in American money
and said, "Just in case." Bruce got his phone out of the safe and
programmed the hotel front desk's number into it and Dad reminded us that he and Mom had to use their romantic dinner
credits that night and were scheduled for a six-thirty sunset on
the beach with champagne.

The plan: A van would pick us up at seven thirty a.m. outside
the resort. We would drive an hour to Tulum. We would tour the
Tulum ruins and then swim in the crystal clear waters below the
cliffs there. The van would leave Tulum at one thirty, and we would
be back to the resort by two thirty p.m. to enjoy the rest of our day.

That was the plan.

That's not what happened.

The van picked us up and I was excited. I'd been reading the
brochure about Tulum at breakfast. Bruce and I had to rush eating
because the buffet only opened at seven. I ordered my omelet entirely in Spanish. *Jamón, queso y dos huevos por favor.* I only got to eat half
of it.

On the walk to the lobby, I assaulted Bruce with Tulum facts.
Tulum was the last Mayan city where people lived. It was a major
port for the area. Diseases brought by the Spanish probably killed
everybody there. It was built between 1400 and 1200 BC. At its

peak, 1,600 people lived there. One of the things traded there was obsidian. I didn't know what obsidian was, so I asked Bruce, but he was just walking fast and trying to find the Amstar representative so we wouldn't miss the van. So I kept saying the word over and over. *Obsidian. Obsidian. Obsidian.* It was a cool word.

We got in the van with six other people.

I was the only little kid, so I knew not to be annoying. Bruce and I sat in the back and there was barely any air-conditioning and it was hot and my seat belt was slashing across my neck because the seat was so low.

The driver started talking to us and telling us all about Tulum. I looked out the window as we drove from the safety of our resort and onto the main road south. It wasn't nearly as pretty outside of the resort. There were a lot of small towns where people hung their laundry on lines strung between buildings. We drove a stretch of road where it was nearly all jungle to the right and I wondered how many howler monkeys were growling there. The driver hit a bump in the road too fast and swore in Spanish and apologized. He said, "No matter how many times I drive this road, I forget this new bump!" The adults laughed. I readjusted my seat belt so it didn't cut into me the next time he did that.

Bruce looked down at me a few times during the drive and asked if I was okay by giving me a thumbs-up and raising his eyebrows. I returned the thumbs-up with a smile to let him know I was fine. Really I wanted to ask him about Mom and Dad getting divorced. But we were in the van—with other people. Probably not the right time.

The driver told us too many facts about Tulum. How fortified it was. How many buildings there were. Something about the Descending God or a diving god or something about a pyramid and then some words I didn't understand. I lost track of every sentence he said halfway through.

We hit another bump too fast. All of us bounced and a few of the adults said something to the driver. He apologized. He said something was wrong with the van. There was a scraping sound under me and Bruce. It had already been an hour since we left the resort, so I thought we were close, but we weren't. The driver said, when he pulled the van over to the side of the road, that we were still twenty minutes away.

He left all of us in the van and went outside to talk on his cell phone. He looked at all four tires and then he leaned over and looked under the van and talked faster into his cell phone.

He got louder. He said, "Okay, okay!" and then he hung up.

"Ladies and gentlemen, we will have to be patient. Our vehicle has had some problem. Help is on the way!"

Adults up front complained. *We need to be back by two thirty! I paid money for this trip! Can't you fix it yourself?* Bruce and I stayed quiet but it was getting so hot in the van that I asked if I could get out, and when I did, all the others wanted to get out of the van, too.

One guy, who we learned was from Michigan, made a joke about how our trip to see ruins was ruined. Nobody laughed.

There was no shade on the side of the road. It felt like 110 degrees and Bruce helped me put sunblock on my shoulders and my back. I had a hat on but I put some on my face just in case. Every Tulum tourist van that drove by after that beeped at us, but they didn't stop to help us.

The driver opened the back doors of the van and handed us each a bottle of water. It was hot. Mom always told Bruce and me not to drink hot water out of plastic bottles, but we figured if there was a time to do it, that was it. I don't know how much time passed before a van finally stopped.

The driver pulled in behind us and I noticed there were already people in his van. Too many for us to fit in with them. I asked Bruce what time it was and he checked his phone and said it was almost eleven thirty.

"Eleven thirty?"

This one guy kept badgering the driver about getting his money back. The driver was too busy talking to the other van driver to answer. They seemed to be figuring out a plan. I tried to follow in Spanish, but I knew *un pocito español*.

I knew what *autobús* meant. I knew it meant a bus. I told Bruce a bus was coming to pick us up.

That's also not what happened.

The van driver told us to get our things out of the van and crossed the road with us all in tow—he held one of my hands and Bruce held the other. He said we would catch a bus. We had to walk about ten minutes in the midday sun to get to the bus stop. Every adult with us, Bruce included, was soaked from sweat. It was past noon. The bus was due any minute. The driver said we would all get a refund, he was very sorry, and we could try to see Tulum again tomorrow.

The Michigan man made his ruined ruin adventure joke again and this time people laughed.

It was a public bus and the van driver took care of our fares. It was crowded and didn't have air-conditioning but the windows were open.

The people on the *autobús* stared at us. Some smiled, but not that many. Most of them glared because the Michigan guy was talking so loud and the complaining guy complained about the *autobús* and wasting a morning of his vacation and I realized that we were the annoying American tourists that give annoying American tourists their reputation. Stupid jokes, expecting luxury, loud—all while riding on a public bus with people who were probably going to work to wash American tourists' sheets and towels or something. The glares made me uncomfortable, but I got to see a part of Mexico that Mom and Dad would never see from their perfectly lined-up chairs over the rims of their never-ending drinks. I got to see a man spit out the window of an *autobús*. I got to see a woman hand-sewing the hem of a baby's white dress. I got to see the driver let a man onto the bus who didn't have enough pesos to cover the fare.

We got back at three. The bus had stopped what seemed like one hundred times. So much for Tulum. So much for seeing pyramids and cliffs and the real Caribbean sea—crystal clear and turquoise.

Bruce said, as we walked into the lobby, "I'm so sorry, Sarah."

"Wasn't your fault."

"I'm going to be in so much trouble."

"You didn't make the van break down," I said. I said it snippy, though. I was tired and hungry. I wanted to talk all day to Bruce about Mom and Dad and divorce. "Can we go eat something?"

"I have to tell them we're back. Mom's probably worried."

We found them on the beach. Under a thatched umbrella, drinking today's drink of the day, a Sea Horse. Mom said, "Back already!"

Bruce and I decided, right then, with a look between us, to pretend that everything had gone just right.

"How was it?" Dad asked.

I said, "It was awesome! But I'm starving, so we're going to go and grab something from the snack shack."

Snack shack. Fried chicken nuggets and hot dogs. I knew this wasn't real. I didn't see one *snack shack* in my two hours on the *autobús*. After being in the real world from seven thirty a.m. to three p.m., I knew the resort was just a lie.

After we ate, we went back to the room and Bruce had a shower because he smelled pretty bad. I sat out on the balcony and watched Mom and Dad on the beach. They just sat under that umbrella and drank and drank and Mom read a book and Dad had a nap and they never went near the water. Day Four and I bet they hadn't even noticed the seaweed. I looked out to sea and asked the sea god to help us. I wasn't specific. There was no need. We needed help in every department, as far as I was concerned.

Later, after the dinner buffet, Bruce and I sat on the balcony covered in Mexican bug spray. I didn't know what to say to him so I did a lot of math while Mom and Dad were fake-loving each other in the tent below, having the romantic dinner they earned for sitting through the vacation club presentation.

The math was coming to me. If Mom and Dad hadn't slept in the same bed since Bruce was eight and I was born when Bruce was nine, then that means they stayed together for an extra year and then—

"I'm an accident!" I said to Bruce.

"Join the club," he said.

"But I'm a *real* accident," I said. "They didn't even want to be married at all by the time I showed up."

"It feels the same. Trust me."

More math. They were married a year before they had Bruce. They stopped loving each other before Bruce was eight. That's maybe seven years they might have been happy. They had me at least two years after they were unhappy and now they're married twenty years. Seven happy years. Thirteen unhappy years.

"How do you know they're getting divorced?" I asked him.

"They told me. I thought they told you, too," he said. "They said they were going to this time."

"It's okay," I said. "I'd rather know than not know."

"They were supposed to tell you," he said.

"It's pretty obvious they hate each other," I said.

"True."

"Last week I heard Dad call Mom the c word."

"They think they're being quiet," he said.

"I snoop."

"You don't snoop. You just live in the same house. They thought I didn't hear it either until I was fifteen and finally said something."

"What'd you say?"

"I was mad because they wouldn't let me try out for a play at that teen theater thing they run over at Arden," he said. "I think I said something like *Just because you two are so busy calling each other asshole every night doesn't mean I have to stay here and listen!*"

"You'd think Mom would say *anus*," I said.

Bruce spat out his mouthful of beer and we both cracked up for about a minute. I think our day surviving the trip-not-trip to Tulum was getting to us because this was an obvious point. Mom would call an asshole an anus.

We used a bottle of water to clean the beer off the balcony tiles. We looked down at the tent set up on the beach where Mom and Dad were eating their pretend-romantic dinner. The resort made a big deal out of these romantic dinners—warm, dim lighting, rose petals strewn around the tent, romantic Mexican music. I wondered if Mom and Dad were trying to figure out what the lyrics to the songs were. Mom speaks a little Spanish because of her job. Dad thinks *bandadigo* means "fantastic" because some guy once told him it did, but he never checked so he says it thinking he's speaking Spanish, but he's not. He's speaking a language one of his frat brothers made up in college.

I said, "What do you think the lyrics are to the song that's playing down there?"

Bruce said, "I can't really hear it."

"No. I mean made-up lyrics. Like, *You're an asshole and I should have never had kids with you.* Stuff like that."

"Oh," Bruce said. "How about, *You're just a bitch because you're on your period and you don't realize it's a medical condition.*"

"Oh, I have one. *One day you're going to realize that I'm a really great guy and you'll stop nagging me all the time.*"

"Great guy, my ass," Bruce said. "How about, *You're a dumb prick and I hate you.*"

"I've heard that song before," I say.

By the time I was sixteen, I'd forget this moment. But then I'd remember it again. And everything would change.

What happens for the next six days is nothing new. What happens for the next six days is unoriginal. I don't want to see ten-year-old Sarah because she wants to talk about Mexico and I don't want to talk about Mexico because Mexico wasn't original. I stay away from Alleged Earl's street because I don't want to see Alleged Earl because he's an original idea and I don't want my dullness to rub off on him. That happens, you know. That happens to people.

One minute you have a guy and he's full of energy and spark and he's ready to take on life and then the next thing you know he meets another guy who likes to sit at home and watch football games and drink beer or something. Then his spark just gets smaller and smaller until he's the same as the other guy. Happens all the time.

On Tuesday morning I leave the house before Dad even gets up. I see the sunrise. I see all the people rushing to work. I see a college girl walking along singing to the music in her ears that no one else can hear. She has a nice singing voice. I see people coming out of the subway stations and I see people running down into them. Subway stations are mysterious from street level. It's as if thousands of people just disappear down there every day. I decide that subway stations are like portals. You leave at eight in the morning, you arrive back at five thirty in the evening in the same clothes, with the same briefcase. It would be a lot cooler if the subway portals took people somewhere original, though, instead of just to work.

I decide not to think about art for a week. I decide art is futile. I decide there are better things than art. I decide not to take any buses for a week. I decide that if I want to go somewhere, I will walk.

On Tuesday, I decide to walk to the Liberty Bell.

The Liberty Bell is at Independence Mall. It's a state park, but it's not a park. It's just another part of the same city I live in. I stand in line and when I get to the room with the Liberty Bell in it, I learn all the things I learned the last time I was here. The crack. The repair. The second crack that ruined the bell for good. The inscription. What it's made of, who made it, and when.

Did you know that no one living today has actually heard the Liberty Bell ring?

I think that's a metaphor for something, but I'm not sure what.

I have to stop my brain from thinking about it because metaphor is art.

I notice the groups of schoolchildren. Some can't stand still. Most aren't listening. Some are trying to reach in and touch the bell and they know it's not allowed but they do it anyway until a chaperone stops them. None of this is original, but I can't figure out what's so important about being original right now. Who cares?

I can't stop my brain from thinking about art. I watch the kids and think: *Those kids are art.*

I think: *That bell is art. It's on display like art and it's viewed by millions like art and it's a symbol of something artistic. Freedom. Freedom is artistic.*

For lunch, I stand by a trash can and wait for someone to throw food away. It only takes a half hour for some tourist guy to buy a vendor hot dog and take a bite, then toss it away. I wait for him to round the corner and I lean in and pull the hot dog out. He put mustard on it and I hate mustard, but I wipe it away with the napkin and then I eat the hot dog by the side of the trash can.

The hot dog is art. The napkin with the mustard all over it is art. The trash can is art.

Outside Dunkin' Donuts, a woman tosses in a bag with half a cruller still in it. It's the nicest doughnut I ever ate even though it had her lipstick smeared on one side of it.

I don't know why I'm doing this. I have money in my wallet. Five bucks. I have a SEPTA pass that could put me on any bus, subway, or trolley in the city. Instead, I hang around tourist areas and eat food out of trash cans.

I think I'm trying to become Alleged Earl.

Which is stupid. I am a boring middle-class girl who has a house and a bed and a favorite umbrella.

But on Tuesday, I learn that other people's food tastes especially nice. That and the thing about the Liberty Bell never being heard by anyone living today. You can learn things by just walking around and listening. Mom asks about dinner with my friend and I tell her my friend is sick. She says, "Maybe next Tuesday, then."

Wednesday I leave for school because Dad wakes me up and makes me pretend. He stands at the door and tells me to have a nice day and to keep our deal and Mom is still asleep even though she didn't work last night, and before I leave, I pack my backpack full of every piece of sidewalk chalk we have.

And I go.

I stop at the food cart where they sell the best breakfast sandwiches. The woman's smile is art. The way she pronounces *oregano*. The way her husband fries the egg so it fits the roll, the way he places the ham and cheese on top—the way he folds it once the cheese is melted, the way he scoops the whole thing up and lays it on the roll is art.

I walk to the corner of South and 4th and I watch the tourists try to figure out which cheesesteak place to go to. Pat's or Jim's? That's the question. That's always the question. Truth is, the difference between these two cheesesteaks is so large that you should try them both. Everyone has an opinion about which one is the most authentic but what does authentic have to do with anything anymore?

Cheesesteaks are art. Some art is Rembrandt. Some art is Rothko.

I find a place on the sidewalk to doodle with my chalk. I'm still in yesterday's clothes. Some people throw me a quarter around noon. They just toss it like I'm a fountain and they made a wish.

Here's what I decide they wished: They wished they knew which cheesesteak place was the right one.

If they would have asked, I would have told their fortune. *Beware of any cheesesteak with bright orange liquid cheese.*

I draw nothing. Just big blobs of color. Nothing comes to me. Did you ever see those people who draw those 3-D masterpieces with sidewalk chalk? I want to draw that. But I don't know how to draw that. I don't even know where to start. So I just rub the chalk against the sidewalk and I make dust. This doesn't feel like art—probably because I'm not enjoying myself at all. At least the breakfast sandwich couple love what they do. Or maybe they have to. Or something. Either way, this doesn't feel like art and I don't care. I am relieved that I've gotten it out of my system. Pesky art. Who needs it?

At dinner, Mom and Dad notice I'm still wearing the same clothing I've had on since Monday. Mom says something about my washing my hair. Dad says that my shirt is filthy and points at the chalk markings on my jeans.

No one asks me where I was all day.

Mom and Dad both look exhausted like they do sometimes. It's not work exhaustion. It's something else. They have exhausted each other. This is clear because they don't make eye contact. Maybe it was one of those parental meetings they do. I assume it's where they make those parental *deals*. From here it looks like they spent the whole day at the tilt, wearing hundreds of pounds of armor and racing toward each other on horseback. If I was to guess the outcome, Dad won.

Thursday and Friday I walk up Broad Street as far as I can and I sing. I sing anything. I sing "Jingle Bells" even though it's May. I sing nursery rhymes. I sing songs I learned to sing when I still took piano lessons.

No one on Broad Street says anything to me. But I'm not listening so it's not like I'd hear it anyway. By Friday afternoon, I think I might have gone crazy. I am not the Sarah I used to be. I am a different Sarah. I don't hear people anymore. I hear birds. I try to figure out what the pigeons are cooing to each other. I eat out of trash cans even though I have five dollars in my wallet. I walk even though I have a SEPTA pass.

I don't care about the pear I couldn't draw. I don't care about Bruce. I don't care about Mexico. I don't care if I stay this way forever.

I wanted to go to my new school one more day this week, but I didn't manage to get there. I have no idea what I'm doing and I don't know why I'm doing it. Part of me wants to stand naked in the middle of Broad Street with pineapple stuffing rubbed all over me while throwing imaginary vegetables at people. Another part of me wants to climb to the top of Liberty One and yodel until my throat bleeds.

I should probably see a psychologist.

I'm halfway home on Friday afternoon when I see a little girl with a dog. I'm too tired to follow them, but I want to follow them because I can't figure out why a girl this young would be allowed out alone with her dog in this part of town.

Maybe I don't understand the neighborhood. Maybe I don't understand the dog. Maybe I don't understand the girl.

Something about the girl is original.

Something about the dog is original.

I ask the girl, "What is art?" and she says, "Art is what you believe no matter what other people think." I grunt at this. I yell, "I don't give a fucking tangerine what you think, girl! You think I'm out here trying to make friends?"

She and her dog recoil, and I try to figure out why I just yelled at her.

I think I might have become Alleged Earl even though Alleged Earl doesn't want me to follow him anymore.

I think I care about art even though I don't want to. I can't get away from myself.

I see ten-year-old Sarah just outside City Hall. I wave to her but she doesn't see me. She's talking to another girl her age. I'm happy she's made a friend. Her friend looks like Carmen did when we were ten.

I think about Carmen and how much I miss her. I don't miss her much. I don't miss anything much. I think this is a side effect of whatever is happening to me.

Carmen knows about the something in "Did something happen at school?"

She's the only one who understands what's inside a tornado.

She's the only one who understands that what's inside me and what's inside everyone who ever wanted to be an artist is a tornado. She seems okay with Miss Smith's idea about no one having original ideas. I don't know how she does it.

She is immune to discouragement.

I stop outside of City Hall and pull out a piece of sidewalk chalk. I draw an enormous tornado. Swirls and swirls of dust and debris. I walk three big steps at the top of the tornado—it's ten feet wide at the top. The only color chalk I have is sky blue and it's a sky-blue tornado and inside the tornado is everything that ever mattered to me and everything that ever mattered to you and every tourist and every Liberty Bell and every hot dog with mustard and every cheesesteak and every song I ever sang and every pigeon that ever cooed. They are all inside my tornado. I don't notice anyone watching me. No one stops to care. No one asks me to stop but if they did I probably wouldn't hear them anyway because I am still deaf to everyone except art—art that doesn't matter. This tornado doesn't matter. Not even with the skin from my index-finger knuckle in it. Not even with the sweat that dripped from my nose.

Then I turn around, City Hall at my back, and face the art museum down at the other end of the parkway and I yodel the best yodel I can as loud as I can. I sound like a bad imitation of Tarzan. If yodeling is art, I suck at it. I take my sucky yodel, put it inside my sky-blue tornado, and start walking home.

I can smell myself. I am so many days old I can smell more than just my sweat, I can smell my own five-day-old dirt. Dirt *is* art.

When I get home, Mom is already at work and Dad is downstairs on the couch watching TV. He says something to me as I walk to the kitchen but I don't hear anything.

I see his mouth move, but I don't hear him at all.

His frown is big.

He makes an animated smile and points to it.

I realize he's telling me to smile.

As if smiling would make my tornado go away. As if what's on the surface matters. That's what Carmen taught me. That's what her tornadoes have always been about.

I smile and I get myself a bowl of Cheerios.

I take it back to my room and smile on my way through the living room and I go to sleep with my five-day-old dirt and I don't feel like art.

When I wake up on Saturday, Mom is heading to bed after her long night. I decide to paint my bedroom. The color in here is awful. It's the worst green anyone ever imagined. No wonder I couldn't draw the pear. I live inside of bile. It's taken its toll.

I look on the computer for nicer colors and I find the perfect one. Vanilla Milkshake. It's not quite white, and not quite yellow or brown. It's warm. But it's a milk shake so it's cold.

That's what color I paint my room.

I move all of my furniture into the center of the floor. I lie on my bed and start by staring into the southeast corner and I see myself on a step stool with a paint roller. *This is too fake.* I go to the hall closet and get the step stool and bring it to my room and I stand on it and roll my imaginary roller into the Vanilla Milkshake pan and then roll it onto the wall. I work my way around the room counterclockwise. Floor to ceiling. When I'm done I sit on my bed and I can see the truth: The truth is that you can't paint over bile in just one coat.

I take a pretend nap and then when I wake up I decide the whole room is dry and I can put a second coat on. A Sarah is sitting on the end of my bed. She's older.

"Forty," she says.

"Oh," I say. "Hi."

"Do you want to talk about what happened in school?"

"No."

"I know you walked in on Miss Smith kissing Vicky."

"So?"

"So you can't paint over that," she says.

I think I can. I think I can paint over what I saw and unsee it and not tell anyone. I think I have to.

"You're afraid to say anything because it would be your word against theirs?" she asks.

"You're me. You know."

"Well, you're wrong. And she should be fired. Trust me. Vicky isn't the first or the last one."

I stop and stare at her. She's calm. Soft around the edges. She's nice and not here to mock me like twenty-three-year-old Sarah. This Sarah looks like she could draw a thousand pears. She doesn't care about how cool her shoes are because she's wearing beat-up hiking shoes. She's telling me information about Miss Smith from the future. I think about how helpful it would have been had she brought lottery numbers instead.

"I don't want to get involved," I say.

"How much nasty shit has happened because people don't want to get involved?"

"Mom and Dad would kill me."

"Mom would respect you. Dad doesn't matter."

She's still calm. I don't know what to say. "How did you get in here?"

She gets up and opens the side window and climbs down the fire escape.

I look back at my ugly green walls and decide a second coat is needed. This time I work clockwise, and by the time night falls and Mom is awake again, I have painted my whole room. I have rid myself of the bile.

In my head, I now live inside a vanilla milk shake.

I put on new clothes on top of my five-day-old dirty self. I decide I am not going crazy. I do not need a psychologist. I decide I am an artist inside of a tornado that will not let me go.

Six days have passed. I still don't want to see ten-year-old Sarah. I still don't want to talk about Mexico. I want to do something fun, but I have no idea what fun is. I am the dull person who rubbed off on me. That can happen, you know.

I leave the house through the back door.

Dad would flip out if he knew I was walking by myself up 17th Street at midnight. *This is art.* I don't even bring my pepper spray. I didn't bring my phone or wallet. Mom is patching people back together again twenty blocks from here. It's a Saturday and the ER is probably busy. I walk to Rittenhouse Square and sit on a bench. I decide to sleep here tonight.

I find a good bench—well lit but out of the way. I lie down and try to sleep but every footstep I hear makes me open one eye.

I take a deep breath and then I take another one on top of it, and then another. I think: *If my lungs burst, I won't be able to tell anyone about Miss Smith and Vicky.* I think: *If my lungs burst, I won't ever have to tell anyone about the headpiece and how I found it and how it made me cry.*

I hear people walking in the park and talking to each other. I hope they don't see me, so I become invisible. I blend into the park bench. Very quiet. Blend. Disappear.

While I'm gone, this is what happens: I remember the fighting.

I see Bruce standing at the edge of the water in Mexico. I see him throwing something into the water. *Art.*

When I open my eyes, it's light, but it's still night.

My face is sweating. I want to sleep but I can't sleep.

I'm in Rittenhouse Square and this is not the place to sleep. When I sit up, I see ten-year-old Sarah standing next to my bench. She says, "Sarah?"

I move over and she sits next to me. There's a college girl sitting cross-legged on the grass across from us. She's looking right at us, a huge grin on her face. Ten-year-old Sarah says, "She's been here for an hour. She keeps looking at her hands and giggling."

I watch the college girl and she doesn't seem original. She's high on something—probably something psychedelic. Giggling at one's own hands is a dead giveaway.

The art club takes LSD. They do it and go to Great Adventure and ride the Kingda Ka—the fastest roller coaster in New Jersey and forty-five stories high. They could be lying but that's what they tell me. Sometimes they drop acid in school, too. Carmen is their weed connection. That's why they keep her around. Carmen doesn't know this. Carmen thinks she fits in, but she doesn't fit in because she's not like the others. Up until now you thought they were just normal art-snob teenagers in high school who steal my ideas. That's because I tell the truth slowly. I think that's how the truth shows up sometimes. Slowly.

I'm sitting in Rittenhouse Square watching a college girl laugh at her hands. I think about my hands. My blind drawings. I wonder if I could draw my hand without looking at the paper or my hand, the way Alleged Earl drew his chicken in University City. I dig in my jacket pocket and there's a small lump of sky-blue sidewalk chalk left. I kneel down onto the brick paving and I start to draw my hand from memory. It's hard to draw on brick pavers, but I go slowly. I keep breathing. In. Out. I hear the college girl giggling. I hear ten-year-old Sarah trying to get my attention, but I ignore her. I keep the image of my hand in my head and my eyes closed and I finish with my thumb and the curve to my wrist and, when I open my eyes, I see a disfigured sky-blue hand.

The college girl comes over to look at what I've drawn. She says, "It's beautiful!"

Ten-year-old Sarah is angry. She's saying, "Listen to me! Goddammit, listen to me!"

The college girl walks down the path toward the frog statue and all I have is ten-year-old Sarah. She says, "What the fuck happened to you?"

I'm not saying anything. My mouth is open. I close it. My eyes are open. I close them. I lie back down. I make myself invisible to ten-year-old Sarah. I don't want her to see me like this. She's ten. She'll think I'm crazy.

She says, "What *are* you?"

I ask myself what I am.

What are you?

I am a human being. I am sixteen years old.

That's it. That's all I have. I don't have any other answers. I am a human being. I am sixteen years old.

I think it's a good start.

I get up and leave ten-year-old Sarah on the bench.

I walk sixteen blocks to Mom's hospital. Past a bunch of people who say hello or don't, and I don't know what to say back so I just say nothing and pretend I'm listening to music in a pair of invisible earbuds. I am good at imagining. I hear the music. It's like nothing I ever heard before. It's traffic and doors opening and closing and it's a siren in the distance and it's got a slow rhythm that is my breathing in and out. In and out.

I don't go into the hospital. I just sit outside in the well-lit parking area near the ER. Being closer to Mom should make me feel safe. Because I don't have my wallet, if I was found right now, I'd be a Jane Doe. Except Mom would recognize me even if I don't.

I am a human being. I am sixteen years old.

That should be enough.

An ambulance comes into the ER bay with its lights on and its siren off. The lights are mesmerizing. Red, blue. Red, blue. Red, blue. It's like light-art. It's the kind of light-art that stops you in the museum and makes your heart beat faster. People move around quickly. I can't see what's going on, but I don't want to.

I wanted to be an artist once. Now I just want to be a human being and be sixteen years old.

I can't see anything wrong with this.

I can't see anything sad about it.

"Sarah?"

It's ten-year-old Sarah.

"I want to walk you home," she says.

I don't know what time it is, but it's too late for a ten-year-old girl to be walking around Philadelphia.

"It's late," I say.

"I want to walk you home," she says again.

We hold hands like sisters and she walks me back to Market, back over the bridge, down through the park, and onto 17th. She doesn't say anything to me. When we get to the front door, she whispers, "I'll see you tomorrow." She doesn't even look me in the eye. When I watch her walk east down Lombard, I can feel her shame. She thinks I'm a loser. She thinks I have shitty hair and no plans and no idea what happened in Mexico.

I stand there.

I am a human being. I am sixteen years old.

I miss my brother.

That should be enough.

132

MEXICO—*Day Four II: The Whole Sky*

Mom and Dad returned to the hotel room after the romantic dinner, and Bruce asked if we could take a walk on the beach.

It was a clear night but we didn't recognize any constellations. We were always looking for constellations because stars are individuals in Philadelphia. It's not like we could look up and see the Big Dipper or Orion or Cassiopeia from anywhere—not even the top of the Liberty Two skyscraper. Not unless there was some sort of blackout, I guess. I wouldn't know. I've never seen a blackout.

Bruce learned about constellations when he was young. He said, "That's the Big Dipper. Or the bear. *Ursa*. That's *bear* in Latin." He squinted around the sky as if he'd lost his dog. "I can't find any others that I know."

"They're pretty," I said.

We sat in the sand near the water and I looked out and saw lights on far out boats.

He said, "If you lie back and look at the whole sky at once, you'll probably see a shooting star. They happen all the time."

"People never see shooting stars."

"That's because they aren't looking," he said. "I'm serious. You'll see one if you look."

I lay back and tried to look at the sky all at once, like he said. He was already lying down, so now we were just two siblings lying in the sand in Mexico on a cloudless night trying to *see the whole sky* and not talking about Mom and Dad getting a divorce.

"Why's Dad so mad at you?" I asked.

"I don't know," Bruce said.

"You know and you think I'm too young to talk about it with me," I said.

Bruce pointed to the sky and said, "Oh! Look! Did you see that one?"

"Shit," I said. "I was looking that way."

"See the whole sky," he said. "Don't focus."

"So why's Dad so mad at you?"

"Dad was always mad at me," he said. "I wasn't the son he wanted."

"What kind of son did he want?"

"I don't know."

I didn't know shooting stars flew so far and so fast. It seemed to last forever and then disappear as if I were imagining it. I gasped and both Bruce and I pointed to it as it traveled from the right-hand corner of our view to the left—all the way across the sky.

Seeing it with Bruce made it real.

"You didn't write me any letters," I said to him. "I liked when you called, but you said you'd write me letters."

"Yeah. I didn't know college was going to be so busy. I'll write you some next year."

Another shooting star.

Bruce was right. It's not that hard to see a shooting star. I'd just seen two in under a minute.

"I'm not coming back next summer," Bruce said. "I'm transferring to another college. Farther away."

"How far away?"

"All the way," he said. We both laughed. "Oregon."

I was relieved. Oregon wasn't so far. "There are direct flights from Philadelphia to Portland," I said.

"How do you know so much when you're ten?"

"I snoop," I said. "And I listen to you because you're smart. And Mom and Dad say stuff right in front of me sometimes because they think I'm thinking about My Little Pony, but I don't really like My Little Pony. And anyway, Salem is the capital of Oregon, not Portland. I'm telling you that so you don't embarrass yourself."

"Don't be a show-off."

I beat Bruce in the capital game every time we played it. He never learned his capitals or his eleven and twelve times tables because his third-grade teacher only believed in states and multiplication up to ten.

Another shooting star. And another.

"Are we out here because Mom and Dad are having sex or something?" I asked.

"I doubt it."

"They're probably fighting or watching TV," I say.

"Do you want to go back in?"

"I'm a little cold."

Bruce handed me his sweatshirt. "I worry about you, Sarah."

Another shooting star, but I only caught a glimpse because I was putting Bruce's sweatshirt on.

"Growing up around Dad," he said. "I mean, and the stuff that's on TV. And the Internet. Not all boys are that bad, okay?"

"Dad's not bad," I said.

"Dad is typical," he said. "I don't want you to end up with some typical guy."

"I know the state capitals and the twelve times tables," I said. "I'm ten. I don't even want to get married."

Day Four: over. Day Four: ruined ruins, lied lies, and shooting stars.

135

I don't sleep. I dream while I'm awake, but my eyes are closed. I am Lichtenstein's sleeping girl. I am a series of dots. I am my own constellation. Sarah—the big question mark.

I dream about Carmen's tornadoes. I dream about all the things I've ever heard when I stand in random places. I dream about all the things I've seen that I wasn't supposed to see. I dream of nothing and everything all at the same time and they cancel each other out. My dots get all mixed up. I am Lichtenstein's mixed-up sleeping not-sleeping girl.

And then suddenly, I wake up, the sun is up, I know I slept, my body aches, my head is fuzzy. My room is not a vanilla milk shake. My room is still the ugliest green ever invented.

I remember the sky-blue hand I drew in Rittenhouse Square.

I remember sitting in the hospital parking lot in the middle of the night.

I remember ten-year-old Sarah walking me home.

I remember Mexico. Parts of it. Enough of it. I remember what I need to remember.

I want to call Bruce but I text him instead. I pull out the scrap of paper from my wallet and enter his number into my contacts. I don't put his name on the contact; just the letter B.

I want to call you later. Will you be home? This is Sarah.

I get a reply almost instantly.

I'm home all day. Please call.

I've never had a more invigorating shower. It feels like I was reborn last night. Like staying up all night changed me. I feel like I am more than I was. I feel like I am less than I was. It's very hard to explain.

Everything fell apart a month ago.

Over silliness and drama. Over something so stupid.

But who's to say what's stupid and what's not stupid when your life falls apart? Some people fall apart over TV shows. Some people fall apart over a breakup. Some people fall apart over someone eating the last bowl of Apple Jacks. I fell apart because of the annual art show. No one noticed I was falling apart before then.

I stay in the shower for a long time—enough time to get the week's dirt off me. I think about asking Mom to find me a therapist or something. I can't talk to anyone about anything. I can't talk to Carmen because she's the weed connection. I can't talk to Dad because he doesn't mind the sliver of tissue stuck to the TV. I can't talk to Mom because she wants us to have fun now. I can't talk to anyone in school because I don't go there anymore. I wanted to talk to Alleged Earl, but I lost my chance, and if I would have taken the chance I would have asked him all the wrong questions anyway.

Bruce.

Maybe I can talk to Bruce.

I decide it's best to talk to him outside of the house.

Dad isn't around when I go downstairs. Mom is just stirring after her night shift and I hope I didn't use all the hot water.

I walk out the door and to Rittenhouse Square. I sit on my bench—the one with the disfigured hand drawn in front of it.

I watch a bunch of kids who are my age walk the path up the middle of the park. They are a pack. Boyfriends and girlfriends. Holding hands. Giggling. Having fun. Too young to be like the college girl in the park last night. Too old to need supervision. I hear one of them mention a movie. I decide they've just gone to see it. I decide they've all been friends since primary school. I decide that they will all be at one another's funerals. They have something I don't have.

It's not as simple as the art club fissure or the shit Miss Smith did to Vicky. It's not about the art show even though it is about the art show.

It's about lies and trust.

I've never had a boyfriend. I've never wanted a boyfriend. Or a girlfriend for that matter. Bruce had it all wrong in Mexico. I won't end up with a typical guy because I'm not going to end up with anybody. Since I can remember, I wanted to live alone and make art. Selfishly. I wanted to make art and not care about anything or anyone else. I know this is abnormal for a sixteen-year-old human being.

I'm supposed to be like them.

I don't trust anyone. Not even myself.

I dial Bruce. It doesn't ring even once.

"Sarah?"

"Hi, Bruce."

"Oh my God, Sarah," he says. And then I can hear him crying— not sobbing because Mom and Dad never taught us how to sob. But he's emotional.

"Hi," I say, because I can't figure out anything else to say.

He sniffles. "Hi."

I decide not to dawdle.

"Did you ever get your degree in psychology?"

"Not quite," he says.

"Oh."

"Are you really a religious freak?" I ask.

"A what?"

"Did you get naked in a river and get baptized?"

"Holy shit," Bruce says.

"Did you?"

"They brainwashed you."

"But did you?"

"To my knowledge, I have never been baptized in a river. Or anywhere."

"Huh," I say. "So I guess the only thing I know about you is that you're a crappy kayaker."

"And an awesome big brother."

"You haven't called me in six years."

He sniffles again.

"Sorry," I say. "I didn't mean it like that."

"Let me talk," he says. So I shut up. But he doesn't say anything.

"Bruce?"

"I should come visit."

"You should call Mom and Dad."

"Not them. You."

"We live in the same house."

"I can stay in the B&B."

"What B&B?"

"I always stay in the one on Pine."

I'm not computing anything Bruce is saying. When has he stayed at the B&B on Pine? "Why don't we start over?" I say. "Why don't I say *How are you?* and then you tell me how you are?"

"Okay."

"How are you?"

"I'm good. Life is good. How are you?"

"That's not an answer. Good? Life is good?" Six years have passed and I get *Life is good*. His voice sounds deeper than it used to. He sounds grown-up. I say, "Are you married? Do you have a girlfriend? A job? What are you doing out there?"

"Not married. I work with kids."

"You're a teacher?"

"I'm a mentor."

This sounds promising. I wait for more, but he doesn't say more. He asks, "What about you? Tenth grade now? Am I right?"

"Yeah. But kinda no. It's a long story."

We are vague. Ten-year-old Sarah would be disappointed. Ten-year-old Sarah likes details. Ten-year-old Sarah will probably never come around anymore because I was so rude to her last night.

"What?" Bruce said. "You're not in tenth grade?"

"It's a long story," I say again.

"I have time."

"I'm only figuring it out," I say. "I'm in some sort of . . . transition or something."

"In school?"

I don't know what to say. Here is a brother I haven't talked to in six years. Now he wants me to tell him how I'm doing when I don't know how I'm doing.

"Do you come back to Philly and not tell us?"

"Kind of," he says. "I came back twice."

"And?"

"And the first time I called Mom, but she said Dad didn't want me in the house," he says. "The second time was for business. I didn't tell them I was there."

"But I miss you."

"I miss you, too."

"What kind of kids do you work with?"

"Mostly at-risk kids. Kids who are messed up."

"Like delinquents or what?"

"All of that. And runaways and kids in the system and orphans and kids who are just bored and don't have much to do. The whole gamut."

"Is that Bruce?" ten-year-old Sarah says. She's appeared next to me on the bench.

"Shhh." I'm elated to see her.

Bruce says, "Are you talking to someone?"

How do I explain this?

I say, "I think I'm an at-risk kid."

"Oh."

"I stopped going to school. Now I'm just walking around most days."

"Do Mom and Dad know?"

"Yeah."

"Is that Bruce?" ten-year-old Sarah asks again.

"Who is that?" Bruce asks.

"My friend from around the corner," I lie. I turn to ten-year-old Sarah and say, "Yes, now quiet."

"Are they freaking out over you not going to school?"

"Yeah. And no. It's weird."

"Are you failing or something?"

"No."

"How was your birthday?"

What a strange question. My birthday was in March. It's May. Maybe Bruce is so far away now that those dates seem closer together to him.

"It was fine," I say.

"Sweet sixteen," he says.

"That's the most unoriginal thing you ever said," I say.

This was probably the wrong day to call Bruce.

The Movies

I said I'd call him back tomorrow. I nearly told him I was having an existential crisis, but it didn't seem fair to him. He's in Oregon and a stranger now. I'm in Philly and a stranger now, too.

Ten-year-old Sarah asks, "Wanna go find Earl?"

"I don't follow Earl anymore." I don't tell her that I think I've become Earl.

"Okay."

"I think I need a nap."

"You *were* up all night," she says.

"Do you want to come to dinner this week?" I ask.

"That's weird."

"Mom says we're having tacos."

"I love tacos."

"I know. I'm you."

"You don't know who you are," she says.

We walk back home and ten-year-old Sarah asks me how Bruce is. I tell her I'll know more tomorrow. It's getting near twilight and I feel like last night made me lose a day. Ten-year-old Sarah says she wants to come in and I let her come in because I know Mom will be working and Dad didn't recognize her last time.

Mom is there when we walk in. She doesn't look at first. Just says, "Sarah? Is that you?" Ten-year-old Sarah and I both say yes. "I got the night off—switched with Georgie for Tuesday. Your father got called into work today. Some weekend insurance emergency,

I guess. Want to go see a movie or something?" She's dusting the mantelpiece, her back to us. We stand there, twins but not twins, and she turns around.

"Hi," we say.

She freezes. She puts her fingertips to her chest. She squints. She frowns. She concentrates. She crosses her eyes. She scratches her head. She finds her way to the couch and sits down, still staring. We stand there.

"Sarah?" she asks.

We both nod.

I say, "Dad said she could come for dinner this week but I forget which day."

"This—this is your—friend? From around the block?"

"Hi!" ten-year-old Sarah says with a wave. Same wave I have. Same wave we've always had. The circular fun wave.

"He said we were going to have tacos," I say.

Ten-year-old Sarah says, "I love tacos!"

Mom is speechless.

"And I love movies!" ten-year-old Sarah adds. "Can we go, Sarah?"

"I need a nap," I say.

Mom says, "I need a glass of water."

I go to the kitchen and get a glass and get her some water out of the water cooler we have because of trihalomethanes. Philadelphia water has some history with trihalomethanes, and Mom avoids cancer when she's not in the ER. Who doesn't?

As the water *glup-glup-glups* from the cooler into the glass, I hear ten-year-old Sarah talking to Mom, but I can't hear what she's saying. When I come back into the living room, they are both sitting on the couch.

"We're going to a movie!" ten-year-old Sarah says. "You can come with us. Or you can take that nap if you want."

I look at Mom. "Isn't that a little weird?" I look at ten-year-old Sarah. "Don't you have to be home by dark?"

"I know who she is," Mom says.

I don't answer.

"How could I not recognize my own daughter?"

This is all happening too fast. And I've stopped thinking about how unoriginal everything is because this is original.

This is original.

MEXICO—*Day Five I: Kids' Club*

We stood at the omelet station at the breakfast buffet—me, Dad, and Bruce. Mom preferred the Mexican yogurt and fresh fruit for breakfast. So far, none of us had contracted Montezuma's Revenge and Mom trusted the fruit even though the guidebooks say to avoid the produce due to it being washed with tap water.

Dad and I had already ordered our omelets. Dad said, "Bruce, what do you want in yours?"

The cook stood waiting, but Bruce wouldn't answer.

Dad said, "He'll have the same as I'm having."

When we left the omelet station with our plates full, Dad turned to Bruce and said, "What the hell is your problem?"

Bruce didn't answer. This was not Bruce's usual behavior. It was as if something were happening to Bruce in Mexico. I don't know if it was the lying, the truth, the seaweed, or the shooting stars that changed him, but he was different on Day Five than he had been.

Dad bragged that he'd reserved two umbrellas on the beach. Up until Day Five, he'd only reserved one umbrella because Mom said it was rude to take up too much space with our rule-breaking. But Day Five he went all the way. He said, "I paid to come here and sit on the beach with my family." He was talking like all the other selfish bastards at the resort now, except when he said *my family* he sounded like he owned us, not like he loved us.

Halfway through breakfast Bruce asked, "So what are we doing today?"

Mom didn't answer because Dad was the vacation planner.

Dad didn't answer because he was giving Bruce some payback in the not-talking department.

I said, "I want to swim, but then I want to do something else."

"What else is there to do?" Mom asked.

"I saw on the daily newsletter that there's a Ping-Pong tournament and stuff like that all afternoon. Games and a nature walk, too."

"I didn't come here to play Ping-Pong," Dad said.

"Okay," I said.

"There's a kids' club schedule at the main desk," Mom said. "We'll go look at it after breakfast, okay?"

She said that to me. But Dad acted like she said it to him. He said, "I don't need to look at the fucking kids' club schedule. I'm not here for games."

Mom said, "Why not let them go and have fun?" I wanted to tell her that the kids' club was for little kids, not for me and Bruce, but I kept quiet.

Dad looked at Bruce. Bruce was pushing his food around on his plate.

"It's not up to *you*, Helen," Dad said. He was acting so cranky, we all just stared at him while he shoved his omelet into his mouth and washed it down with the watered-down orange juice they were passing off as fresh-squeezed when anyone with taste buds could tell it was mixed from powder.

Mom got up and I got up and Bruce got up. We all went to look at the kids' club activity schedule for the day.

Mom and Bruce had a conversation while I asked a balloon man in the lobby to make me a dolphin. When I came back with my balloon dolphin, Mom said, "Okay?" to Bruce. Bruce said, "Okay," to Mom and then they hugged.

They both made a big deal out of my balloon dolphin.

When Mom headed back to the room, she looked at Bruce and said, "Ten minutes?"

He said, "Okay."

But we didn't wait ten minutes.

We stood outside the door and listened to them fight. Dad said Mom was undermining his authority. Mom said "What authority? This is vacation!" Dad said she knew damn well what he was talking about. Mom said, "I think you're going deeper, Chet. I think you need to stop and remember why we're here."

"And why are we here, Helen?" he yelled.

"To help you," she said. "To help you learn how to relax."

"And you think I'll relax when you undermine me? You think I'll relax when you're a bitch to me in front of my kids?"

That's when Bruce touched his room key to the doorknob with his shaking hand and we walked in. It hadn't been ten minutes. Probably more like five.

Mom was sitting on the sofa. Dad was standing above her with his arms wide, making his point. When we walked in, he put his arms to his sides and walked toward their bedroom. His fists were clenched. He didn't even look at us.

Mom said, "Oh, hey, kids! Get ready for the beach!"

I said, because I was ten and excited for the kids' club, "After the beach I can still go to the kids' club, right?"

Mom said, "Sure, honey."

Dad came in from their bedroom and just stood there.

Bruce said, "When are you going to just be nice to her?"

Mom has met ten-year-old Sarah. This is what goes through my head as I stand there and look at the two of them. Mom is a new mom. She isn't the same mom ten-year-old Sarah had. She now wants to have fun and *do things*. Right this very minute, she wants to go to a movie with ten-year-old Sarah.

I admit I feel oddly jealous.

I finally got my mother back—just a tiny bit—by having an existential crisis, and now ten-year-old Sarah is going to reap the benefits of my hard work.

"Are you sure you don't want to come with us?"

"What movie are you seeing?" I ask.

"Whatever's in," Mom says.

"I really could use a nap," I say.

Ten-year-old Sarah is holding Mom's hand. I remember that. I remember holding my mother's hand. There is a thin membrane between that time and this time—so thin I can't see it, but it's here. I don't know what I'm supposed to do.

When Mom asked me last week what I wanted to do to have fun, I couldn't think of anything. I don't know what fun is. Fun is going to the movies, I guess.

Mom is on her phone checking show times. Ten-year-old Sarah walks into the kitchen for a glass of water. I'm left in the living room with my mother and the sliver of tissue that's still stuck to the TV.

Mom looks up at me and says, "I don't understand what's really happening here."

"It's weird."

"It's a second chance," she says.

"I still need you," I say.

"We'll have more fun this week. We'll go to a museum or something."

I like museums. I love museums. But I can't find the answers in a museum.

My answers are somewhere else.

Maybe in Bruce.

Maybe in ten-year-old Sarah.

Maybe just inside myself because I'm the only one who knows all the details of me. But there's a thin membrane between me and myself, too. It's like I'm a little me inside the big me and I'm holding an umbrella and the rain is bullshit and I am the rain and I am the bullshit.

HELEN'S GLUE

There is nothing I hate more than bullshit. Especially in a busy ER. I have to work with people who've been nursing longer than I have who try to bullshit me. They don't write down every detail but they say they do. They take breaks to check their phones or post something on The Social and say they were just taking a bathroom break. The only thing I hate more than a bullshitter is a lazy person bullshitting about being lazy. And yet look at my life. Look. At. My. Life.

You think I hate Chet because he's lazy around the house. Because he shrugs. You think it's because he doesn't really vacuum right and because he won't scrape off the sliver of tissue Sarah put on the TV. And while I don't respect lazy people, I don't hate Chet because of this.

You think I'm hard to please.

But I haven't told you the whole story.

I'm not embarrassed to tell you about my feelings, but I'm embarrassed to tell you where they came from. I'm embarrassed about my bad choices. I'm embarrassed by being stuck and being the glue all by myself.

Nineteen years old. I had never been hit before. Not by a kid in school, not by my parents, not by anyone. I was in nursing school. Chet was in college—living off-campus in an old house near Temple. It was a bad part of town and he wouldn't let me walk home by myself. He bought me a small can of pepper spray that fit on my key chain after the second night I stayed over and I thought that was sweet. A lot of things about Chet were sweet. He loved to cuddle and we liked the same TV shows and he loved walking around Center City holding hands and talking about everything.

We lived in that apartment near Temple for three years. We got married at City Hall and Chet didn't tell his mother. I was pregnant with Bruce when we moved out. But before that. Before that there were bad times. Chet could get too drunk and be surly. He'd tell me off and I would chalk it up to his being drunk. He was a college guy and only drank on weekends. He didn't know how to be drunk yet. He was just messing around. He'd tease me about something too much. His favorite subject was how I'd run off with a doctor one day.

"Only reason girls become nurses is to marry a doctor," he said.

A lot. He said it a lot.

I have no idea why I didn't see he was going to be a problem right then. Instead, I figured it was his way of showing insecurity. It was my job to prove to him that I loved him, not some unknown doctor.

He wasn't drunk the first time.

I'd made dinner for just the two of us. He came home from class and though he didn't seem like he was in a good mood, when he saw the candles lit and smelled the beef roast I'd overcooked, he was pretty nice.

It was something I said.

It's never really something you say. Remember that. But at the time I thought it was something I'd said. At the time, it's always the fault of the person who isn't swinging. But it really isn't.

He asked how my clinical rotation was going. I was working in geriatrics that month. I said that the old men flirted with me.

"Dirty old guys," he said.

"Nah. They're nice. Just bored."

"What about the doctors?" he asked.

"They're okay. One of them actually asks questions instead of telling us what to do all the time. He's nice."

"Nice?"

"Yeah."

"Do you like him?"

"Like, do I like him? No. He's—too—he's too tall."

I picked tall because I had to pick something. I was going to say bald. I was going to say hairy. I was going to say a bunch of things when I stuttered but I said tall.

Chet is five foot ten. Nothing wrong with that. I had no idea that his frat brothers called him "Half Pint." I had no idea that tall was the worst word I could have used.

Except it wasn't. Remember that. It wasn't because I said the word tall.

"He's too tall?"

"Yeah. Can we talk about something else? I love you. I hate when you think I like doctors. It's weird."

This was not the thing to say after just saying the word tall.

Chet put his hands on the edge of the table and pushed it. He was trying to push his chair out. That's what I thought. But instead he pushed the table right into my ribs. Broke one. I doubled over. The candles fell over and went out. The plates smashed into each other. My glass of water spilled onto my lap. I stayed doubled over because the pain was intense. I think I was crying.

When he came over to me, I thought he was going to say, "Oh my God! I'm sorry! Are you hurt?" I couldn't breathe. My rib was broken. I'd heard it snap. He was going to be concerned. He loved me.

But that's not what he did.

He slapped the side of my head as it was down near my knees. His fraternity ring got caught in my hair. He pulled the hair out. He slapped me again—right on the top of my head. Then when I looked up, his fist was closed and he slapped me across the face with it and I was crying already from the pain of my rib and he didn't get a good hit. He pulled his arm back to try again.

I didn't know what to do.

I didn't expect him to be hitting me.

I didn't know that I shouldn't say *tall*. I didn't know what I'd done.

He was screaming. *I can't trust you to leave this fucking house! You want a doctor? I'll get you a fucking doctor! See how this fucking works!*

This was not Chet. That's what I kept telling myself. This was not Chet.

I didn't understand. What had I said? What had I done? I'd made roast beef. I'd lit candles. I'd candied carrots just like he liked them.

As I sat, doubled over, I lost count of how many times he slapped my head. I don't remember him landing one on my face, but later the mirror reflected a woman with a faint bruise.

Who was she?

What had she done?

I didn't go to school for two days after that night.

I could cover the bruise on the side of my face easy enough, but I couldn't do the work I had to do with the pain. I'd taken as much Advil as I could. I'd wrapped my chest as tight as I could. I walked around the apartment standing up as straight as I could. I wanted to look normal. That was what I did. That is not what I recommend anyone do, but it's what I did. I walked around and tried to stand up tall.

Chet had already apologized. He said he was stressed out over an exam.

He didn't say it right then when the roast beef was on the floor. He said it the next day. That night, after he'd hit me enough times, he just went out. Stayed out all night.

That was the routine. That became the routine because I let it become the routine. I am the glue.

When I went back to my rotation, the tall doctor noticed I couldn't do my work without wincing and he asked me what was going on. How was I supposed to tell him? Him? He was nice and cute and concerned and the longer I waited before answering his question, the more he knew without me having to tell him.

I can spot a battered woman at twenty paces now.

They're always the ones not saying anything about how they got that bruise or how come they can't reach above their head or why they can't walk without limping.

I was nineteen years old.

How was I supposed to tell anyone what happened?

I couldn't move back in with my parents. I couldn't even tell my best friend what happened. I just brought Chet to Thanksgiving and Christmas that year and showed him off like a prize dog or something. I don't know why. I don't know why I didn't leave before it happened again.

He said he was just stressed out. He hadn't done it again since.

But he still asked me questions about the doctors.

That only stopped once Sarah was born. Six months after we buried Gram Sarah. I hated him by then. What he'd done to me and Bruce was unforgivable. I'd kicked him out twenty times. He never left.

And now, we're here.

It's like putting a movie on pause for twenty-six years.

I'm stuck, eating staples, on pause, glue.

But meeting ten-year-old Sarah changed everything. I can see my Sarah in her. I can see what she used to be like. Though, at ten, Sarah had already seen what Chet could do. She saw in Mexico. She saw before Mexico, I bet.

My Sarah? My Sarah doesn't see shit. She's all conflicted. She stopped going to school. Something happened but she can't talk to us. Why would she ever trust us? Chet and I have been lying to her since she was born.

Kids are smart. I've said that my whole life. In the ER when we have to give bad news to the parents before we give it to the kid, I say to my nurses, "You can't bullshit a kid. You have to tell the parents first, but the kid knows." And there I was bullshitting a kid when I know you can't bullshit a kid.

I don't go to the movie. I open my umbrella and balance it on my headboard. It's dangerous if I sit up fast, but I don't plan on sitting up fast. I plan on napping. Except I don't nap. It's impossible to nap if one's mother is out with oneself and one is not there with them. It's very confusing.

I think about calling Bruce again tomorrow. I think about him staying at the B&B on Pine. I want to be honest with him, but more than that, I want him to be honest with me.

I get up and manage not to poke my eye out with the umbrella. I put on a thick sweatshirt and I leave. Dad still isn't home and no one has said anything about it. Maybe his weekend insurance emergency will last all night. Maybe he got mugged on the way home and is lying in a puddle of his own blood. Maybe he's seeing someone on the side.

I leave the house and decide to stand in random places. On 16th and Pine, a guy says to his friend, "It'd be really cool if you had a bed that makes you shrink because then when you sleep you'd take up less space."

On 16th and Locust, a woman tells her partner that his shampoo smells like Lysol.

On Broad and Locust, I hear the beginning of a conversation between two middle-aged women and I follow it.

"It was a great book."

"I didn't like it."

"Come on. Didn't you think Gregory was hot? I mean, I just read it for the scenes where he'd take his shirt off and chop wood."

"I thought the Gregory character was a douche."

"He was confident."

"He was a douche."

"He was hot."

"I thought the most interesting part of the book was the wife who took shots of Jägermeister as mouthwash."

"She was weird."

"Not as weird as Gregory chopping wood shirtless. Creepy."

"Hot."

"You're forty going on sixteen."

That's where I stop following them. Halfway between Locust and Walnut. I'm sixteen and I think I'd have liked the Jägermeister-mouthwash wife better than Gregory.

I stop listening to people and walk down Walnut. It's a nice night. Ten-year-old Sarah and my mother are at a movie. Dad is AWOL. Bruce is in Oregon and he might be coming to see me. He can't be my therapist. I will be my own therapist.

Twenty-three-year-old Sarah says, "What's the first thing you would talk to your therapist about?"

I say, "Oh, hi. This isn't weird at all." I notice she's carrying my favorite umbrella again. I left mine at home. I wonder can the two exist in the same place at the same time. "It doesn't look like rain," I say.

"I always carry it just in case."

"Always?"

"Always."

I look at her well-done hair and her stylish boots. I can't tell if she's an artist or someone who works in the mall, at the Gap or something. "You don't realize that carrying an umbrella on days when no rain will happen is a bit weird?"

"We're weird. We can handle it."

"Don't say we."

"So? What would you talk to your therapist about?"

"None of your business. Unless you're a therapist."

She shrugs.

"You know what I'd say. You're me. In seven years. You know what I'd say."

"I don't remember what I thought when I was sixteen. I don't remember if I knew yet," she says.

"Well, it's none of your business."

"You don't have to be so immature," she says.

"I really don't need your judgments right now."

"Get over yourself."

She walks down 17th Street with her umbrella.

I'd talk to my imaginary therapist about a bunch of things, really. But I'd never tell the therapist about the Sarahs.

I'm pretty sure I'm going crazy. And if I'm going crazy, then Mom is too because right this very minute, she is in a movie theater with ten-year-old Sarah but I'm pretty sure Mom doesn't think she's going crazy because she seemed perfectly fine with it. Maybe this has something to do with the fact that she sees real mental illness all the time and she knows it's no different than a broken arm.

When Mom comes home she is by herself. She tells me that ten-year-old Sarah had to go home. She said she offered her to stay with us, but ten-year-old Sarah said that would be too weird. I agree. One Sarah is plenty.

"I don't know what to say," she says.

"About what?"

"This is a lot to take in."

"There are other ones," I say.

"Other whats?"

"Other Sarahs," I say. "Like, tonight I saw twenty-three-year-old Sarah."

She looks at me very seriously.

"She was the one I saw first. At the bus stop. When I started skipping school."

"Twenty-three-year-old Sarah?"

"Yes."

She looks relieved. "I'm so glad to hear this."

"She's kinda snobby," I say. "Thinks she knows everything."

Mom nods.

"Do you think I should see a therapist or something?"

She says, "Let's make a snack."

I follow her into the kitchen and she pulls out bread from the cupboard and cheese from the fridge and I sit at the little round table and watch as she makes a cheese sandwich and then piles it high with potato chips, puts the second piece of bread on top of the potato chips, and then smashes it down.

"Want one?"

"Nah."

"A slice of cheese?"

"No thanks. I'm not hungry," I say.

She sits in her usual chair and I move back into the corner chair and she says, between crunchy, cheesy bites, "I think I can get you excused from school. I have a friend. A doctor."

"You're going to tell him I'm crazy?"

"I'm going to tell him that we're having a family crisis and that you're in need of some time."

"You're not going to tell him about ten-year-old Sarah, are you?"

"No."

"Are we having a family crisis?" I ask.

"I think so," she says. "I'm pretty sure I am."

"Okay," I say. "Where's Dad?"

"Who knows?"

"Aren't you worried?"

"About what?"

"I don't know. That he's not home?"

"Not really."

"Okay," I say.

"Do you really think you're going crazy?" Mom asks.

"No."

"Good."

"Did you know that sixteen is a popular age to have an existential crisis?" I ask.

"No."

"Well, it is," I say.

"Good to know."

Dad comes home about a half hour after I go to bed. I know this because he slams his bedroom door. It's past midnight. I wonder was he out with the person he was saying sorry to last week—if he has some sort of girlfriend or something. I wonder if he slammed his door to wake us up on purpose.

I'm not paranoid. I'm remembering.

Dad has not been the kindest man on the planet.

I'm going to call Bruce again tomorrow. We'll talk about it. We'll talk about everything.

MEXICO—*Day Five II: Edgy*

By the middle of Day Five, things got edgy. Edgier than normal. Very, very edgy. Bruce was edgy because Dad was edgy and Mom was edgy because Dad was edgy and I was edgy because everyone was edgy. I think that's why I ended up making friends with the fish I couldn't see and the sea god I'd never named.

I think, really, if Dad was the one making everyone edgy, then we had always been edgy and would always be edgy.

He drank all day under his selfish bastard thatched umbrella. It seemed normal in Mexico to do this, but by Day Five, it also made him act like a complete asshole. Mom said please and thank you to waiters. Dad just barked orders. Mom tried to have fun with us in the water despite the seaweed, which stuck to her exposed bikini belly. Dad just rolled his eyes and said that wasn't his idea of a good time. Dad was—and I knew it that day for sure—the pervasive seaweed in our family's ocean. No matter if his surface looked calm from the shore, once you got into the water, the waves of crap just crashed and crashed.

I remember wondering what his idea of a good time was. I remember thinking it while floating faceup on the water. I even asked the sea god. I know it's hard to understand and it was hard for me to understand it when I was ten, but I think Dad's idea of a good time is sitting in one place, doing nothing. It reminded me of the commercials on TV for depression pills. I remember asking the sea god if Dad was depressed. The sea god didn't have an answer. I remember asking the sea god if Dad could be helped. The sea god rose out of the water, forty stories high, and reached onto the beach and plucked Dad out from under his thatched umbrella and held him up by the leg. Dad was screaming. Then the sea god turned him into a chicken and swallowed him whole. I felt bad for that daydream, but who was I to control the sea god?

Anyway, Dad drank all day. He snapped at Mom a few times. When we all ate together he kept telling Bruce to stop eating so fast. He kept telling me I would turn into a tortilla chip. He kept looking at Mom like she'd caused him these problems—a son who ate too fast and a girl who was a tortilla chip.

Those days in the middle of the vacation were too long. Bruce went for long walks down the beach by himself or stayed in the room watching TV. Mom and I went to a movie at the resort. But during the day, we just hung out on the beach and it got boring. I was ten. I didn't have a problem saying that I was bored.

Dad said, "Figure out something to do. We're on vacation, for Christ's sake."

So I drew more pictures in the sand and let the tide wash them away. I built a sand castle. I talked to the fish. I floated in the seaweed and talked to the sea god.

Here's one thing the sea god told me after he turned Dad into a chicken and ate him. The sea god told me that I should make sure to make myself happy. I don't know why he told me this, but he did. I remember floating there thinking about it and wondering how the sea god knew I wasn't happy.

The sea god told me that no one else would make me happy. Only me.

And then later that night, when Mom and I were coming back

from a movie, she said it to me in the elevator. The exact same thing. She said, "Just remember, Sarah, only you can make you happy."

I had no idea how when I got back to school I would put this into the "What I did on my summer vacation" travel report for the first week of fifth grade.

Day Five: over. Day Five: more selfish bastards, Dad turning into a chicken, *only you can make you happy.*

Document *everything*. It's the golden rule. Every single thing I do when I'm with a patient, it goes on the record. For their sake, for my sake, for the hospital's sake. Documenting saves asses and I am a born documenter. When the kids were small, I could tell you the last time I changed a diaper, the last time they ate, and the last time they burped. It's something drilled in. Even in the chaos of the ER, I write everything down. In the chaos of life, I had a little book. Since I was nineteen and Chet broke my rib, I wrote down the dates and times of his moods. Not like it helped me not marry him. Not like it saved my ass.

You could always tell about two weeks out when Chet was going to blow up. Two weeks. Almost to the day. He'd be a mix of quiet and trying too hard. Hot and cold. Chet ran hot or cold. Black or white. 0 or 10. Chet has no in-between except silence. It made him look like he could be in-between, but really, he was just building to the next 0 or 10.

A week out, he'd become a half-assed taskmaster. Taking out trash, cleaning little things. Making dinner. If you'd ask him to do anything at that point, he'd give you a look. He'd start picking and disappearing. Like a mosquito.

Two days before, he'd start staring at things. At nothing, really. Just staring.

It was like he was a drunk, but he's not a drinker. It's one thing to reach for a bottle and become a monster—a mean drunk—but it's another thing to have that bottle inside you. A rage organ.

I think it would be easier to understand if Chet was a drunk, but he's not one. But when he drinks, the process speeds up. In Mexico, he drank all day every day. In Mexico, two weeks compressed into one week.

I saw it coming. I didn't know who was going to get it, me or Bruce. Or Sarah.

I stopped drinking so I could stay on my toes for when he blew up. So I'd know what to do. But when it happened, I didn't know what to do. It never changes. Not since I was nineteen and the roast beef fell on the floor. I never know what to do.

Pity Shower

This is what happens when Mom wakes up the next day. She knocks on my door and asks to come in. She lies down in bed next to me, but on top of the covers, and she puts her hands behind her head. She is clearly not herself. This is just weird.

"Did that really happen?" she asks.

I'm just waking up.

"Did I go to a movie with my daughter last night? When she was ten? You? When you were ten?"

I try to move, but she's taking up so much of the bed that I can't turn over because the quilt is so tight across my chest. I grumble.

"Was it real?" she asks again.

"Yes."

"You said there were others?"

"Yeah. A few, I think."

"She's coming for dinner tonight," Mom says. "We're having tacos."

"Yeah. I know."

"We have all day," she says.

"Okay."

"What do you want to do?"

"I kinda want to be by myself."

"We can go to the museum," she says.

"I'd rather not."

She rolls over and looks at me. "Are you mad at me? About last night?"

"No. I just have stuff to do."

"Can I do it with you?"

I sigh.

"Let me get up and get a shower. We can do some stuff."

As she's leaving my room, she says, "I don't get it. Does she go to school during the day? I mean. I didn't mean that you don't and she might. I meant—shit. I meant what does she do all day?"

"I don't know," I say. "I was pretty sure she was just a hallucination until you took her to the movies last night."

"Is that why you asked me if you were crazy?"

"Maybe," I say.

"We'll talk later. Go shower. I'll make breakfast."

"Okay."

Dad's bedroom door is closed, but I hear him in there. This is weird. Dad should not be home. Dad should be at work.

I take a shower, my second in two days—a change from the dirty teen-Earl I was trying to become last week—and try to figure out how to talk to Bruce. Try to figure out how to explain to him that I was in some sort of mental hibernation for all this time. Try to figure out how to tell him that Mom went to a movie with ten-year-old Sarah last night. How she loves that Sarah more than she loves me and she's only known her for a few hours.

It's a pity shower.

I am awash with pity.

I don't want my umbrella. I don't want to be Umbrella. I just want to stand here and feel for once, even if I'm pitiful.

Eleanor Rigby

"Your father is working from home now," Mom says during breakfast.

This is not going to work out. I know it. She knows it. My scrambled eggs know it. My turkey sausage knows it.

"They did some restructuring at the office," she says.

I applaud their restructuring. If they were trying to get rid of lazy assholes, they picked the right guy. The sliver of tissue has fallen off the TV and is now lying on the carpet right in front of the entertainment center.

After breakfast Mom pays bills on the computer in the study. The piano is still there but I never play it anymore. I decide to play.

I sound like a girl who hasn't played the piano in three years. It's slow and though I'm reading the right notes, I'm also hitting the wrong keys. When I was ten I went through a major Beatles thing. I pull out the book and look over the music for "Eleanor Rigby." If you don't know the lyrics to "Eleanor Rigby" then you can't understand why it's relevant. In the end Eleanor Rigby dies. Nobody comes to the funeral. Nobody cares.

It's a little like ruin porn.

The piano is electronic. The house was always too small for an upright. The house was always too small for a lot of things. Maybe that's why Bruce moved out and never came back. Maybe the house is too small for any of us to be who we are. Mom can only listen to metal on headphones. Bruce had to practice his lines for drama club in the garage. When I think of this, I realize Dad watches his baseball games with the volume way up. He is the only one allowed volume in a house with thin walls. I don't know what this means, but I want to play the piano.

I plug in a pair of earphones and, while Mom sits with her back to me entering numbers into her bank account to make sure the lights stay on, I relearn "Eleanor Rigby." I am surprisingly good at this song. After three practice runs, I unplug the headphones and play it and sing, too.

I have a good singing voice. I've always hidden it because it's something I like to enjoy by myself. At home. In the study. When I was ten-year-old Sarah, I would sing for my parents and Bruce and they would look as if I were Aretha Franklin or something. But I am not Aretha Franklin. I just have a decent singing voice when I play "Eleanor Rigby."

So I sing it.

Mom stops doing the bills. I hear the chair swivel. I hit the keys as if I'd never stopped practicing. I hit a few bum notes, but it doesn't hurt the song. It almost helps the song. It's "Eleanor Rigby." It's supposed to be sad. It's supposed to make Mom cry. Last night, she went to a movie with ten-year-old Sarah. Today, sixteen-year-old Sarah is singing her a song. It must be weird for her.

When I finish, we are both crying a little. Not like sobbing or anything, but we have tears in our eyes.

She is remembering a daughter she once had.

I am beginning to remember where I really came from.

She turns and goes back to the bills and says, "I'll only be another minute or two."

"Okay."

"Why don't you want to go to museums anymore?" she asks.

"I don't know. I think art is everywhere or something. And the art in museums is just art people paid a lot of money for. It's depressing."

She swivels around again to face me. "You used to be so excited about art."

"I grew up, I guess."

"Christmas was only five months ago. You were excited then. You were talking about ceramics class. You were talking about getting into the art show this year. It's like you're in some sort of shell. I miss you."

Mention of the art show makes me shiver. "I miss me, too."

"I want my daughter back."

"We'll talk about it later."

When I say this, I don't know what I'll talk about. I can't tell her about the headpiece. It's stupid. I'll look like a whiner or something. It was just one mean person, probably. Just one person who decided it. That's what I keep telling myself.

I've wanted to ask Carmen for months now. I've wanted to ask Carmen *again* because I already asked her, and when she answered, she was like one of her tornadoes. She looked like one thing from the outside, but inside, she had hidden other things. The answer is in her tornado.

She knows who did it.

But now it's been so long that if I bring it up, I'll look like a girl who can't let go of things. Teenage girls always have to let go of things. If we bring up anything, people say we're bitches who can't just drop it.

Anyway. There's nothing we can do about it.

That's what Miss Smith said when I found it. She said, "Well, there's nothing we can do about it now."

I'm sixteen years old and this is the main idea the adults in my life have given me. Whether it's seaweed in Mexico, missing art projects, or Dad shrugging, the message is clear: The older people get, the less they can do about things. They seem to be stuck. They seem to be glue.

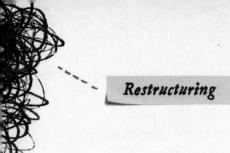

Restructuring

Dad comes down for lunch and makes himself the same lunch he always makes himself and then takes it back upstairs to his room. He doesn't say hi to Mom or me. I think we're supposed to be understanding that he is a man who has been restructured and that he is pretending to be in his office at work, with us not there. So we don't say hi to him, either.

Mom says she's going to the grocery store for a few things. I say I have to call a friend.

Since Dad is in his room—or office or whatever it is now—I can't call Bruce from my room. I have too much to say.

I decide to go outside and sit in the spring sun and talk to him there.

He picks up on the first ring.

"I'm so glad you called back."

"Me too," I say.

"I thought about you all night," he says. "I should have said so many other things yesterday. I just didn't know what to say. It's been six years. You don't know anything about me. I probably don't know anything about you."

"I sang 'Eleanor Rigby' this morning," I say. "I haven't changed as much as you think."

"I can't believe they told you I got baptized in a river."

"It was Dad, I think."

"How's Mom?"

"Still working the night shift. She told me this morning that she can get me an excuse for not going to school. So that's cool."

I don't want to tell him it's a mental health break because even though I know that breaking your brain is the same as breaking your arm, I'm still ashamed that my brain is broken.

"And Dad?"

"He got laid off or something this weekend. As of today, he's working from home."

"Hm."

"I have a lot to say about Dad," I say. "I have a lot to say about everything."

"So?"

"Lately, I've been connecting with the old me—the girl you knew," I say, careful not to somehow spill that ten-year-old Sarah is real and is coming to eat tacos at my house tonight. "I think I'm remembering some stuff about how Dad is. Or was. Or maybe why everything fell apart with you and him and us. I mean, I can't really remember it, but I'm starting to."

"He has a lot of problems," Bruce says.

"He came downstairs to get lunch today and didn't even say hi to me or Mom. We were sitting right there."

"He's probably freaked out over his job. Shit. He worked that job since college. He doesn't know anything else."

"Yeah. That's what I figured, too."

"So why are you skipping school? Can you tell me that?"

"Nothing ever really happens," I say.

"Meaning?"

"Meaning nothing original or new ever really happens and school is just a place where we all pretend like we're new and original and we're not. We're all the same."

"Did something happen?"

I wish people would stop asking me this question. "Yes. Something happened."

"Did a guy do something?"

I think: *Why does everyone think a sixteen-year-old girl's problem has to do with a guy?* "No. It's nothing like that." See? This is the other reason I can't talk about the headpiece. In the weekend that passed between showing up at the annual art show and the day I found the headpiece in the art room, so many horrible things happened to people in my school. Not like I know the details, but I know the statistics and I hear the rumors. Between violence, depression and suicide, rape, bullying and all of those really heavy things, my problem is like a hangnail. I wonder if this is how Vicky-the-grand-prizewinner feels. I wonder if she even realizes that what she's doing is illegal. Miss Smith treats it like a hangnail, anyway. Miss Smith treats everything like it's a hangnail.

"Do you want to tell me what happened?"

"Not really."

"I was looking at flights this morning and I can be there tomorrow or the next day depending on whether I can get a guy to cover me at work."

"That would be awesome," I say.

"But you'd tell me if I came there?"

"Yeah. It's not all that exciting, though. So don't think it's a big deal or anything."

"It's a big deal if you stopped going to school because of it."

"Nothing ever really happens. That's why I stopped going to school."

"We'll talk about it when I get there," he says.

"So you're twenty-five and you don't have a girlfriend?" I ask. "I mean, I'm not trying to pry, but what's with that? You're a cool guy."

He laughs. "Well, I've *had* girlfriends. I thought I even wanted to get married a few years ago but it didn't work out. Twenty-five isn't old. I'm sure I'll find someone one day. I don't know. I just like to work a lot. It keeps me happy and busy and probably too busy for having a girlfriend who needs me to be around a lot."

"You must like your job."

"I love it. Every day I get to help kids like—kids like . . ."

"Like?"

"Like me," he says. "Every day I get to help kids like me."

Do you see how we skirt around it? How we maypole dance? We're not tilting at windmills—we're talking about a real monster. We're just not allowed to talk about it. Which makes my stupid headpiece story even more ridiculous.

"I'll text you later once I buy tickets. I already called the B&B and they have a room. I'll stay for a while. We'll do some stuff. Maybe take me to the art museum!"

"Christ," I say.

"What?"

"I don't want to go to the art museum."

"How about the Mütter?"

The Mütter Museum is the grossest museum on the planet. It's filled with medical oddities and skulls and Civil War amputation kits and the livers of the most famous conjoined twins in history. There are centuries-old gynecological tools. There are babies in jars. Parts of Albert Einstein's brain. Seriously. Albert. Einstein's. Brain. It's the perfect place.

"Yes. You're on."

"I'll text you," he says.

We say good-bye and hang up.

We make tacos. Chicken and black bean mix—extra spicy because Mom and I both know that's how ten-year-old Sarah likes them.

"Did you know that she only got back from Mexico about a month ago?" I ask Mom.

"No," she answers, and she looks concerned.

"That's why she's still peeling," I say. I feel like I'm still peeling, too, six years and one month later.

Mom pours the taco sauce over the chicken and the beans. She mutters something about wishing she'd had time to make it homemade. "Your father didn't recognize her when he saw her last week, did he?"

"I don't think he'd be able to believe it."

"I hope he's ready," she says. She stops and laughs to herself. "Maybe I should just take dinner to him upstairs."

"Nah. I think we should have dinner as a family."

This is a joke. It's a joke on Dad. He's the one who always said to me, when I wanted to eat in the living room, "We should have dinner as a family." Not like it ever helped much. He called Mom "Mom" and she called him "Dad" and they never held hands or smiled and they never talked to each other. It was just his rule. Dinner as a family. I think he should live by it as we all have had to live by it.

"We never got to do anything fun today," Mom says. "Tomorrow? I have to work at seven, but I'd love to go somewhere fun during the day."

I think about Bruce. I think about the Mütter Museum. I think about what's fun. I have no idea where she could take me. "Yeah, sure."

"Also, I talked to the principal today," she says. "You're all set for a break but you have to do a little summer school."

"God," I say. "Summer school."

The doorbell rings. As I walk to the door, I realize how weird it must be for ten-year-old Sarah to ring the doorbell to her own house.

When Dad sits at the table, ten-year-old Sarah is taking a bite out of her taco. This is against every one of Dad's rules. He's very strict about table manners. You eat only once all people are sitting and served. But we did wait five minutes for him and his tacos have been getting cold, so Mom, ten-year-old Sarah, and I decided that his rules didn't count if he was five minutes late for dinner.

He appears to be a different person. Unshaven and in a pair of sweatpants. His hair looks greasy. He doesn't care that we're eating. He doesn't make eye contact. But he's as cheery as he can be about ten-year-old Sarah.

And out of the three of us, it's ten-year-old Sarah who has planned for his first question. Mom and I never even thought about it.

"So nice to see you again . . ."

"Katie."

"Katie! Yes. Now I remember!" Dad says.

"Thanks for having me to dinner," she says. "I love tacos."

Dad looks at her, sitting in my seat—her seat—our seat for the last sixteen years. I'm sitting in Bruce's old seat. Mom and I planned it this way.

"It's our pleasure, isn't it, Mom?"

Mom says, "Dad and I rarely get to meet any of Sarah's friends."

Ten-year-old Sarah nods as she chews on her taco. Dad takes a bite. Mom looks at me and smiles.

Dad says, "Wow! You made these spicy! Katie, I'm sorry if it's too hot for you."

Ten-year-old Sarah says, "I like tacos spicy. They're perfect."

Dad stares at her for a minute and Mom and I watch him, checking for signs of impending brain implosion. So far, he's clueless.

"Could you pass the tortilla chips, please?" ten-year-old Sarah asks.

I push the bowl closer to her so she can refill her side plate.

"My dad once told me that I'd become a tortilla chip because I eat so many," she says.

This is where I choke on my taco. I mean, I literally choke. A piece of taco shell lodges in my throat and I cough and clear my throat and my eyes are watering and I can't get it out or inhale and Mom tells me to sit forward and I'm panicking and she tells me again, "Sit forward!" and I lean forward and Mom pushes the table toward Dad and ten-year-old Sarah/Katie and they back up and I sit forward and Mom slams me hard on the back and I know I'll get a bruise and I don't care because she hits me again and I can feel the chunk of taco shell unstick itself from my throat and she pounds one last time and it's out, on the floor, and I'm gagging and coughing and Mom is handing me water and there's snot coming out of my nose and my adrenaline is high and I'm embarrassed.

But everyone around the table looks calm when I look up. Calm as if I weren't just choking on my taco shell. Calm as if this were just another night at the dinner table. Dad is staring at ten-year-old Sarah. Mom is rubbing my back as I drink water and get my breath back.

"Sorry," I say.

No one tells me I shouldn't be sorry for choking.

180

"You okay?" Mom asks.

I nod.

"Wow. That was close!" ten-year-old Sarah says. "I never saw someone choke before."

"Glad Sarah could give you your drama for the night," Dad says, but no one laughs at his joke.

He tries again. "If I had a dollar for every dramatic episode in this house, I'd be a rich man."

No one laughs at that, either.

Mom and Dad didn't wear their wedding rings to the beach. I noticed this because every day before we left for the beach, they opened the little safe in their closet and asked us to sacrifice our electronics. On top of those, they would put their wedding rings.

This was our last day in Mexico and we wanted to enjoy it. We got to the beach early to claim our thatched umbrellas. We left towels and one beach bag under each one before we went to grab a quick breakfast. Dad went to the resort's lounge for a cup of coffee and a few Mexican pastries while Mom, Bruce, and I went to the buffet restaurant.

None of us talked about Dad. Looking back, we should have. We should have talked about Dad.

Bruce came swimming with me after breakfast. We didn't play catch. We waded out past the larger lumps of seaweed and I showed him my imaginary fish and they said "Hello, Bruce" in my head but I didn't tell Bruce that because I could tell he was getting annoyed by my stories about the pretend fish. Bruce suggested snorkeling and we got some gear from the resort and we swam near the jetty where there was less seaweed and some fish, hiding in the shady water.

I could feel my skin getting hot but I didn't think anything of it. The Mexican sun was different from the Philadelphia sun. I finally got to see real fish in their real environment, even if it did look like we were swimming in a sewage treatment plant.

We stayed in the water for almost two hours, peeking under the jetty, looking at coral and fish, and we even had a swimming race in deeper water and Bruce won because he was twice my size so of course he won. I didn't mind. It was nice having him in the water again after a few days of him not coming to the beach.

We were out deep—Bruce couldn't even stand—and we looked back to shore and saw Mom and Dad under their umbrella. They were talking to each other, but not in a good way. Dad was flailing his arms the way he does when he tries to make a point. Mom was making gestures with her arms that said "Calm down."

"God. I wish they'd just split up already," Bruce said.

"Yeah," I said, but I didn't mean it. I wasn't ready for that. They were normal parents. That's what I kept believing.

"What kind of guy brings his whole family to Mexico and then just sits around and complains the whole time?"

"I don't know." I was treading water fast and it was getting tiring.

"He's not right in his head, you know."

"He's not crazy," I said.

"You just don't know all the facts yet."

"So tell me the facts."

We swam to where we could stand and I waved at Mom once I was chest high in the water again so she wouldn't worry. She waved to me and then went back to talking to Dad.

Islands of brown seaweed bobbed around us. The seeds stuck to our skin like tiny ticks.

"The facts are, they should get a divorce. Now. They keep putting it off. It's not doing either of us any favors to live with that guy. I don't want you to be around him. He's dangerous."

"Dad isn't dangerous."

"You don't know him."

"I've known him for ten years."

"You don't know him like we know him."

"You're like talking to a puzzle," I said. "I know they fight, but Mom says that's normal."

"She used to say that to me, too. But it's not normal the way he fights. There is good fighting and bad fighting."

"I don't know," I said. I looked back to Mom and Dad and they were just sitting there now, watching us. I didn't want them to get divorced. They were my parents. I was ten. I didn't know what life looked like without both of them.

When we got out of the water and walked back to the thatched umbrella, Mom got up and held my towel for me. She wrapped me in it and did that thing where she rubbed her hands over the towel to dry me off and that's when the pain hit me.

My shoulders and my back were on fire. When I said "Ow!" she stopped rubbing and put her sunglasses on her head and squinted at my skin.

"Oh, shit," she said.

"Ow," I said again.

"Honey, we have to get you inside." She grabbed her beach bag and rifled through it, found the key card, and put her sunglasses back on. Dad lay there with his hands across his belly and didn't even open his eyes, but I knew he couldn't be asleep. Mom fast-walked me to the door and for the first time in a week she went to the elevator and didn't make me walk the three flights of steps to our rooms.

"I have sunburn, don't I?"

"I don't think it's too bad," she said.

Nurse translation: It's really, really bad.

We got into the room and she told me to take my bathing suit off. She ran warmish water into the bath and put in all the teabags she could find in our rooms. Six tea bags. She ran the water hot for a while to let the tea steep into the bath.

As I watched the tub fill up I noted how all the teabags kept rushing toward the water and getting sucked into the stream and when one of them broke I said, "Mom! One of the bags broke!" and she said, "It's probably better that way."

I didn't think being covered in tea leaves was better. I had no idea what tea had to do with sunburn.

"Why are you putting tea in the bath anyway?"

"It cures sunburn."

"Cures it?"

"I can't believe I forgot to cover you up, Sarah." She came back into the bathroom with shorts and a T-shirt and put them on the sink counter. She checked the temperature of the bath and when she leaned over, her Mexico tanned belly separated into three sections. I leaned over to see if my belly did the same thing. It kinda did, but it wasn't the same. She started adding cold water to the bath. "I'm a nurse, for God's sake."

"It's okay. It's not bad, right?"

She looked at my shoulders and my back and made a wincing sound. "Let's get you into the bath."

The bath wasn't like a cup of tea. It wasn't brown. It was just tan with the leaves floating in it. It was weird. I got in and sank down and got my shoulders in like Mom told me to.

She sat on the sink counter and called the front desk and ordered aloe vera, more tea bags, and a Mango Tango. She asked them to please hurry up. She said, "I'm going to change here.

Close your eyes, okay?" But I didn't close my eyes, really. I watched Mom take off her bikini and stand there naked for a few seconds, brushing the sand off herself. I hadn't seen Mom naked before—not like this. It felt weird but okay, too. She was my mom. I wanted to know what I'd look like when I grew up. She didn't seem to care or notice that I didn't have my eyes all the way closed. She looked at me and smiled. There was something in that moment—me in the tea bath and her being naked—that made me want to hold on to her forever.

I asked, "Is this the kind of sunburn that causes cancer?"

She slipped on her shirt first and then her underwear and shorts. "No. It's fine. It'll hurt for a little while but it'll go away."

"We heal fast," I said. That was Dad's line. *We heal fast in our family.* Every scraped knee, every stubbed toe, everything that ever happened to me, that's what he would say. *We heal fast.*

"I'm so sorry," she said.

"I should have remembered," I said. "I was just so excited about our last day."

"I know. And I was—distracted."

She sat while I soaked and someone knocked at the door and brought her the stuff she ordered from room service. She drank her Mango Tango in about two gulps and sat back on the sink counter in the bathroom.

"Are you guys really going to get a divorce?" I asked.

"What?"

"Bruce told me that you were supposed to tell me that you're getting a divorce. Is it true?"

"No!"

The tea leaves were making a design on top of the water. I swirled

186

the designs with my fingers and made spirals. "Well, Bruce doesn't lie," I said. "He wouldn't make that up, would he?"

"It's a long story," Mom said. "But no. We aren't getting a divorce. You need two parents. A mom and a dad. I'll talk to Bruce later. I'm sorry he said that to you."

"Don't be mad at him. He thought I already knew."

"Just don't say anything to Dad, okay?"

"Okay."

"Everything is fine. I mean it." Nurse translation: *It could be worse.*

"Okay."

"Nothing bad is going to happen to us. I promise." Nurse translation: *We'll probably have to amputate that leg.*

I kept making designs in the tea leaves. The hotel room door opened and Dad came in and Mom shut both doors to the bathroom and left me in there alone. I heard them talking low to each other. I remember hoping that I didn't get Bruce in trouble. But I somehow knew I'd gotten Bruce in trouble.

After my choking episode, we're all relatively quiet as we eat. Ten-year-old Sarah isn't her usual happy, talkative self. I find that weird because she can leave anytime she wants and there's no reason to be careful. She looks up at Dad a few times, and he just eats his food like he's a food-eating machine and doesn't say anything. We finish our tacos. Mom rinses dishes and I put them in the dishwasher. Ten-year-old Sarah is in the study looking at her painting above the piano. She asks Dad, "Do you mind if I play?"

Dad says, "Please do!"

She plays a rusty early version of "Eleanor Rigby." Mom and I come in to see if Dad will recognize her. He doesn't.

When ten-year-old Sarah goes home—wherever home is—Mom and I are left in the living room alone.

"If Bruce came to Philly right now, would you let him come over?" I ask.

She looks at me with a very dubious face.

"Hypothetically," I add.

"Of course!" she says. With the exclamation point. With vigor.

"I know his phone number," I say. "I've been meaning to call him."

Mom starts plumping pillows. This is probably the first time I have ever seen her plumping pillows. "That would be great!" she says.

I decide not to say anything else. I decide that if Mom didn't work at the hospital four nights a week, she'd probably become a crazy pillow-plumping lady.

It's when she sits on the couch, hugs a pillow that she's just plumped, and starts to cry that I decide to say more.

"Are you okay?"

She says, "They say the number one rule of parenting is to never let your children see you cry."

"Who says that?"

"I don't know. Everyone."

I grab the box of tissues from the side table and put it next to Mom's leg. "So why are you crying?"

This makes her cry more.

"If it's because I brought up Bruce, I'm sorry," I say.

"No, no. It wasn't that. It's not your fault." She blows her nose. "It's just—everything."

Here's what I'm deciding. I'm deciding that Mom is crying because of Dad being restructured. She's crying about Bruce, even if she denies it. And she's crying about ten-year-old Sarah because she saw how little ten-year-old Sarah had to say at dinner. Ten-year-old Sarah has only been home from Mexico for a month. I think that's why Mom is crying.

That is Mom's *everything*.

She shoos me upstairs with her free hand. The other hand is hiding her face.

I tell her I love her.

This makes her cry more, so I go upstairs. There is a text on my phone from Bruce. **My flight lands at 4:15 pm in PHL tomorrow. Dinner?**

Mom and I go shopping. At least it's not a museum. We go to the underground mall in Center City, and on the walk there, I see two other Sarahs but I don't point them out.

In the misses' area of one department store, forty-year-old Sarah shows up. Her hair is perky and shorter. I say, "Hi, Sarah."

She says, "Hey there," and does the circular fun wave. "You still haven't told them, have you?"

I am talking to myself in twenty-four years. I'm ignoring her question. I look her up and down, and she smiles and tousles my hair with her hand. "You're a lot cooler than twenty-three-year-old Sarah," I say.

"Ya think?"

"She thinks she's better than me. And everyone. But especially me."

"The twenties are complicated," she answers.

"She thinks I'm stupid."

"But she's you. Think about that for a minute."

She walks through the racks and picks out clothing and drapes it over her arm. She stops periodically to look at me, then grabs more items. I have no idea what she plans to do with the clothing until she hands them all to me and points to the dressing room.

"How are you with bras?" Mom asks me through the dressing room door.

"I hate them."

"Necessary evil," she says.

The clothes forty-year-old Sarah picked out for me are cool, but not me. I think of Alleged Earl. I wonder when he went shopping last. I wonder when he wore a new shirt last. I think it was probably a while ago.

Thinking of Alleged Earl makes me feel like a coward. I sit on the little bench in the dressing room and I think about the day in the café across from 30th Street Station and how I could have met him. When I walked out of the café, I'd have felt stronger or prouder or like I'd done the right thing.

I haven't thought much about original ideas in the last week, though.

I haven't thought about how nothing ever happens because things happen. Or they have happened. I am shopping in the mall with my mother. We had ten-year-old Sarah over for dinner. My mom got me out of school for a "mental health break." I called Bruce. Dad restructured. Things are happening.

Some of those things are original.

Some of them happen every day.

Some of them are art.

Today it doesn't seem to matter anymore. Or it matters less because I will tell Bruce about what happened at school.

I put all the clothing back on the return rack.

"I didn't like any of those," I say to Mom. "I think I'm better off at a thrift shop or something. More my style."

Mom says, "Bras?"

"I really hate them."

Forty-year-old Sarah is over in the accessory section looking at wallets. She holds up a sign that says, TELL MOM. I notice that she's not wearing a bra.

"Let's skip them today, then," Mom says.

We eat lunch at a crepe place across from the mall and it's good. Mom doesn't have a lot to say. I don't have a lot to say. We just eat and look out the window at the people going by. On the two blocks between the crepe place and Walnut, we pass three homeless people and Mom gives them each a dollar.

She says, "You really have Bruce's phone number?"

"Yes."

"Have you called him?"

I don't answer this. I just keep walking. Then I say, "Do you remember in Mexico when I asked you if you were going to get a divorce?"

"Yeah."

"I know Bruce got in trouble for telling me, but why was it such a big deal? People get divorced all the time."

"I don't know. Your father can't handle it, I guess."

"Dad can't handle dusting the TV screen."

"True."

"I just don't understand why he had to hit Bruce because Bruce told me."

"He didn't hit him!"

I stop on the sidewalk and she takes a step to notice and then steps back to where I am. "Don't lie for him, Mom. I remember. Ten-year-old Sarah remembers. She's still scared of Dad. Didn't you see that at dinner last night?" We're in front of a palm reader's door. Mom looks at the image on the glass—a woman with a mystical-looking scarf over her head, blowing stars out of her hand. The rest of the glass is covered by stars, a graphic of an upturned hand, three tarot cards, and the words PSYCHIC READINGS BY TIFFANY.

"Your father is a complicated man. He goes inside himself." She says this while still staring at the door.

"So?"

"So, he had a rough childhood. He does what he can."

He does what he can, my ass. That's what I want to say. But I don't say anything. A minute ago she denied Dad even hit Bruce. She's still staring at the door to the palm reader's place.

"Want to go in?" I ask.

We open the door. The first thing we see is an overturned trash can. This is not a good sign. A man comes into the hallway from a first-floor apartment with a trash bag and starts to put the spilled trash into the bag. He asks, "You here to see Tiffany?"

We nod.

He yells something foreign up the steep staircase in front of us and says, "Go ahead up. She's there somewhere."

Tiffany appears and she looks as if she's been napping. There are little children running around. I want to ask Tiffany where her family is from, but she doesn't seem to want small talk. She's wearing a long blue skirt with tiny bells at the bottom. When she walks, they jingle. When we get into her palm reading room, there are three chairs. This is the waiting area. She looks at us and frowns. "Who's first?"

Mom says, "How much?"

"Depends on what you want."

"A palm reading?" Mom says.

"Twenty-five."

Tiffany looks at me when she answers Mom. She doesn't smile. She doesn't not smile. She could still be napping in her mind, but it doesn't look it.

"I'll go first," I say.

"Yes," Tiffany says. "That would be best."

Her accent is extraordinary, her voice strong, and she's scary, but in a comforting sort of way. She could be a drill sergeant. A drill sergeant of your future. She opens a door to a tiny room where there's a table covered in thin, brightly colored scarves and on it is a deck of tarot cards. She sits down in her chair and I keep standing.

It's now I realize I don't want to know my future. I don't want to know anything. I just saw forty-year-old Sarah at the mall. What else do I need to know?

"You need to know your present," Tiffany says. Shit. "Your name?"

"Sarah."

She says, "Give me your hand, Sarah."

I give her my left hand and she looks at it for about a second. Then she looks at my face. Then she grabs my hand and pulls it closer to her. She looks at my face—right through it—and she says, all in one breath, "You're healthy. You'll live a long life. No illnesses or anything like that. You're hiding things from other people and from yourself. This isn't good for you. You want to live an honest life. You have little faith in people. You have little faith in yourself. Something happened to you."

I nod. I wonder why she isn't looking at my hand. How can a palm reader read your palm if she doesn't look at your hand?

I think about how many times I've drawn my left hand without looking at it. Two hundred times at least. I think back to the magician in Mexico. I wonder if this is all a scam.

"You are unhappy and lost. You have no home," she says.

"I have a home," I say.

"A home is more than a roof over your head."

"Can you see marriage and kids and love and stuff?"

"How old are you?"

"Sixteen."

"You have talent," she says. "You already know with great talent comes great pain. Something happened in the winter that changed you. Spring, maybe. It was cold. It changed you. For the worse."

"Yes."

"You're surrounded by negative energy. Black magic. I could cleanse this from you."

I find myself wondering if I want to be cleansed from black magic. After five seconds, Tiffany realizes that I'm not the one with the money.

"I'll do your mother next," she says. "Just send her in."

"That's it?"

"Send your mother in," she says.

I feel like I was only in the room for about two minutes.

"Why can't I draw anymore?" I ask her.

"It's the black magic. I can cleanse that for you. Just pick three cards."

I try not to laugh. This must be how fortune-tellers make their money. I'm sixteen, not stupid.

"I'll get my mom." I get up, nod, and say thank you, and go to the door to tell Mom it's her turn.

As I sit in the waiting room, I try to remember what Tiffany said to me. *I don't have a home. I'm unhappy. I saw something when it was cold and it changed me. With talent comes pain. Black magic. Negative energy.* She never answered my question about love.

I try to remember the positive things she said. *Long life. No illnesses. Talent.* That's all I remember. I take her ignoring my question about love to mean that I won't ever find it. This isn't a positive, but it feels like one. I don't know why.

Mom stays in the room for about the same amount of time. A little longer, maybe. Four minutes, tops. I hear them laughing at the end before the door opens. Then I see it's just Mom laughing and Tiffany still looks like a drill sergeant. Mom hands her some money and says thank you. She has tears in her eyes.

"Come back one day," Tiffany says. "You both need a cleansing."

We say we will and we walk through the chaos of little children and an old man toward the staircase and leave the place and walk south to Pine Street.

"Holy shit," Mom says.

"Yeah."

"What did she tell you?"

"A bunch of stuff. But then at the end she said I had to get cleansed of the black magic."

"Me too," Mom says. "I told her that the black magic was working for me, so I didn't want her to cleanse it. What a shyster."

"She said some good stuff, though," I say. "She read me."

"Me too," Mom answers, and her face is a block behind us. Far away. Somewhere else.

I didn't want to tell Mom that I would never find love. I didn't want to tell her that I'd never been looking, either. I didn't know why this idea was so new to me. I knew I'd never cared. Since second grade when kids got married at recess, I never got married at recess. Kids had passed me will-you-be-my-girlfriend? notes in fourth and fifth grade and I always checked the NO box. No one ever even assumed I was gay, which is saying a lot because everyone is assumed gay at some point if they never say yes to those notes. All anyone knew about me was that I drew pictures. All the time. Got in trouble in class for it, won primary school competitions for it, was the middle school art teacher's pet for it. No one ever expected me to be anyone's girlfriend.

Not even me.

And I don't know why. Tiffany knew why. The answer is on Mom's face, now two blocks away.

"I'm hungry," she says. "Those crepes were small."

"Yeah," I say.

We are a scribble—two people stuck in a dark scribble of black magic—walking home to eat a snack. We are not ourselves. Tiffany just changed us. We don't know what to do with this.

When we get home, Dad is in the kitchen making a snack of queso and tortilla chips. He says, "Want some?" He's dipping the chips right into the jar. He's double dipping. He double dips right in front of us so we'll say something. This is called bait. What he's doing is fishing. I watch Mom watching him. *He's a complicated man.*

HELEN'S LYING

I lie. I lie. I lie. I lie.

I lie. I lie. I lie. I lie.

All I want is a quiet place. Six days in a quiet place. I need some sort of head space so I can figure myself out.

My parents died before I was twenty-five. I've been alone in the world from long before that, though. I've been busy. Too busy to listen to my own heartbeat. Too busy to look at my own hands. Too busy to figure out what I'm doing wrong. I'm doing a lot wrong.

I just want to listen for a while. Stop lying. Stop talking. Stop pretending. I just want to listen for a while and see if I can hear my heart beating.

Chet provides the noise. Even when he's not here, his noise is in my head. Sometimes it's so loud I scream and when I sleep I can't escape it and I clench my jaw and bite my cheeks until they bleed.

I never get to listen. I never get to stop and figure out this puzzle. I don't have a table big enough to fit the puzzle.

If I could listen to the quiet for just a day. If I could listen closely to the quiet for just an hour, I could figure everything out. I'd make a plan. I'd know what to do.

A complete stranger looked at me today and said, "You are living a lie, Helen."

Why did it take a complete stranger to get me to hear this? The noise. The noise. The noise.

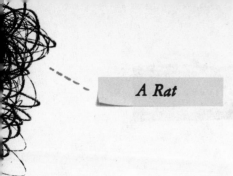

A Rat

My father is not who he seems. He's a complicated man.

Last week, he was processing insurance claims in a cubicle in a skyscraper. This week, he is an unshaven, greasy man who locks himself in his room. He doesn't even come out for baseball. He doesn't say hello.

Mom says that he goes inside of himself but Mom doesn't know that I remember. Not everything, but I remember enough.

Dad has been a grizzly bear. A prizefighter. He's been a bully. A rat. Outside of that, he's been a blank space.

He's some sort of time bomb—Mom and I can feel it every time he walks by us and we can smell his two-day beard and his anger. You can smell anger. That's what they say. They say you can smell anger and danger and I smell it now.

It smells like trash day in mid-August.

It smells like burning rubber.

It smells like the day before the end of the world.

Bruce texts me when he's in the B&B. **Unpacked. Where do you want to go to dinner?**

I reply. **I'll come to the B&B. We can decide from there.**

Bruce: **I have stuff to tell you. I want to know why you left school, too.**

Me: **We can talk about that.**

Bruce: **I want to get it out of the way. So we can just hang out.**

Me: **Sure. We can talk first if you want. I'll come early.**

Dad is back in his room. Mom is taking a nap. I leave a note on the study table. I say I've gone to Katie's house for dinner and that I'll be home later. Of course there is no Katie. Katie was invented for Dad's sake on the night we ate tacos.

I bet if Bruce came to dinner for tacos, Dad would pretend not to see him, either, the same as he didn't see ten-year-old Sarah.

He might call him Jimmy. Might crack a joke about how me choking on my taco shell was drama to imaginary Jimmy. Imaginary Jimmy wouldn't laugh, either. Do you know why? Because anyone can see through Dad's complicated-man shit. He's just a big hole. A big hole who takes up space and doesn't mind being a big hole because he doesn't know what else to be since he stopped being a rat.

MEXICO—*Day Six II: Finding Bruce*

We couldn't find Bruce anywhere. It was lunchtime and I'd been sufficiently steeped in my tea bath and Mom put aloe vera on me and helped me put on the most comfortable shirt I packed—a loose-fitting thing with tiny straps.

When I saw myself in the living-room-wall mirror I said, "Holy shit!"

Dad said, "Sarah! You can't say that."

"Did you see my back?"

"You still can't say that!" Dad said. "You're ten!"

"I have blisters on my shoulders," I said.

Mom said, "It's okay. They'll drain."

The idea of draining blisters was not what I wanted to think about.

"I'm hungry," I said. "Can we go to the restaurant? I want some of those tacos."

"We need to find Bruce first," they said.

"Bruce can get lunch by himself. He has all week."

They talked again in hushed tones and Dad said he was going to find Bruce on his own. Mom said we could go to the buffet. I ate the soft corn tortilla tacos again and Mom had some, too. She didn't talk much. She just kept asking how I was feeling.

"You're not dizzy, are you?"

"No."

"Do you have a headache?"

"No."

"Okay. That's good."

I didn't know if that meant it wasn't good. She had her mystery nurse face on.

I just ate more tacos because if I was going to die of Mexican sunburn, I wanted to at least eat more tacos before I died.

She kept looking at the entrance of the restaurant as if Dad and Bruce would walk in any second, but after an hour they still weren't there.

"It's our last day," I said. "I still want to do stuff. It's just a sunburn."

"They have a siesta movie today. *Finding Nemo.* We should go!"

"I want to be outside," I said.

"You need a break from outside until at least after three or four," she said.

"I wanted to bungee jump at the kids' club. That's at four."

"I don't think you can bungee jump."

"It's just a sunburn!" I said. But I saw the looks on people's faces as they walked past our table. This was not just a sunburn. "And it's not a real bungee jump. It's like a mini-really-safe bungee jump for kids. It'll be fun. I can totally do it. The sunburn doesn't really hurt that much. I promise."

"We'll see," she said. Nurse translation: *You will not be bungee jumping.*

When we got back to the room, Dad was freaking out and yelling into the phone. "Well, *somebody* had to steal them! I didn't steal them myself."

Mom went into the room where Dad was and I looked in our adjoining room to see if Bruce was back, but he wasn't there.

I went out to the shady balcony and sat on the chair. I left the sliding door a little bit open so I could hear what Dad was yelling about. But he just said, "If you won't call the police, I will!" and hung up.

I sat on the balcony and pieced together the story. Someone

came into our room and robbed our safe. They took Mom's and Dad's wedding rings. They didn't take anything else. I decided this was the reason they didn't wear their wedding rings on the beach. Maybe in Mexico, gold is really valuable or something.

Mom came to the door of the balcony. "How you feeling?"

"Good."

"Do you see Bruce out there?"

"No."

"Keep an eye out for him."

"Okay. Are the police coming?"

"No. It's not a big deal."

"Dad thinks it's a big deal."

"He's never been robbed before," Mom said. "It always makes a person very angry when someone takes their things."

"Okay."

"I'm going to close this door now so the air-conditioning doesn't leak out."

I stayed on the balcony and looked for Bruce. His swimming trunks were drying in our little bathroom so I didn't worry that he'd drowned. He was probably at the restaurant or something. That's what I thought.

The manager came to the room. I heard all the adults talking. Dad was talking louder than anyone so I could hear things he said. He said thief. He said housekeeping. He said police. He said I'll sue you! I kept looking out to sea. My shoulders were on fire again. The heat out there wasn't helping but I couldn't go back into the room.

By the time the manager left our room it was four o'clock and I could hear the kids bungee jumping over at the kids' club and I didn't get to see the movie with Mom and Bruce wasn't back yet because I saw him walking on the beach.

I saw him stand at the water's edge in the no-swimming coral reef area, and I saw him throwing rocks into the water as far as he could throw them. One after the other, he just stood there and threw little rocks.

Except they weren't all rocks.

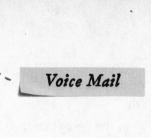

Bruce hugs just like he always did except now he doesn't have to pick me up anymore. I can barely look at him without getting tears in my eyes.

I remember the Christmas when he pulled out his old car-racing track and set it up for me and we played for days even though he was seventeen and I was eight.

We just look at each other and hug and then look at each other again.

I remember him babysitting me one time when Mom and Dad went out and he fed me four milk shakes. Four. Two chocolate and two vanilla. He made popcorn. He let me stay up until eleven.

The B&B has a small foyer and we move to the small living room lobby and sit on the couch. We talk about where to go for dinner and Bruce makes a reservation at his favorite Italian place. We sit there awkwardly for a minute. I have this mix of sheer happy and a little bit of fear that I'm doing something wrong by seeing him. I don't know why I'm so emotional. It's just—he's my brother.

"I have no idea how to start this conversation," Bruce says.

"Me neither."

"Shit," he says. "I want to just tell you everything now and then you'll know and I won't have to carry around secrets anymore."

I look around. "Shouldn't we go somewhere more private?"

"The owners are out. It's just us."

The couch is bright colonial blue. The wallpaper is insane. The room looks like the Victorian era threw up.

"How are you?" Bruce asks.

"Fine."

"How was school?"

"I didn't go. I went shopping with Mom." I don't want to talk about Tiffany so I don't mention her.

The gaudy clock on the wall chimes gaudily. It's four thirty.

"Could this be any more awkward?" Bruce says.

"I want to know about Mom and Dad. I want to know about everything," I say. "I just don't know anything so I don't know what to ask."

"And I don't know where to start."

"It would have been easier to have this conversation through voice mail."

Bruce laughs.

"I'm serious," I say.

I hold my hand to my ear in the pretend-phone position and start. "Hi, Bruce! It's Sarah. Why did you really leave? And why don't you call?"

Bruce holds his pretend hand-phone to his ear. "Hi, Sarah! It's Bruce! I left because of a bunch of reasons. Mostly because Dad was abusive to us and it really messed me up and then he hit me again in Mexico and I couldn't really forgive him, you know? And then Mom said—"

"Beeeeeeeep," I say. "My voice mail doesn't have all day. But did you say he hit you *before* Mexico?"

"Let me try again," he says. "Hi, Sarah! It's Bruce! I left because Dad was abusive to Mom and me and, yes, before Mexico."

"Hi, Bruce, Sarah here. But why don't you call me?"

"Sarah, it's Bruce. I don't call because after the whole thing in

Mexico, he told me I wasn't ever allowed to contact you."

"Hi, Bruce! It's Sarah! He told you that you couldn't contact *me*? Me specifically? I wonder why he did that."

"Hi, Sarah! It's Bruce! Yes, he had this paranoia that I would tell you that he was a wife-beating jerk. So he told me he'd call the police if I got in touch with you."

"Hi, Bruce! It's Sarah!" But then I don't know what to say. Dad said he'd call the police. That's harsh. "But you're my brother. What could he tell the police?"

"Hi, Sarah! It's Bruce. I really don't want to repeat what he said because it makes me want to vomit, but I'm a male and you're a far younger female and I think you can figure it out if I just say this and hang up now. Click."

"Hi, Bruce. It's Sarah. I can't believe he said that. I mean, I can believe he said that. He's so schizo, you know? Is that how he was when you were little? Did he just lose it and then hit you? I'm sorry he hit you. I feel bad about that. I feel bad I never knew. I feel—I—"

"Beeeeeeeep! Never feel guilty for not getting hit. It wasn't your fault I got hit. It wasn't my fault I got hit."

I think back to Mom's face after we came out of the palm reader's today. I think about what Tiffany must have said to her. "I worry about Mom."

"Hi, Sarah. It's Bruce. Welcome to the club."

"Hi, Bruce. It's Sarah. I'm pretty sure Mom and Dad hate each other. So why are they still married?"

"Hi, Sarah. It's Bruce. They agreed to stay together for our sake. Didn't you ever hear Dad go on and on about what it was like to grow up with no father? They didn't want us to come from a broken home."

"Hi, Bruce. It's Sarah. A wise woman once told me that *home* is more than a roof over my head." I take a deep breath. "Anyway, Dad doesn't talk to me much, so I never heard him say anything about him coming from a broken home."

"It's like we had two completely different sets of parents," Bruce says.

We sit there for a minute just looking at each other. Bruce has filled out. He used to be so skinny and now he has something inside all that skin. He looks like a man. His phone dings and he looks at the text that's come in and then looks back at me. I put my phone-hand back in place.

"Hi, Bruce. It's Sarah. How bad did Dad hit Mom?"

"Hi, Sarah. It's Bruce. Pretty bad. One time he broke her arm. You're probably going to ask how often this happened, and since I was a kid, I can't quite remember, but I know it was at least once a month. Sometimes every weekend. They fought verbally all the time."

"Hi, Bruce. It's Sarah. And how often did Dad hit you?"

"Hi, Sarah. It's Bruce. Dad hit me a lot. If you count slapping and hair pulling, then it was every day sometimes. I was nine when he stopped, but I never stopped being afraid of him."

I don't have anything else to ask. I feel so guilty. I want to cry but I don't know how. I just feel like I wish I had been there to help him or to help Mom. But I wasn't even born yet.

"Hi, Sarah. It's Bruce. Can we go out to dinner now? I'm starving. Plus, when is it my turn to ask the questions?"

"Hi, Bruce. It's Sarah. Let's go. I'm hungry, too."

We hang up our pretend hand-phones and Bruce asks, "Do you need a hug?"

I nod and we hug. I remember a hug he gave me once when I was tiny—maybe three or four—and he was sweaty after getting yelled at by Dad for over an hour. It might be my earliest memory, that hug—that sweat. He rubs my back and I cry a little because even though I was never hit by my father, I feel as if I just got hit by him a hundred times.

I say, "I hate Dad."

"Don't hate Dad."

"Don't you hate Dad?"

"I used to. But then I figured him out. I'm still angry, though. I'm really, really angry."

"He didn't really change," I say. "He just stopped hitting people, I guess."

"I meet little Dads all the time. Angry. Abandoned. Scared. If you see Dad as a kid, it really helps with not hating him."

We walk up Pine to the restaurant. We're a half an hour early, but they don't mind. It's Tuesday and the place is nearly empty.

When he orders lasagna and a Caesar salad, I laugh.

"I don't understand why she stayed," I say. "He broke her arm. He hurt you. She's put up with him for twenty-six years. That's too long."

"She wanted what was best for us."

"I hate to kill the forgiving mood, but this was not the best for us," I say. "Not for her, not for you, and not even for me."

"I can't deny that."

"I feel like I'm living a huge lie inside of a huge lie inside of a huge lie."

The waiter brings us a basket of bread. I eat some and try to figure out what's really going on.

"I'm the last to know about everything," I say.

"I know. I'm sorry."

"Not your fault."

"I'm so glad you called me."

"What are we gonna do? I can't stay there anymore."

I feel like running away. I feel like going home with Bruce and living in Oregon. I feel like I'm two different people. Maybe three. Maybe ten.

Bruce finishes chewing his piece of bread. "So why'd you leave school?"

"It's a long story."

"You keep saying that."

I realize that it really isn't a long story. Not if I just say what happened. But it's not about what happened. It's about how I pointed at what happened and said, "Look! That happened!" How do I even bring it up in the middle of a conversation that includes both my mother getting her bones broken and Bruce getting hit every day of his life until I was born? It just makes me feel the pervasive feeling of being sixteen—silly and dramatic. It's not a long story. It's an unimportant story.

I am saved by a steaming hot plate of goat cheese ravioli.

"Hi, Bruce? It's Sarah. Did he ever break your bones?"

"Hi, Sarah. It's Bruce. Yes. Two times we know of for sure."

"Hi, Bruce, it's Sarah. Why didn't Mom help you? I don't understand why she didn't help you."

"Hi, Sarah. Bruce here. I think when you've been abused by someone for a while, it's like being in a cult. The longer you stay, the more brainwashed you get. It's not her fault. She didn't have anywhere to go."

"Hi, Bruce, it's Sarah. So, they were going to get a divorce? You told me that in Mexico. That they were getting divorced."

"Hey, Sarah! It's Bruce! Yeah, they were always going to get a divorce. At least four times a year. Probably more. But it never happened. As you know."

"Hi, Bruce. It's Sarah. I don't know if this is normal, but I feel guilty because, out of all of us, I'm the only one who wasn't beat up."

"Hi, Sarah. It's Bruce. Please don't feel guilty. It's normal to feel this way, but there was nothing you could do about it. They put you in a role and you had to play that role."

I hang up my hand-phone. "That's the problem," I say. "I'm acting."

I have no idea who I am. I'm a character in a sad movie about my parents. I'm a character in a sad movie about an art show. I thought I knew what I was doing.

I had no idea what I was doing.

When you learn the truth late, you doubt everything that ever happened in your whole life because your whole life was a lie.

I try to imagine going home tonight and seeing Dad. I think about Mom and I know I shouldn't be angry with her, but I am. I am so angry with her.

"I can't go home tonight," I say.

"You have to," Bruce says. "They'll worry."

"You've been gone six years and they don't worry about you," I say.

"I'm not sixteen."

"Mom took me shopping today. She was so normal."

"She *is* normal. All this stuff we just talked about is old. It all happened a long time ago. I've healed. Mom's healed. It's—"

"Mom hasn't healed," I say. "She's still living there. She has to deal with him all the time." When you learn things late, you put everything you ever knew through a completely different meat grinder and you end up with totally different meat. The sliver of tissue was a test. This is what abuse looks like. It looks like weeks of waiting for your wife to say *Why can't you vacuum up that sliver of tissue?* so you can tell her she's a bitch. It's a trap. Everything Dad does is a trap. Every shrug, every night he sat and watched TV when there were dishes in the sink—everything was a trap. And Mom knows because after twenty-six years, how could she not know?

I think back to every time Dad was cocky around Mom. I try to picture her reaction. She would shrink. I understand now. I understand that hitting a person is the same as screaming at a person, is the same as head games and traps and bait and all that hard-to-define emotional abuse. This is why I never said anything about Miss Smith. It's why I never took my headpiece seriously. It's sneaky. It hides under other words and other actions. It's power. That's all abuse ever is. That sliver of tissue is power.

We lighten the conversation for a while. I try to see Bruce as my brother again, not a victim. He's the kid who let me win half of our Ping-Pong games in Mexico. He's the brother who showed me shooting stars.

He tells me about Oregon and how much he loves it out there. He tells me the people are different—he can't explain how, but they're just different. He tells me it rains a lot. I contemplate telling him that I am Umbrella, but I decide against it. He tells me about his job and his kids. That's what he calls them—"my kids." He tells me about an eleven-year-old girl who's addicted to meth and a fifteen-year-old boy who keeps getting arrested for arson. He talks about these things the way Mom talks about retrieving random things from patients' rectums. He seems happy—with his job, with his life.

"It must be so cool to know what you want to do with your life," I say.

"You're only sixteen. You'll figure it out."

Bruce asks to see the dessert menu even though I didn't eat but half of my ravioli. It was delicious, but I'm not hungry. He insists on cake.

"It's the best chocolate cake, Sarah. Trust me."

I take a deep breath. I think about Mom with a broken arm. I think about the number of times I've heard Mom say "Would you just let me sleep?"

"You will come to terms with this," he says. "I promise."

I'm still putting my entire life through a meat grinder. The meat that comes out makes no sense. I just sit there, grinding meat.

"Hi, Sarah? It's Bruce. I want to know what happened at school."

"Hi, Bruce. It's Sarah. I'm kinda preoccupied right now because my entire life is a lie."

"Sarah? It's Bruce. I think it would be a good idea to talk about school. And you're being so quiet about it I'm starting to worry."

"Hi, Bruce. You don't have to worry. It wasn't a big deal. It was just a stupid art show."

"And?"

I take a deep breath again. "It feels so stupid now."

"What does?"

"You used to get beat up. My problems are stupid." I am putting myself through the meat grinder. My own meat doesn't look the same anymore.

"Don't compare," he says. "If it made you leave school, it's not stupid."

"It didn't make me leave school. I left school because nothing ever really happens. Nothing new. There is no such thing as an original idea. That's why I left school."

"You said something happened."

"I'm having an existential crisis," I say.

215

"Shit."

"Yeah."

"That's a big deal."

It is. It's a big deal. It's an even bigger deal now that I realize everyone I ever knew has always been lying to me since I was born. Maybe I was built to get screwed over. Maybe I was trained to be omitted over and over and over again. Exclusion: not at all original.

The cake is warm. It's fresh. I concentrate on the cake because it's not a lie. I bond with the cake as I eat it. I decide that eating the cake is my first action as a real human being. I have been reborn. Baptized by a chocolate cake. The cake is proof that ingredients matter. Anyone can put flour and cocoa and butter and eggs into a pan, but it takes the right mix to make this cake. It takes the right temperature, the right amount of time, the right whisk. If parents cared as much about raising kids as the chef cared about making this cake, the world would be a completely different meat grinder.

Bruce can't take a bite of his cake without moaning a little. We let it melt in our mouths. We don't talk. I stop putting my life through the meat grinder. I feel lighter even though the cake is making me full.

By the time Bruce pays the bill I feel happy. Like—content-on-the-other-side-of-the-meat-grinder happy. Not the fake happy. Not the pretending happy. Not the playing-a-role happy. Exhausted but happy for real.

We walk slowly and quietly back to the B&B. We sit on the stoop and Bruce burps. This makes me laugh because Bruce always had the best burps. If I try to burp, I give myself a stomachache.

"I don't have the energy to pretend to leave voice-mail messages," he says. "I ate so much I can't even lift my arms."

We're sitting side by side looking across the street. "I made this headpiece out of wire for sculpture class. I wove it. It's hard to explain but it was cool. I got an A plus. Miss Smith was impressed, you know? She said she wanted it in the annual art show."

Bruce nods for me to go on.

"I didn't tell Mom and Dad about any of it. My plan was to go to the opening on Friday night and then bring Mom and Dad over the weekend to see the show. I think I might have thought I had a chance to win a prize, I guess. Dumb, but I thought I had a chance."

"It's not dumb to think you might have won. Sounds like it was awesome."

"It was," I say.

"So you didn't win?" he asks.

"No, I didn't win." I can leave it here. I can leave it here in the place where I didn't win and Bruce will console me and he'll say that it's normal to feel this way and I'll go home. As we sit there, still looking across the street as we talk, forty-year-old Sarah walks west on Pine. She doesn't look over. She doesn't have to.

"That's not all that happened, is it?"

"No."

Bruce burps again and excuses himself. "So? What happened?"

"I went to the opening. I even dressed up a little. It was my first art show and I wanted to look like an artist, right? So I dressed up," I say. "I got there and walked around and saw the ribbons on the winners and mostly it was the seniors in the art club who won and their work was great and all, so I was happy for them, you know? They're my friends. Or they were then—or whatever.

"I couldn't find the headpiece anywhere. When I realized it wasn't there, I found Miss Smith and I told her it was missing. She said, 'Oh, I'm sure it's here somewhere.' And then she went back to shoving those mini quiches in her mouth and laughing it up with the seniors." I think of forty-year-old Sarah. "Especially with Vicky-the-grand-prizewinner."

"Well, where the hell did it go?"

We're still sitting side by side, looking across the street. It's easier this way. I don't really want to look at Bruce. I feel pathetic, really.

"It was just gone. But I saw the Styrofoam head I'd mounted it on used as a decoration in some stupid display. *Our Art Is Out of This World!* They made the Styrofoam head into an alien head. I went back to Miss Smith and told her that the Styrofoam head was there, but my headpiece was gone. She told me to calm down, but I wasn't freaking out or anything. She just said, 'Calm down. I'm sure we'll find the answer.' But the judging was over and the whole point of being in the show was over and the headpiece was gone."

Bruce puts his hand on my shoulder. I continue to look forward like we're at a baseball game and I'm telling him this story with my eye on the game. In reality, I'm watching forty-year-old Sarah walk east down Pine now, trying to get me to talk about the right thing.

"So you never saw it again? Someone just took it?"

"I went early to school that Monday and went to Miss Smith's room and started looking for it. She was kinda rude about it. Told me *good luck* and *have fun* and stuff. She told me I could search the whole room, which I thought was weird because I was only going to search the obvious places."

"She sounds bitchy," Bruce says.

"The seniors came in for first-period class and they laughed at me the whole time I searched. No one offered to help. It was so weird. They were my friends the Friday before. Now they just seemed to be Miss Smith's friends. Even my sophomore friends wouldn't help. Not even Carmen during second period. She just played it cool."

Bruce squeezes my shoulder.

"I found it in the end," I say. "No one expected me to find it."

I feel deep shame. I have no idea why. I didn't do anything wrong. I didn't hurt anyone. I wasn't being mean or weird. I just wanted to find it. Why am I so ashamed of wanting to find it?

"It was in the bottom of the big trash can behind Miss Smith's desk," I say. "It was crumbled into a ball and someone had taken a wire cutter to the middle of it. It looked like they were trying to cut it in half but then gave up."

Bruce took his hand off my shoulder and put his hands in front of him. "Hold on. Hold on. Someone took your art project and tried to cut it in half and then crumbled it into a ball and threw it in the trash?"

"Yep."

"That's the weirdest shit I ever heard."

"I know, right? And they had to do it Monday morning because the janitors would have emptied the trash on Friday night."

"So what'd you do?" he asks.

"What could I do?"

But I know what I did. I said, "I found it!" and pulled it out of the trash can. When I saw someone had cut it up, I said, "Oh my God," because I guess that's just what came out of my mouth. I remember sweating then. I remember feeling like someone had cut me in half and never finished. I remember wishing someone would have put *me* in the trash. It was the day I first saw ten-year-old Sarah, only I didn't let myself see her. She was sitting on a bench outside school chewing bubble gum and blowing bubbles. At the time I thought it was a hallucination, but now I know she was real.

Bruce doesn't know any of this. He just knows I found it. I don't know how to explain my breaking to someone else—not even him.

He asks, "Did you ask if anyone knew who did it?"

I shrug. "No matter who I talked to about it after that day, they said I had to 'let it go' or 'stop obsessing.' I tried to talk to the guidance counselor. He said, 'There are always other art shows, Sarah.'"

"Not if someone cuts up your freaking projects! What kind of psycho does that?"

"Then the art club stopped talking to me. They wouldn't even hand me tools in class if I asked. They pretended I was invisible. So I stopped going to school."

I wasn't going to tell him about the pear. There was more to it than I *couldn't draw the pear*. There were a lot of reasons I couldn't draw the pear.

"The principal should know about this," Bruce says. "That's bullying."

"Nobody beat me up."

"They destroyed your art project."

"They just ignored me."

"Exclusion is bullying. I should call."

"Don't. Seriously. I don't care anymore."

"I do."

"It'll just make things worse."

"You're talking like Mom. Yeah, maybe it'll make things worse, but in the end it'll make things better. Maybe we can get that teacher fired. Or we can find the kid who stole the project. A lot of good can come from this."

"Just hold off, okay? I'm already excused from school until next year and I don't want to go back there and I don't want more shit from the seniors."

"Fuck them," Bruce says. "Fuck them!"

He's all riled up and he stands and looks at the sidewalk like he's trying to figure out a plan. I know if I told him about Vicky and Miss Smith—about seeing what I saw—that he would be able to get Miss Smith fired. But I don't want to tell. They already hated me. How bad would they hate me if I told about *that*? As if he knows what I'm thinking, he says, "I want to get this woman fired."

"I really don't want to talk about it anymore. It's not the only reason I left school. It's a big part, but not the only part. Okay?"

Bruce paces and burps for a while. He says he misses Philadelphia and says Portland smells different. He talks a little about how he's thought about moving back home one day. I yawn. I don't mean to, but I guess I'm tired and I want to go home, too.

My home. I live in ruins. I have always lived in ruins, but I only found out today. "I missed you," I say. I say this because I realize Bruce is probably the only person who ever really saw what I am. I am a human being. I am sixteen years old.

"I wish I could go back six years and change everything," he says.

I consider telling him about ten-year-old Sarah, but I don't.

But I decide they should meet.

The Whole Stupid Story

I can't figure out how I'm supposed to look my parents in the face today. How do I do that? How do I look at them? Two chefs who made this lie-stew I've been simmering in for sixteen years.

The clock says 6:55 a.m. I don't hear anyone awake in the house. I slept in my clothes again. I get up and pull my hair into a braid and tiptoe out the front door to find ten-year-old Sarah.

I walk around the block a few times. I walk to Broad so I can sit in a bus shelter. I loop back through Rittenhouse Square. I can't find ten-year-old Sarah anywhere.

I lose my breath thinking about never talking to her again. I don't know where to find her. She can't just leave.

"I'm not going anywhere," ten-year-old Sarah says.

I am so elated, I hug her. She's not fond of hugs. I know this because I'm not fond of hugs. She squirms a little until I let her go.

"I want to see Bruce."

"You can't see him yet. But maybe later. Tonight."

"Why'd you hug me so hard?"

"Because I thought you were gone."

"What do you care if I'm gone?"

"I don't know," I say, but I think about it for a few steps. "I guess because I wouldn't have remembered anything about when I was you. And I wouldn't have figured out what was wrong with me."

"There's nothing wrong with you," she says.

"There's a lot wrong with me," I say. "And you know it."

"Does this mean you'll go back to school and not throw our future down the toilet?"

"Not going back to school until summer," I say.

"Will you tell me what happened?"

I stop walking. I sit on the sidewalk with my back to the side of a building and she sits down next to me and I tell her the whole stupid story.

"Sounds like some asshole was jealous."

"Yeah."

"Sounds like that whole art club is full of bitches."

"Carmen is nice," I say.

"Carmen didn't have your back, though. Did she?"

I look at her and try to figure out how she's so honest and how she's me but not me. I remember being honest. I can't remember when I stopped.

"Do you remember Bruce getting hit?" I ask.

"How could I not remember that? It was a month ago. Dad knocked his tooth out."

"I mean before then."

"No. I do remember Dad being nasty, though. To Bruce, I mean."

"And Mom."

"And Mom," she says.

"I have to get home," I say. "See you later?"

"I can't wait to see Bruce."

I say, "He can't wait to see you, either."

When I get home, Dad is locked in his room and Mom is up and doing things. She says, "There you are!" She looks so happy to see me. Looking her in the face isn't as hard as I thought it would be.

I say, "Want to go for a walk?"

She says, "Fun! Yes!"

When we get outside, she says, "I want to see—um—the other Sarah. You know what I mean."

"Later," I say. "She's busy."

Mom looks concerned. "How do you know?"

"She's me."

"This is very hard to take in, you know."

"It's easier than some stuff I can think of," I say. "It's easier than a lot of stuff, really." I'm cranky. I want to call her a liar. I want to ask what Tiffany the palm reader said to her yesterday. I want to forgive her.

She doesn't say anything. We just walk. I wonder can she see I've been through the meat grinder. I wonder can she feel Bruce four blocks away. I wonder if she knows that ten-year-old Sarah is about to save our lives.

Somehow, I know this.

Mom and I take a left up 15th Street. When we round the corner onto Spruce, I see Alleged Earl drawing on one of the plywood rectangles covering the window above where he sleeps. He's using oil crayons. Mom sees him, too. I stop and watch. He's in some sort of trance and I remember that trance. I remember weaving the headpiece that way. It was tedious work. Tiny, thin strands of wire in and out and in and out of the spokes.

"That's Earl!" Mom says.

I look at her. "You know him?"

"Yeah. He comes into the ER some nights. I haven't seen him in years, though."

"His name is really Earl?"

"Did you think it was something else?"

"I don't know," I say.

"I bet he's hungry," she says, and crosses Spruce to talk to him.

I follow her a few seconds later because I have no idea why.

Mom has a quick conversation with Earl. He looks over at me. I wave in my circular me-wave. He puts his oil pastel in his coat pocket.

Mom says, "Earl, this is my daughter, Sarah. Sarah, this is my friend, Earl."

"We finally meet," he says.

"Yeah."

"You stopped hanging around," he says. "I kinda missed you."

"I kinda missed you, too."

Mom says she's going to the pizza place for a few slices for us. She crosses the street and leaves me standing here with Earl. No longer alleged. No longer painting on the plywood. No longer jumping up and down or throwing imaginary fruit.

"Your brother is in town, eh?" he asks.

I say, "Mom doesn't know."

He looks at me sideways.

"My parents don't talk to Bruce anymore," I say. "So his visit is a secret."

"Huh."

"Yeah."

"That's uncomfortable, I bet."

"Not as uncomfortable as sleeping in that hard doorway every night," I say.

He doesn't say anything.

"There has to be a better place to go," I say.

"I like to be where the action is."

"But in winter, you could die."

"I haven't yet."

"But there's no action here. It's all just the same old thing. Nothing ever really happens."

Mom arrives back with three slices on paper plates. The grease is seeping through them already.

"Nothing ever really happens?" Earl says. He laughs a little.

"Not around here, no," I say.

"You know Sarah is an artist," Mom says. "Just like you."

I say, "See? That's the problem. I'm not an artist. And I'm not like him."

"I got three sodas. What kind do you want?" Mom says, holding up three cans.

226

"I'll take the cola," he says. "Thank you." He turns to me. I finally get to see his eyes. They're brown.

"You know the truth will set you free, right?" Earl says.

"That's why I was following you," I say.

"I don't have your truth!" he says and laughs again.

"You're a real artist," I say. "I want to be like you." I don't tell Earl he is Spain. I don't tell Earl he is Macedonia.

"You see me in the art museum?"

I shake my head while taking a bite out of my slice.

"You see me at the art sales? With the college kids? Up in the galleries in Old City?"

I shake my head again.

"You know what art is?" he asks. "Art is the truth. Maybe you don't feel like an artist because of, because of"—he swirls his hands around—"because of all this."

All this.

My life.

Mom is completely lost because she doesn't know what Earl is talking about. Earl is trying to wipe a drip of greasy cheese out of his dusty beard and Mom holds his Coke can for him.

"I can't say I miss you in the ER, Earl, but I worry about you."

"My son's up at Drexel now. He's doing great."

"College already?" Mom says. "My God. It's been a long time."

"He's going to be a teacher," Earl says. "Just like his old man."

"You're a teacher?" I ask.

"I was. Twenty-five years. Taught middle school."

"An art teacher?" I ask, thinking of Miss Smith. Thinking of how much I want Earl to be my art teacher.

"History," he says. Then he turns to Mom. "Helen, you know

I think I saw your boy down on Pine Street? He looks good!"

Mom stops eating her pizza. I stop eating my pizza.

Earl keeps going. "He filled out. Last I saw him he was scrawny. How old is he now?"

It's like they're two old friends. I ask, "How long have you guys known each other?"

Mom says, "Bruce lives in Oregon now. You must have seen his double."

Earl looks at me. I can't say anything. I take a bite of pizza. Earl takes a bite of pizza but he keeps looking at me. Mom's frown is deep in her forehead. It looks like a scar between her eyebrows.

Earl says, "The first time I met your mom you probably weren't even born."

Mom says, "You had pneumonia. You let it go too long."

"Your mom saved my life," he says.

"She saved your life?"

"Saved my life," he says.

Mom eats her pizza. She knows Bruce is in town; I can feel it. Maybe mothers have an extra sense or something. Maybe they can tell when their son is in town and no one has told them.

Earl looks back at me. "I'd be dead."

"You *were* dead," Mom says.

"That's when I saw the light. When I got my calling."

Mom nods. "Thank God I walked in. That other nurse had no idea you were about to tank." I think about this. I wonder if Mom has noticed that I'm tanking. I don't think she does.

"So, you were a history teacher," I say. "So how'd you end up—um—here?" Mom and Earl look at me funny. I add, "If you don't mind my asking."

"I gave up all my possessions. I freed myself from all my responsibilities."

"Oh," I say.

"I got laid off. I sold everything I had to pay hospital bills."

"The other way you said it sounded nicer," I say.

"The truth will set you free," he says again.

"But aren't there places that could help you? You could totally get a job at one of those learning centers," I say.

"I have a job," he says. "You know I have a job. You've been following me around watching me do it."

"You've been following Earl?" Mom says.

"Her and her sister. I didn't know you had another one," he says.

I look at Mom. "Ten-year-old Sarah."

She goes to say something but she just eats another bite of pizza instead. Earl does, too. I pick my slice up and am about to shove the crust into my mouth but I say, "Mom, Bruce is here. He's staying at a B&B. I had dinner with him last night. Sorry I lied. I just didn't want to make you angry."

I don't know why I'm sorry. I don't know why I'm scared to make my mother angry. My emotions are smaller than they should be. I'm the one who should be angry, but I'm *cranky* or *upset*. As if a sixteen-year-old can't be angry for real.

A tear crawls down Mom's cheek. It moves so slowly I can't figure if it will drip onto her pizza or if it will be absorbed into her skin before it does.

Mom says, "So while you're skipping school, you follow Earl around?"

"Just for a few days."

"Other days she goes up to places she shouldn't," Earl says. He looks at me. "That's a dangerous place, that old school."

Mom is entirely confused.

"It's better than real school."

Earl chews and thinks on this a minute.

Mom says, "Something happened in school and she won't tell me."

They both look at me. I shove the crust into my mouth and when I'm done chewing, I say, "There is no such thing as an original idea."

Earl says, "Who told you that?"

"My art teacher."

He shakes his head. "Is she an artist?"

I never thought about this before. I've never seen anything she made. Mom goes back to eating her pizza. I want to tell Earl everything. Instead I just answer his question.

"I don't think so, no," I say.

He nods, slowly.

Mom says, "How long has Bruce been in town?"

"Yesterday." Earl and I say this in unison. He says it calmly. I say it with anger. He looks at me and smiles and I have no idea why. It doesn't make me any less angry. I wonder if Earl was following me and not the other way around. And this is art. Everything is art.

Here's why I like making things. I like making things because when I was born, everything I was born into was already made for me. Art let me surround myself with something different. Something new. Something real. Something that was mine.

I don't know if this means I could also be a competent architect. Or a car mechanic. Or a carpenter. I just like constructing new things that are real.

I believe this is a side effect of growing from seed in soil made of lies.

I believe this is a side effect of being born into ruins—this need for construction.

Mom is quiet on our walk up Spruce. I say, "I think you and Dad should get a divorce."

"You're sixteen years old," she says.

I am sixteen, I am ten, I am twenty-three, I am forty. After last night with Bruce, I understand everything. "That doesn't make me stupid."

"It means you don't understand divorce."

"Do you even love him?" I ask.

She sighs. "I don't think so," she says. "In fact, no. I don't. Isn't that horrible?"

"It's not that bad."

"It's horrible," she says. She has tears in her eyes.

"Not really," I say. "The truth will set you free, right?"

"Easy to say."

She's walking too quickly. I decide to slow down to see if she'll notice. She doesn't. She just keeps walking. Doesn't look back. Doesn't do much else but look both ways at intersections and then crosses streets. I lose sight of her and stop walking. I just stand on the corner of Pine and 17th and nobody is around, really. No chatting friends walk by. No random art students on their way to class carrying large black portfolios, nobody walking their dog, nobody at all. I look up at the sky and feel like someone has me under a microscope.

I am safe—squished between two glass slides. I am easy to read, easy to identify. I am a human being. I am sixteen years old.

Inside my brain lives the image of a woven wire headpiece. It's the only place it exists—in my brain. If we focus in a little closer, there are many images of the headpiece. Partially made, wire sticking out from many angles. Finished and polished and mounted on a Styrofoam wig stand covered in black linen. Crumbled into a ball, pieces severed with wire snips, in a trash can behind Miss Smith's desk. If I could go back in time and figure out who did this, if I could go back and stop them, who would I be now?

Look. This isn't a temper tantrum. I'm not some teenager you can blow off because you made a myth about teenagers being dramatic. You go work hard on something you love. And you find it in the trash like it's garbage. Tell me how you feel. Tell me what's missing when you're done. I can tell you what's missing. You. You are missing.

I stopped going to school because I was missing. I was either in the past or in the future everyone always talked about. I stopped going to school so I could focus on the now. But the now is my mother telling me she doesn't love my father. The now was always feeling like something was wrong, only I didn't know what. The now is one of Carmen's tornadoes. Since the meat grinder, I am trying to adjust.

Ten-year-old Sarah walks toward me on 17th. Next to her is twenty-three-year-old Sarah. They look well adjusted.

I wave to the ten-year-old Sarah and then focus on twenty-three-year-old Sarah. I ask her, "Do Mom and Dad get divorced?"

"Yes."

"When?"

"Right about now," she says.

"About time," ten-year-old Sarah says.

"Yeah," I say.

"I want to see Bruce," twenty-three-year-old Sarah says.

"Me too," ten-year-old Sarah says.

"Maybe tomorrow," I say.

"We can meet at the house," they say.

"Bruce isn't going to the house," I say.

Twenty-three-year-old Sarah says, "Yes he is."

They are the glass slides on either side of me. They keep me safe under the microscope. Both Sarahs are carrying the umbrella. The umbrella can exist in two time periods and in one space. I can exist in three time periods in one space. Living for the now suddenly seems pointless.

"Do I ever get to find out who stole the headpiece?" I ask her.

"No."

"Do I stop caring?" I ask.

"No."

"I have to go," I say. They both know I'm going to see Bruce. They might even know we're going to the Mütter Museum. "Please don't just show up, okay? I really love you both but I want to just be in the here and now for a day."

"Sure," they say. "We're going to the park anyway."

They walk north. I walk south toward home, where a divorce is waiting for me. I'm oddly happy for Mom.

I am a human being. I am sixteen years old.

She is a human being. She is forty-seven years old.

This should be enough.

Last night Bruce talked in therapy words. He said, "I was abused." He used the term *domestic violence*. These aren't terms I can relate to. I've lived in an abuse-free domestic-violence-free lie for sixteen years. And yet I live in a house with both a victim and abuser. Until I was ten I lived in a house with two victims and an abuser.

If I think about it too hard, I end up in the meat grinder again. Earl said to me today that the truth will set me free. I don't feel free yet.

MEXICO—*Day Six III: Tooth Fairy*

Mom and Dad went to look for Bruce. Day 6—last day. I was sun-
burned and stuck inside watching Mexican television. They told me
not to open the door for anybody. They told me to lock the door
with the inside door lock that nobody could open from the outside.

But when Bruce came about ten minutes after they left, I let him in.

"Did you tell Mom what I told you?" he asked.

He was angry and I didn't know what to say. "Maybe?"

"About them getting a divorce?"

"Yeah," I said. "I'm sorry."

He sighed. "God, Sarah. Mom told Dad. He yelled at me so bad."

"I'm really sorry. It just slipped out when Mom and I were taking care of my sunburn. I don't know. It just slipped."

Bruce plopped on the couch next to me.

"I don't want them to get a divorce," I said. "They're my parents."

Bruce didn't say anything.

"I'm really sorry," I said again.

"It's okay. I just know I'm never coming back home now. I can't
live with him."

"You'll still come home for holidays like last year," I said.

"No."

"What do you mean no? Of course you will."

"No."

"I'm sorry, okay? I didn't mean to get you in trouble."

"After this, I can't come home."

"It'll be fine. Dad's just mad because the housekeeper stole his ring."

"I took the rings," Bruce said.

I looked at him hard for a few seconds. He didn't look guilty or ashamed. He looked satisfied somehow. "You?"

"I probably shouldn't tell you. You'll tell them."

"I will not!"

"Just don't tell Mom. Or Dad. It was about time someone stopped pretending around here. I'm just mad I was the one who had to do it."

"Mom and Dad are out looking for you," I said.

"I guess they'll find me here, then."

"I didn't get to go bungee jumping."

He looked at my shoulders. "Wow. Your sunburn is *bad*, man."

"Mom says the blisters will drain. Gross, right?"

"Totally gross."

"Why did Dad yell at you if he's the one who told you that they were getting a divorce?"

"There's a lot of things you don't know about them," he said. "There's even things you don't know about me."

I turned off the TV. "So tell me."

"He'll kill me."

"He won't kill you."

"He could."

"Anyway, we'll be home tomorrow and everything will go back to normal."

"I'm moving. I told you."

"To Oregon?"

"Probably."

"Tomorrow?"

"As soon as I can."

I started to cry a little. "It's dinnertime. I hope they come back soon," I said. "I'm hungry."

"You just want tortilla chips."

"I wish you weren't moving away. It'll just be me and Mom and Dad. I won't have anyone to hang out with this summer."

"Do you know what I think?" Bruce asked. But right when he said it, Mom's knock came at the door and Bruce shut up and got real tense and I got up and undid the lock on the door so Mom could come in.

She took one look at Bruce and shook her head. She produced a huge handful of single-packaged Earl Grey teabags and told me I had to have another tea bath for my sunburn. She said we were meeting Dad at the restaurant. She said he had things to take care of before we left the next morning.

Last dinner in Mexico. You know what happened at the end. You know we all told Bruce to shut up because he was so mad. But before then, I got to eat a lot of empanadas (actually good) and taquitos (mostly flavorless) and piles of tortilla chips. Mom and Dad kept drinking fancy Mexican drinks. The drink of the day was a piña colada, Dad's favorite.

During dinner, we didn't talk much and it was awkward. My back was on fire and freezing cold at the same time. Mom put so much aloe on it that it never dried.

Finally, Mom said, "So, let's talk about our great vacation. Who has memories?"

"I do!" I said. That's when I talked about the fish and how they were my friends and how we said hello to each other every day and how I'd remember them forever. Complete lies. I have no idea why I told them.

Mom and Dad said some stuff about how nice that was.

Bruce said, "They aren't your friends. All the people here see them."

Mom and Dad told Bruce to shut up. I said, "Yeah. Shut up, Bruce."

Bruce said, "Fish don't like humans, Sarah. Not even you."

"I think they like me," I said.

"You're delusional," he said.

"She's ten," Mom said. "Can't you just pretend to have a good time?"

"Why pretend?"

"Jesus Christ, son. We brought you here. We paid for the whole week. Why are you such a pain in the ass?"

That's when Bruce got up from the table and went back to the room.

You know I ate cake. You know Mom thanked Dad ten times for the vacation. She looked scared, that's what she looked like. Scared. I'd seen that look before and I'd heard Dad be rude to Bruce before and I felt bad right then for telling Bruce to shut up. I guess I was just used to everybody ragging on Bruce. It was a tradition in our family. But when I ate the three cream cake and cried, I wasn't crying because the cake was so good. I was crying because I'd goaded Bruce the way he'd been goaded his whole life. Maybe I was why he was moving so far away. Maybe I was one-third of it, anyway.

I was ten. I knew better than that. We had no-bully rules in our school. We had be-kind rules in our school. I vowed to be kind to Bruce from that moment forward. In my head I vowed this. I couldn't tell Mom and Dad because they were too busy being mad at Bruce.

But I vowed it.

What happened next went as fast as I'm going to tell it.

I didn't tell Mom and Dad about the rings.

Bruce did.

I was on the balcony again. Mom closed the door all the way again. It was a clear night and I could see the stars. It was a quiet night at the resort—no pool parties or beachside romantic dinners—and I could hear them all fighting through the sliding door to the balcony. The people in the room next door even called the manager about how loud they were. The phone ringing made Dad madder.

I didn't hear whole sentences. I heard words and phrases. I heard *divorce, Sarah, liar, you're the liar, divorce, rings. In the ocean now. Because you're living a lie. It's not helping her. Oregon. Never giving you another penny. Stay away from this family. Never coming back.* Bruce was right near the sliding door when he said this last thing. He said, "You think because you stopped beating on us that this isn't the same? It's the same, Dad. You're the same psycho you've always been."

I heard that.

Then I heard the unmistakable sound of a punch. Just like in movies or cartoons—I heard it land and I heard Bruce fall and scream out and I heard the reading lamp go down with him. And I heard Mom yell, "Stop!" and the phone rang again and Dad let it ring and Mom tried to answer it and he said, "Don't you dare, Helen, or you're next." And Bruce said, "See? See?" from on the floor. You must know that a part of me had to make up another story right there and right then when I was sitting on that balcony by myself with my sunburn and looking out into the sea where the sea god had no idea how to help me. You have to know. You have to know that this crisis didn't start with the headpiece in tenth grade. You have to know that from that moment when I turned around and saw my brother on the floor, spitting blood and my mother held tight by Dad's hand as the phone rang and rang and rang that I was alone and life meant a little less than it ever would mean again.

Bruce lost a molar. He showed it to me before bed. Mom had given Dad something to sleep. She packed our bags herself and didn't fold anything. She just threw in the clothing—wet and dry together. She threw in our souvenirs. She used the foot of my double bed for each suitcase—packed all of Dad's things and her things and then zipped everything up, looked under the beds one more time, and then zipped our bags up, too.

Bruce had a huge plastic bag of ice on his jaw. Mom said it wasn't broken. Mom said she was sorry. Mom said Bruce was wrong for taking the rings. Mom said anything she could to get Bruce to talk but Bruce wouldn't talk.

I went over to the side of his bed and I knew he was awake but he had his eyes closed. He was crying. I said, "I'm so sorry."

"It's not your fault," he said, but he sounded like his mouth was full.

"I love you. Please don't go."

He said, "You can always come stay with me, no matter where I am."

I stayed until he fell asleep. Mom had given him something for pain and it didn't take long. She checked on him one last time and I was back in my bed pretending to sleep. I opened one of my eyes and watched her pull out a string of cotton from Bruce's mouth. It was soaked with blood. Instead of putting it in the trash, she flushed it down the toilet.

When Mom went to bed and closed the door between our rooms, I went to my suitcase and found some shells I'd collected. There was some loose American change on our table so I grabbed that, too. And the notepad and pen with the resort's logo. I went to the bathroom and I wrote two notes to Bruce. One said "I'm sorry." The other said "I love you." Then I sneaked back into the room and slid the items under his pillow as he slept. His pillow was soaked from either the melting ice or tears—I couldn't tell.

My sunburn didn't hurt at all that night. I didn't feel a thing.

Day Six: over. Day Six: sunburn, a molar, *you can always come stay with me, no matter where I am.*

HELEN'S IN MOURNING

Last week I met a woman. Her name was Rose. Rose was eighty-five years old and she came by ambulance to the ER after the police found her. They found her on the floor of her bedroom.

Rose lived with her new husband, who was spending her Social Security checks on prostitutes. Two nights ago, the new husband, twenty years younger than Rose, brought home a prostitute who heard moaning from the bedroom where Rose was and the new husband told her to ignore it. She tried to go in, but he stopped her. She did her job. She got paid. When she left, she called the cops because, she said, "Something very weird is going on in that house. He has someone locked up or something."

The police had to break the door down. They found Rose and called the ambulance. She told them the story. A year ago she fell, broke her hip, and this is what her new husband did: He came into her room and found her on the floor. He put her pillows under her head and left her on the floor. For one year, Rose lay on the floor eating food the husband threw in to her once a day. She scraped the food from the floor into her mouth. She pissed and shat where she lay. He threw a bucket of cold water over her every month or so. Her hair grew through the pillowcase. Her fingernails were long and curly. Her toenails had been rotten for at least a half a year. A lot of her body was necrotic.

I was lucky I even got to meet Rose before she died later that night.

It's hard to believe that some people can be so cruel to other people. But then, it's not. I work here. I see things. I know things.

And then I look in the mirror and there I am.

Pretending. Always pretending.

Carmen lives at her mom's house one week and her dad's house the other week. She has a bedroom in each house. At her mom's she has to share with her little stepsister. At her dad's she doesn't have to share with anyone. She has two of everything. Two hair dryers, two flattening irons, two favorite cereal spoons, two sets of paints, two easels, two toothbrushes, two makeup kits, two pairs of slippers, two bathrobes. Her life is like Noah's Ark. She still has two parents, but they still don't get along. When I asked her about it back in sixth grade, she said, "It's not like anyone died or anything."

I thought that was a smart thing to say. Carmen has always handled life as it comes. If it had been her headpiece, I think she would have just shrugged it off and never looked for it. She'd have rolled one of her joints and forgotten it even existed.

If she'd have walked in on Vicky-the-grand-prizewinner and Miss Smith kissing like that, she would have kept her mouth shut.

I want to call her. I want to tell her I am about to walk into a divorce and I want to know if it's anything like her tornadoes. I want to know what will be inside my divorce. Will there be a box of corn flakes? A family dog? Will there be a place for Bruce? Will we survive or will this be the end of our family?

It's not like anyone died or anything.

Bruce is staying at the B&B on Pine. I'm walking down 17th Street. Dad is at home, being restructured. Mom is probably at home by now, too. Maybe she is restructuring Dad even more than he's already been restructured.

When I think about it, I figure maybe it's good timing. Maybe Dad can just take off and do something cool. Maybe he can move to California or Mexico or Wisconsin or something. Maybe he can figure out a way to stop being so angry inside. Or maybe he'll just find some other sucker who lets him do all that stuff he did to Mom and Bruce and repeat the whole nightmare again. I already pity her, whoever she is. I already want to send her a letter and tell her about the sliver of tissue on the TV and how he doesn't really care about baseball even though he pretends to care about baseball.

When I walk into the house, it's silent. I go to my room and grab a hoodie because it was chilly last night. I don't hear Dad in his room, talking, typing, nothing. I don't hear Mom in her room. The door is open. I peek inside and she's not there. I stop by the kitchen and they aren't there, either.

The door was unlocked when I came in, but I decide to lock it on my way out.

On my walk toward the B&B, I decide that Mom and Dad went out for a divorce. It's better than getting one delivered, I guess. I decide that it's not like anyone's dead or anything.

On the street I find a name tag. It's blank except for the preprinted part on top that says HELLO MY NAME IS. I pick it up and put it in the pocket of my hoodie. When I get to the B&B, I use the pen next to the guest book to write my name on the name tag.

I write: UMBRELLA. I stick the name tag to my hoodie.

Bruce doesn't even see it until we're in the Mütter.

245

I tell Bruce, "You're wearing too much aftershave."

He says, "I am not."

"Do you plan on picking up a date at the Mütter? Because that's creepy."

"You're my date. And aftershave isn't for dates. It's for feeling fresh after you shave. That's why they call it *aftershave*, smart-ass."

"What'd you do this morning?"

"I slept off my jet lag and then ate a really stellar breakfast. You?"

I think about telling him about meeting Earl and how Mom saved his life and how everything is art. Instead, I say, "We should get going. They close at five."

"Can't leave the skulls waiting."

"But I have to tell you this one thing," I say. "I think Mom and Dad are getting a divorce right now."

"Right now?"

"Like—right now."

"People can't just get divorced," he says. "You can get married fast, but you can't get divorced fast."

"Well, they are. Right now."

"Did you hear this?" he asks. "I mean, did they tell you or something?"

I think about telling him about the Sarahs. There is no way to tell him about the Sarahs. So I say, "Mom told me today was the day."

I don't want to get him too excited. I'm not even sure if I'm right. And Mom didn't tell me anything. But she told me she didn't love him. I never thought I'd wish for something bad like this. But then I realize that the only person who thinks divorce is bad is me. It's my idea. But sometimes divorce can be good.

I think about playing tooth fairy to Bruce in Mexico. I ask him, "Did you ever get your tooth replaced?"

He presses on his cheek with two fingers. "No. I wanted something to remember him by."

It's a hole. In his mouth. A hole where a rat used to be.

The Soap Lady

Bruce pays my admission fee to the Mütter and we both stop at the entrance to breathe in the familiar smell. Old, weird things. That's what the air smells like. Old, weird things.

Albert Einstein's brain is as cool as it always is but this time I feel bad for Einstein. What's his brain got to do with anything? I mean, take it out of his body and it's just a blob of tissue. It can't do anything without Albert—especially when it's sliced twenty microns thin and slapped between slides so we can look at it.

The wet specimens are Bruce's favorites. Just the name is awesome. *Wet specimens.* Babies in jars. Brains in jars. Tumors in jars. Body parts that can't be used anymore being preserved so we can see weird shit on a Wednesday afternoon.

"Does that say *Umbrella?*" Bruce says as we walk from one exhibit to another. He points to my name tag.

"Yes."

"Is that your name now?"

"Yeah. I think so. Do you like it?"

"It's got something," he says.

I want to tell Bruce that I am the layer between him and a sky full of potential bullshit but I don't think saying that in front of the soap lady would be appropriate.

The soap lady is like a mummy. She's just lying there in her case with her mouth wide-open like she's screaming. But she's not really screaming. She's just dead and encased in an alkaline substance that gave her the name the Soap Lady. They dug her up in Philly in 1875. Some expert doctor said she'd died from the yellow fever epidemic around the 1790s. That expert doctor died a long time before someone discovered he was wrong (because she was wearing buttons that were not manufactured in America until the mid-1800s). I wonder if we'd have sliced the expert doctor's brain into twenty-micron-thin pieces and slapped them between slides if we could find out that he was wrong about the soap lady. I bet we couldn't.

I can't pull my eyes off the soap lady's mouth. Her scream is so familiar. I want to touch it the way I've wanted to touch great paintings . . . except what would I get from touching a scream? I wanted talent from the paintings; maybe if I touch the soap lady's scream, I could feel better about everything without having to actually scream. Either way, I wish they'd bury her somewhere so we didn't have to look at it. She doesn't look at peace right now, screaming in a glass case being ogled by anyone who can afford an admission fee.

I can't remember why I used to love this museum.

I used to love all the oddities and the science, but now it just seems like humans showing off shit they know very little about. Like: Here's a museum of the things that went wrong and the ways we did things that were wrong and the facts we got wrong.

I have grown up around people who can't talk about what's wrong, so maybe I'm just stuck in my own hang-ups.

Bruce says, "You look uncomfortable."

"I am. I don't know why."

"We can go."

"No. You go ahead and look around. I'm going to check out the garden."

There are benches around the medicinal plants in the garden.

Mom used to grow some of these in the little yard behind our house. She used to grow lemon balm and sage and wormwood, only she called them by their Latin names because she's Mom. Now she doesn't grow anything anymore. I try to remember when she stopped. I'm pretty sure it was right after Mexico.

Eventually, Bruce comes out and sits on the bench next to mine. We're the only ones here.

"So, why Umbrella?"

"Why not?"

"Did you just pick a name out of thin air?"

"Sarah is a boring name anyway."

"It is not," ten-year-old Sarah says. She's sitting on a different bench on the other side of the garden.

Bruce looks over to see who said that and I think twice about explaining, but I think he'll figure it out on his own.

She says, "Sarah is a cool name. It means *essence*."

Bruce looks at me. He looks at ten-year-old Sarah.

"I know," I say. "But what am I the essence of, you know? After last night, I guess I'm the essence of bullshit."

"I don't think I understand what's happening," Bruce says.

Ten-year-old Sarah says, "You will." Then she walks back behind the hedgerow and doesn't come back.

After the Mütter Museum, we go to the famous cheesesteak place on South Street and it's crowded for no particular reason other than it's the cheesesteak place on South Street. Bruce and I try to find a quiet table but there is no such thing as a quiet table so we find any old table and we eat. After last night, I don't have that many questions. I don't feel like talking.

We walk home slowly because we both ate too much.

"That girl in the garden looked exactly like you," he says.

"She is me."

"Does she show up a lot?"

"Only lately. She's the one who was talking to me when I was on the phone with you."

"Who is she?"

"I told you. She's me. When I was ten. About a month after we got home from Mexico."

"Stop."

"Mom sees her, too. She took her out to the movies on Sunday night."

"Mom took—I—"

"It's cool. You'll meet her tomorrow. She wasn't supposed to just show up like that, but I think she just misses you a lot."

We don't say a word for a few minutes. I can't tell if Bruce believes me or not, but he will.

He says, "I'm going into the school tomorrow to talk to the principal about your art project."

"Waste of time," I say. "That's a complete waste of time."

"You're coming with me."

"Why?"

"If you can't face your demons head-on, you're fucked."

"In that case, we have bigger demons to face head-on than some dumb principal."

Bruce walks me to the corner so he can see that I get in okay, then he waves and goes back to the B&B. Mom is waiting for me in the living room. She looks worried.

"Were you out with Bruce?"

"Yeah."

She pats the couch for me to sit down.

"How is he?"

"He's great. Loves Oregon. Looks good."

"But he's okay?" Six years. And all she wants to know is if he's okay?

"He's fine," I say. "How are you? You don't look fine."

"It's been a day," she says. Her hair looks like she was in a tornado. Or a joust. Her eyes look like they've been crying.

"I want to bring Bruce over tomorrow. He wants to see you." She shakes her head and her eyes dart around the room like she's looking for a reason Bruce can't come over. Her own son. "Why are you punishing him for something he didn't do?" I ask.

"It's very complicated."

"It's simple. I know everything. I know what Dad used to do to you and to Bruce. So you're scared—so what? Bruce isn't. He wants to see you. He's your son. It's not complicated."

"You know everything?"

"I know what Bruce told me. He's the only honest person around here, so that's all I got."

"Why are you so angry?"

"I'm angry because no one ever told me any of this before and you all thought I could grow up here and not know something was wrong. I feel like I've been festering in rotten water for sixteen years."

"We didn't want you to suffer," she says. "We made a deal."

It's Thursday morning. Like all other Thursdays before June 17th, I should be in school. Instead, I am about to watch a divorce. Or a tornado.

Bruce and I walk toward home slowly.

"Are you scared?" I ask.

"A little."

"Do you think he'll punch you again?"

"He better not," he says.

"He won't."

"He might."

"He thinks you're in Oregon. He believes you were baptized in a river and you don't call us because you're a God snob now."

"I think that's very convenient for him," Bruce says.

"I don't think he'll punch you," I say.

"What's he like on a normal day?"

I think about Dad on a normal day. "He's like—blank."

"Blank?"

"Just blank. I mean, two weeks ago he was lecturing me on going to school, so he's like—a dad or whatever. But he doesn't do anything. He goes to work. He watches baseball. He doesn't want to talk to anyone. Doesn't say *Time to make the art!* or anything like that. Blank."

"Blank."

"He's just a hole where a rat used to be," I say.

Bruce nods. "And he's never hit you?" he asks. "Never?"

I shake my head. "Mom said he made a deal."

"We had a family meeting about that deal."

"But he hit you in Mexico."

"He broke the deal," Bruce says.

When we walk in the door, it's eleven in the morning. Bruce leaves the front door open but locks the screen door. It's a beautiful day. I figure he wants to let some light and air into the house. It's a row house and the only windows are in the front and back. It's an old house. It could use some fresh air. We find Mom in the kitchen, Black Sabbath pulsating from her headphones. Dad is probably in his room.

Mom screams at first—a startled scream, not a scared one. She takes her headphones off and the music still blares from them—a tinny sound of something larger. Then, the house is quiet but for the sound of Bruce and Mom talking to each other. Mom is hushed. Bruce is not.

I decide to sit on the couch. It's like being in the water in Mexico all over again. I can decide the pillows are my friends. I say, "Hello, pillows," and they say, "Hello, Sarah." We are friends, the pillows and me.

We are spectators, today. That is our role.

From here, Bruce's voice has the male bass that Dad's has. It permeates the walls and the floorboards and I wonder when Dad will notice that there is another man in the house. I decide it will be five minutes. I decide that Dad will come downstairs and he will be wearing his pajamas at noon on a Thursday.

The thing about decisions I make in my head: They are not real.

Dad comes down in less than a minute. He is in a pair of sweatpants that have to be from 1985. His legs are too long for the pants because his middle has grown and he wears them higher on his waist. He looks ridiculous.

"Who's here?" he asks.

I shrug.

He walks into the kitchen quickly. Something is wrong with him. He isn't himself. Or he is himself. Or he's the rat. He left his hole upstairs.

Before anyone can say anything, there is a crash. Since I'm on the couch, I have no idea what the crash is, who caused it, or anything. It sounds like someone threw something and it hit a wall and fell to the floor.

There's another crash. It's definitely glass. Sounds like he just threw something through the window. Another crash. Furniture. Wood hitting wood.

Mom and Bruce head through the study and toward the front door. Bruce unlocks the little screen door lock.

Mom says, "Come on!" to me. I don't know where I'm going, but I grab my umbrella from the handle of the coat closet and follow them.

We close the front door behind us and we sit on the front step.

There is a tornado in our house. The sounds are scary, but the three of us are okay. Mom is shaking her head. Bruce is sighing a lot. I'm just numb.

I pull out my umbrella and open it. There is a tornado of bullshit in our house. When it's over, we will be okay.

Bruce says to Mom, "You can stay with me."

"I work tonight."

"He needs to be gone by the time you come home, then."

They look at me. I'm watching two cockroaches scurry across the drain cover on the street. "What?" I say.

"That's been the problem all along," Mom says. "I can't leave her alone at night." This makes me feel like the problem-all-along but I decide not to think about it. Judging from the tornado in our house right now, I know she doesn't mean it that way. We all know who the problem-all-along is.

Bruce says, "I can stay here. I mean, if that's okay."

"But you have to get back. You have a job, right? Or a family?"

"Mom thinks you got baptized in a river," I say.

Mom looks confused.

Bruce says, "I'll take a few weeks off. Not a problem."

Mom says, "This is too much."

A loud crash comes from inside the house. It sounds like Dad just pushed over a bookshelf or maybe the TV. We can hear him yelling. Cursing. *Goddammit!*

I think of Earl and his screaming and cursing. Dad is art.

We hear Dad approaching the door and we all instinctively stand up from the step. He yanks the front door open. He says through the screen door, "I'm sorry."

We stand there. I decide we're all thinking the same thing. I decide we're all asking *Who is he?*

"Will you come in? Can you give me a chance?" This is art.

I decide that if I go in, I'm keeping my umbrella open.

Mom says, "I want you out by tomorrow morning."

Dad says, "Give me a break! I just got fired."

"You didn't get fired," she says. "You got restructured."

"I got fired."

Mom sighs. "So you lied to us?"

"It's embarrassing when a man gets fired," he says. Art. Art. Art.

"Where are you from, Chet? The 1950s?"

"I need you guys," he says. He means me and Mom. He is pretending that Bruce isn't here.

"Out by tomorrow morning," Mom says.

"I still don't hit you!" he says.

Mom says, "You don't get it."

I get it. *The absence of violence is not love.*

Bruce says, "Do you want to go inside and talk about this like adults?"

Dad ignores Bruce. He says, "Helen. Please. You can't kick me out now. Sarah has two more years."

"I'm fine, Dad." I keep telling myself that I'm not the problem-all-along.

"You're a kid! You don't even go to school!" He pushes the screen door when he says this. He is fistfighting anything that isn't human.

"I'm not coming in if you're like this," Mom says. I look at Dad-behind-the-screen-door. He's scary. Scarier than I've ever seen him. He looks a little crazy, too. I wouldn't go in if I were her, either. I've never been scared of Dad, but now I am. I can't tell if it's because of the meat grinder or the present situation. He did just beat up my house.

He says, "Then you go find another place to live. This is my house."

Mom sighs. "Chet, you're acting like a child."

Dad mocks her with an exaggerated sigh. "Helen, you're acting like a bitch."

Bruce pulls out his phone and dials 911.

I can see through the screen door that Dad wrecked the living room. The coffee table is broken into two pieces. He's pushed over the bookcase. He's sweating and out of breath. His pants still look stupid.

Mom looks pained that Bruce is calling the police. Her hand is on her head—fingertips on her forehead, her thumb on her cheek like she has a headache. She stays in front of the door so Dad won't stop Bruce from calling.

Here's the thing, I think. You hope that you can get the rats out of your own house with things you can buy at the hardware store. But eventually, if they don't leave, you have to call the exterminator.

None of us ever wanted it to come to this.

I look at Dad, now back in the living room looking for things to smash. He picks up the ceramic owl I made in elementary school and before he throws it, I scream, "No!" but he throws it anyway and it smashes against the tiles in front of the woodstove.

I loved that owl. Mom loved that owl. Dad loved it more than anyone.

The owl was the beginning of the dream. It was the night when we all sat around the dinner table and talked about how good I was at art.

First grade. That was the beginning of the dream.

Maybe before Lichtenstein painted *Sleeping Girl* he made an owl that was superior to his classmates' owls. Maybe it was made out of dots. Maybe in that owl he kept his muse—the beginning of his dream. Maybe before the soap lady got buried in alkaline she had her own dreams, but now she's just screaming forever over on 22nd Street encased and on display like art.

This isn't like the headpiece. The headpiece wasn't the beginning of anything. The headpiece mattered but it was the end. The owl was the beginning. And now that it's gone, I want to draw a picture of it so I can remember it. All the ruined things in my life, I want to draw. It's like Carmen's tornadoes. I suddenly understand her more than I ever have before. I get this feeling bigger than just anger—I think it's rage. I think after so many years numb and quiet and smiling and faking, I am finally feeling something uncontrollable.

Let him hit me. The police are on the way. Let him smash *me* on the tiles in front of the woodstove. Let him just be a rat.

I push past Mom and walk into the house. Dad is standing by the shelf with all of our DVDs on it.

"You're going to end up in jail, Dad."

"I'm already in jail."

"Okay."

"Put that umbrella down!" he says. "It's bad luck."

"You think?"

"What's that supposed to mean?"

"I don't know, Dad. I just know that you're acting like a crazy person."

"I'm not the one calling the cops."

"Can you see yourself?" I ask. "Can you see what you just did? Look around, Dad. You have problems. Okay?"

"At least I have a high school diploma."

I shake my head. If this is what living with Dad was like for the last twenty-some years for Mom, I don't know how she did it. "Touché, Dad."

He stops looking at the movies and walks toward me. Fast.

I brace myself for whatever he's about to do but he stops short. He puts his hands in the air. Laughs. "Didn't work. You're just a kid. You can't make me hit you. Bring your mother in here. She's the one who did this. She's the one who wrecked all your stuff."

He reaches over and grabs my umbrella. He twists my wrist to get me to let go. He turns it inside out, rips the fabric from the metal spokes and bends the handle over his knee until it breaks.

I realize now that all my older Sarahs must have a different umbrella from this one. I could never tell the difference. I guess it doesn't really matter what kind of umbrella you have—as long as it keeps the bullshit off you.

I hear talking outside.

I leave Dad in the living room breaking my umbrella and go to the door. Two police officers are there asking Mom about what's going on.

I say, "He's lost it."

Bruce says, "Everything will be fine. Trust me. I do this all the time at work."

The cops go inside. I am now without my umbrella. And my owl. And my dream. And my headpiece. And soon, my dad.

"I'm calling off tonight," Mom says. "I think this qualifies as a family emergency."

MEXICO—*Day Seven: The Windmill*

The drive to the airport was fast. We got picked up by a man in a white Mercedes-Benz with an off-white leather interior and it was just us—not like the van we had to take to get to the resort. We were the quietest family in Mexico inside that car. None of us said one word. Not a word. Dad sat in the front seat. Bruce had another ice pack on his jaw. Mom had slathered me in enough aloe that it wouldn't dry and I had to sit forward in the leather backseat so I wouldn't stick to it. Mom sat in the middle. Bruce sat to her left. I sat to her right. We both stared out our windows and Mom looked straight ahead.

The driver started talking about ten minutes into the drive and he told us about things that happened in the news in Mexico and when we passed by a part of the road that had a lagoon to the left side, he told us stories about people who go fishing in the lagoon for small crabs. "It's so stupid!" he said. "These crabs are so small they are not worth being eaten by a crocodile." The whole stretch of road where the lagoon was, there were white wooden crosses to mark the places where people got eaten by crocodiles—just like the way we mark places along the road in America where people died from car accidents. But there were so many. Maybe twenty. The driver told another story about a man who got drunk and fell asleep at the side of the lagoon. Crocodile ate him. Another white wooden cross on the side of the road. A tourist who stopped to take a picture of a crocodile in the lagoon. Eaten. Another cross. As we drove by a crocodile farm and zoo on the right—a tourist attraction —he told us how the workers there hold a live chicken above where the crocodiles are so the crocs jump and people can get pictures. He said twice a worker at the zoo lost his hand just so people can take a picture. He said that there was an American man suing a golf course because he played from the rough that was a swampy area near the lagoon and got his leg chewed off by a crocodile.

I was fascinated by this man's crocodile stories, but I didn't ask any questions. We were the quiet family. I watched the overgrown wilderness pass by me to the right. Then the entranceways with what looked like gates but with no gates—just the pillars, some crumbling and many only half standing and covered in aggressive vines—one after the other. The houses I saw were smaller than an American garden shed. There was a billboard for Coca-Cola. Stone walls around a small roadside kitchen. A cement truck. I loved the road signs. The signs for *bumpy road ahead* looked like boobs.

The driver said, "Do you see the windmill over there? This big, expensive windmill is not generating electricity. It's only for that small office building there. Do you see it?" None of us answered. He kept going. "That's what electricity it provides. Just for that building. That's it. Three years ago we had a global market meeting. There were people from all over the world. Dignitaries, diplomats, presidents, ex-presidents, et cetera. They all stayed at the nicest hotel over there in Cancún. The meeting lasted a couple of weeks. Then, the Mexican authorities decided to put up the windmill. To show to the world and to our visitors that we are, you know, using this kind of energy. But in this part of the country, we cannot use this type of energy because we are next to the Caribbean Sea and we have rainy season also called hurricane season." This was when I fell in love with this man's accent. The way he said *hurricane*. The way he said *season*. The way he said *windmill*. "So this kind of windmill is very risky here. But in the meantime the Mexican government spent thirteen million pesos, or one million dollars. Which means that I have to work and pay taxes for a windmill that will never do me any good."

When none of us responded to this story, the driver clammed up. He'd worked for his tip. He'd told his crocodile stories. He'd told us about the windmill. Now he shut up and moved into the fast lane and I could see the signs for the airport showing fewer and fewer kilometers and I could see planes in the air—taking off and landing. And I thought about how badly Bruce's jaw must hurt and how badly my sunburn hurt.

Stop signs in Mexico read ALTO. That's what I wanted to scream. ¡ALTO! ¡ALTO! ¡ALTO! But I didn't scream anything. I went to the airport, stood in the security line with my quiet family, saw a girl wearing a T-shirt that said ALL MY FAVORITE RAPPERS ARE DEAD. Saw another girl in a T-shirt that said I'M IN CANCÚN, BITCHES.

After security, Mom took Bruce and me to buy souvenirs from the trip. Bruce dug into the pocket of his shorts. He said, "I already have a souvenir." He held up his tooth.

"I want this," I said, holding up a toy cube that unfolds that said ¡*Viva la Muerte!* on the package. The cube was magical—like a Mexican puzzle. It folded and unfolded in different directions and on each panel there was a different drawing by José Guadalupe Posada. The poster next to the display said that Posada lived from 1852 to 1913 and was well-known for his representations of Mexican life and people. It said he was prolific. It also said he lived in poverty his whole life and was buried in a grave that eventually was claimed by someone else, at which time his skeleton was removed and tossed into a mass grave alongside other poor skeletons.

The pictures on the cube game were all skeletons. Dancing skeletons. A skeleton playing a small Mexican guitar. Skeletons at war. Skeletons in love.

Mom said no at first. "Too morbid," she said.

I begged and explained the artistic relevance. She bought it.

When we boarded the plane, Mom said I was supposed to sit with Dad and she would sit with Bruce.

"I want to sit with Bruce!" I said. "That way you and Dad can sit together."

"I'm sitting with Bruce," she said.

It didn't make any sense to me then.

It was the beginning of what I would eventually end.

The answers were never on the airplane. The answers were right there in Dad's fist. In Bruce's jaw. In Mom's eyes. The answer was there. I didn't see it because how do you even guess that kind of shit about your own family? How do you even guess that you will be the last to know about everything? How do you even guess that your parents were stupid enough to build a thirteen-million-peso windmill for people who would never be able to use it?

The flight home—Mexico Day Seven—was the last time I would see Bruce until I was sixteen years old. Dad didn't say a word the whole day. Not in the plane, not in baggage claim in Philly airport, not in the taxi on the way back to our house, not even when I showed him my magic José Guadalupe Posada Day of the Dead cube.

I didn't want to talk to him really. Not after what he did to Bruce.

I wished he would have been eaten by a crocodile in Mexico—a white cross on the side of the road.

I was ten. This was a reasonable wish.

Be Reasonable

Whatever is going on in the house sounds a little like Dad getting eaten by a crocodile. He's not fighting the police or anything, but there's a lot of noise. I think they're moving the furniture back into place.

"I don't think he can get arrested for wrecking his own house," I say.

Bruce says, "I told them what's going on."

"I can't believe you went in there," Mom says.

I can't believe I went in there either. This is going to sound crazy, but I think I went in so Dad would finally hit me. So I wasn't left out. So I wasn't the last to know.

Bruce says, "Let's go in and talk. If we do it with them here, then it will go on record, they can arrest him, and we can get on with our day." Mom sighs. Bruce hugs her lightly.

We find Dad and the two cops putting things back together. One cop is taking a picture of the broken kitchen window. The other one is talking to Dad about his temper. He asks him if he's ever hit Mom or us. Dad lies. Dad says no.

Bruce says, "He's lying."

"What the fuck are you even here for?" Dad says. He almost growls. "I kicked you out six years ago for what you did to your sister."

"Don't believe a thing that man says," Mom says. She's ER-night-nurse calm—she knows the cops and the cops know her.

The adults move into the kitchen to talk. I sit on the couch and hear random words. *Pack. Paperwork. Divorce. Sarah. Safe.* Dad paces with his arms crossed, taking advice from the police officer to stay quiet and let his wife talk. I can see him only when he passes by the door. He doesn't notice that I'm sitting here. Mom stays in clear view of the doorway. I think she does it on purpose so I can see her. She is expressive and stands as if she were dealing with a hospital family who needs assurance. *Out. One day at a time. Pack. Safe. Sarah. Lies. Bruce. Lies.* This is the Mom Earl knew.

Dad sounds like a crocodile. "You can't kick me out of my own house!"

More muttering. More calm talking from the police, from Mom, and even from Bruce. *Ruined the house. We were outside. Sarah's owl. Safe. Sarah.*

"I didn't hit her!" Dad says.

I pick up the pieces of my umbrella and my owl from the living room floor and walk into the kitchen.

"That's what he did to my umbrella," I say, dropping the shards of evidence on the kitchen table. "And that's what he did to my art project." I point to the pieces of the ceramic owl. I don't tell them he twisted my wrist because I still can't believe he twisted my wrist.

Maybe that's why I never said anything about Miss Smith and Vicky-the-grand-prizewinner. Maybe I still can't believe what I saw.

The police stand in the middle of the tiny kitchen. They are huge in every way. They are both over six feet tall. They're filled out with muscles and uniforms and guns. They wear hats and badges and shiny shoes.

"You made that stupid owl when you were a kid," Dad says.

Mom tells me to go back outside. I sit on the stoop and watch the cars go by. I stand up and stare at the doorbell and think about

267

ten-year-old Sarah and how she had to ring the doorbell to her own house last week. I feel like ringing it now—over and over again—until everyone inside goes crazy.

I still hear pieces of the conversation from inside because there's only a screen door between us. The cops tell Dad to stay somewhere else tonight. They tell him to be reasonable. To come back tomorrow when he's calmer. I don't think that's a good piece of advice, frankly. Dad resists it anyway. The cops say they can arrest him now, and Dad says he didn't make threats against anybody. And then I hear the recording of Dad saying what he said to me only a half hour ago. *You're just a kid. You can't make me hit you. Bring your mother in here. She's the one who did this. She's the one who wrecked all your stuff.* Bruce recorded it on his phone. I didn't ever want to hear that recording, but now that I have, it sends chills up my arms and I'm cold on a hot afternoon.

Dad yells at Bruce for a minute—mostly unintelligible stuff—and then the cops bring it back to the present. One tells him to go cool off for the night. Dad suddenly sounds panicky, like he knows this is really happening now—as if he didn't know when he smashed my umbrella and my owl and the house. As if he didn't know that he is a tornado. He says he has to fix the kitchen window that he broke. Mom says she can fix it. She says she's been fixing his broken windows for twenty-six years. I look inside.

Dad sighs and says, "Shoot me now."

"Don't say that, sir."

"Why not? I want to die."

"Sir, really. You shouldn't say that."

"My whole life was wasted on this family. On her," he says, glaring at Mom. "Just shoot me now. You can say I tried to take your gun or any of that other shit. I'd be out of my misery."

This is art.

The cops look at each other. Mom shakes her head and asks all of them to step outside again while Dad stays inside. I get up and they arrive in front of me and no one seems to notice that I'm there.

Mom says, "Either you arrest him now and take him for a psych eval, or skip the arrest and just take him straight to the ER so he doesn't do anything stupid. You know the rules."

"He probably doesn't mean it," a cop says.

"I know he doesn't mean it," Mom says. "But he said it. If he does something dumb to himself tonight, you two are liable same as I am as an RN. But it probably isn't a good idea for me to be the one solving this problem right now if you get my drift."

Fifteen minutes later, Dad is in the back of a squad car and being driven away. When we walk back into the house, three Sarahs are in the living room. Ten-year-old Sarah has collected all the pieces of the ceramic owl from the kitchen counter where I left them and from the living room floor. Twenty-three-year-old Sarah is trying to make sense of the disemboweled umbrella. Forty-year-old Sarah is putting the books back onto the bookshelf in some sort of order.

I have no idea what to say. Not to any of them.

Bruce is outside waiting for me to go to the school with him.

Mom says, "You girls must be hungry. How about lunch?"

Bruce doesn't know what I'm doing, but he follows me anyway. Three buses, a block of walking.

He says something about wishing he'd have dressed more for the weather.

He says, "It's good to face your demons. You can't throw away your future over this." Future, future, future.

He doesn't say anything about how we're not anywhere near the school he expected to visit today.

It's about sixth period so the art room should be full of my class. As we approach, I hear glass breaking from upstairs. Someone else must be here. Someone came in since last week and tagged the entire hallway in bright pink graffiti. Words that don't seem to fit together. ATTENTION. DIGEST. EXPLODE.

"Can I help you?" Miss Smith says.

"Hi, Miss Smith," I say. "This is my brother, Bruce."

Bruce doesn't say anything. Bruce's eyes show he is worried. Probably rightfully. The floor could collapse under his feet. We could get shot.

I look into the art room and Carmen is there and she says, "What up, Sarah?" and I wave and she gives me the code for call you later.

"Nice to meet you, Bruce!" Miss Smith says, smiling so wide bats could fly out of her mouth.

I decide Bruce says, "Sarah told me the whole story. I want an explanation. I'm about to become her guardian and plan to talk to the principal and the administration about what happened in your room. All of it. Not just the disappearance of her art project but the things you've said to students about her."

Miss Smith doesn't say anything. I am still waiting for bats to fly out of her mouth.

I imagine Bruce says, "I think we should start with the art project, though. Did you steal it or did a student steal it?"

"I assure you I didn't take your sister's project."

Bruce turns to me. "Do you have any idea who stole it?"

"I can only guess. Miss Smith is hooking up with Vicky. So it was probably Vicky."

Bruce looks at me. "She's having sex with a student?"

"Is this even legal?" Miss Smith asks. "How did you get in here?" The bats have arrived. "You can't just come in here and accuse me of things."

Bruce says he has to pee.

I walk him to the men's room and he asks me to come in with him. I'm not scared, but he is. There are four urinals. Each one has a letter painted in black on it. The letters spell D-U-M-B. He pees in the one with the M. Two rats skitter from the back corner of the stall with no door and past me into the hallway.

We walk through the halls and Bruce seems concerned. "So this is where you go instead of school?"

I say, "Don't worry. I come here all the time. It's my new school."

"Um—I don't know what to say."

I stop at another locker with a cool diorama. "Never saw anything like this in my old school."

He doesn't say anything.

I take him to the room that says HEED on the wall. I point to the word.

"This place is art. My kind of art."

"It's derelict," he says. "And dangerous."

"I feel at home here. Ruins. Lies. And look," I say, running to the end of the hallway where there's a two-story-high spray-painted windmill. "There's even a windmill!"

Bruce kicks a can of spray paint by accident and startles himself. I lean down and pick it up. Half full. Gold. Seems right. I shake it so the ball inside makes that unmistakable noise.

I walk into the nearest classroom. I go to the front of the room where the chalkboard used to be, but someone has pried it off the wall and left a big rectangle of clear surface.

In gold spray paint, in all capital letters, I write, THIS IS ART.

When I'm done, I find a desk and sit there and look at what I wrote.

There's the sound of footsteps in the hallway and before Bruce or I can move, forty-year-old Sarah comes into the room. She takes a deep breath and says, "God, I love the smell of spray paint." I want to ask her how she got here because she was supposed to be eating lunch with Mom and the other Sarahs, but instead I study her. Still in her hiking shoes—but this time I notice the tiny spots of paint on them.

"Me too," I say.

"You haven't told anyone about Miss Smith yet." She turns to Bruce. "Hey, Bruce."

"Hey," he says, but you can tell from the look on his face he doesn't know who she is. He's standing there and his body is trying to walk toward the door. He's going to say "Let's get out of here" any minute now.

"You have to tell someone," forty-year-old Sarah says.

"Bruce knows."

I don't know what else to say. It's hard to be honest about this. I haven't told anyone because when I walked in on Miss Smith and Vicky, they looked so happy. They looked in love. They looked right for each other. Back when it happened, we were all still friends. Miss Smith was still nice to me. Vicky and the whole art club always said I was the one who would make it for real. They said I was weird enough. Miss Smith often talked about the pain in my work.

Ruin.

There was always ruin in my work. Whether it was color or feeling, or something surreal like an animal with no head. Something was ruined. Painful.

Only I didn't know why until the meat grinder.

But why hurt two people who're in love, you know? Why spread ruin?

Forty-year-old Sarah says, "I can take care of it my own way if you want. I can call the school."

"They seemed so happy," I say.

"You're mixed up. I understand. But a grown woman preying on a teenager isn't happy."

"What's going on?" Bruce says. "Who is this?"

I pace, my shoes landing on broken pieces of everything, and I explain who forty-year-old Sarah is. Bruce looks at her and smiles.

Bruce says, "Let's get out of here."

The two of them start to leave. I put the can of spray paint down and realize that ruin has done me a favor. Ruin is why I will be able to draw the pear. Ruin is why I'll be able to sculpt another owl. Ruin is why my work has *pain*.

When we get back outside, forty-year-old Sarah says she's going to take the next bus and I ask Bruce if he'll walk with me instead.

On our walk back to home, I explain the Sarahs to Bruce.

"It's impossible to explain," I say. "But they're real."

He looks at me as if I'm some sort of mentally ill kid and maybe I am. I just had an existential crisis. Last week I ate other people's food out of trash cans. The week before that I was following around a homeless man because I thought he was Macedonia or Spain. The week before that, and all weeks before that, I was living inside of a giant, useless, windmill-shaped, bile-colored lie.

The walk home is nice. There's a breeze. It feels more like spring than summer. Bruce doesn't say much except for how he misses things he passes—which is nearly everything. I realize that he was exiled. More ruin. More pain.

I tell him, "You can always move back, you know."

The Sarahs and Mom are all sitting around the big table in the study and they're having a conversation about me. I know this because when Bruce and I walk in the door, they stop talking.

I walk Bruce over to the windowsill where he sits in front of the last geranium Mom ever bought. I say, "Bruce, this is ten-year-old Sarah. You remember her, I'm sure." Ten-year-old Sarah waves her circular wave and has tears in her eyes.

"That's twenty-three-year-old Sarah. She thinks she knows everything but she really doesn't. But she means well." Twenty-three-year-old Sarah gives me the finger and I give it back to her.

"And that's forty-year-old Sarah. You've already met."

Bruce leans against the windowsill and smiles. I don't know why he's smiling. On the table is a large bowl of tortilla chips—already half empty—and a little bowl of homemade white queso dip. "Sarah made that," Mom says, pointing at forty-year-old Sarah.

I try some. "Wow. That's good," I say.

"Nice to know I improve," twenty-three-year-old Sarah says. "Last time I made this it was runny and tasted like plastic."

"You used the wrong kind of cheese," forty-year-old Sarah says.

"Okay, so this isn't a joke," Bruce finally says. "You're all really . . . you."

I say, "Yeah." I look at my three other Sarahs and I don't feel as numb as I did yesterday. I feel like doing something with my hands.

Ten-year-old Sarah says, "I'm so glad you came back!" and gets up from the table and hugs Bruce. Of the four of us Sarahs, she is the most traumatized by what happened in Mexico. I am most traumatized by what happened before Mexico. Twenty-three-year-old Sarah is most traumatized by having once been me. I have no idea what forty-year-old Sarah is most traumatized by.

When I ask her, she says, "Traumatized? I don't know."

I go to the kitchen and open the bottom drawer and retrieve the tinfoil. I return to the table with it and start ripping off pieces that are long enough to fit around my head.

Mom sits at the head of the table. She smiles—like maybe it's cool to have four daughters instead of just one truant sixteen-year-old. I start to scrunch the tinfoil into strong bands that will act as the base of my crown. I add shapes every few inches by molding the foil into itself.

Bruce says, "It's like I suddenly have four sisters."

"We didn't want to freak you out," twenty-three-year-old Sarah says. "We came to help Mom pack Dad's things."

"He has to pack his stuff by himself," Bruce says. "He'll probably be back tomorrow. We should all stay."

"That would make me feel a lot better," Mom says.

"I can make dinner," forty-year-old Sarah says.

I say, "I'll help."

All Sarahs head for the kitchen. Ten-year-old Sarah sits at the study table with my tinfoil pieces. She adds beads and foam stickers to what I'd started. Then she grabs a few pieces of paper and my box of colored pencils and comes into the kitchen at the table. She draws all of us making dinner.

Bruce and Mom talk about divorce in the living room. I'm glad to have a wall between me and divorce. I'm glad it's happening, but I'm glad the adults are taking care of it. I want to be sixteen. I want to be a human being. Or four human beings. Or whatever I am.

Twenty-three-year-old Sarah is surprisingly less judgmental around forty-year-old Sarah. Neither of them talk about art, which I find strange.

"So, did we become an artist?" I ask them.

"We can't tell you that," they say. "We can't tell you what happens with you."

I point to ten-year-old Sarah. "She knows that in six years her parents will get divorced."

"And look at how well she draws!" they say. Ten-year-old Sarah looks up and grins. "She's so talented!"

"I'm having an existential crisis and you guys show up and you can't tell me how it's going to work out?" I think back to Tiffany and what she said. *With talent comes pain* or something like that.

"You live," they say. "See? We're proof that you'll figure it out."

"Doesn't help," I say.

"But it's original," they say. "Isn't that what you wanted? To be original?"

"You're original," I say. "I'm still just me."

"If you want to see it that way, that's up to you, Umbrella."

The phone rings. Mom answers it. She takes the call upstairs and stays there for a while. Bruce comes into the kitchen and sits with ten-year-old Sarah as she draws. After half an hour, I decide to see if Mom's okay. Her bedroom door is open a crack. I can't hear any talking.

When I peek in, she's curled on her bed with a box of tissues in her arms. A thousand scenarios go through my head.

"Is everything okay?"

She looks up, nods, and beckons me inside while she blows her nose.

"I'm sorry, Sarah."

"For what?"

"I'm sorry we're getting a divorce."

"It's not like anybody died or anything," I say.

She laugh-cries at that. A little bubble of snot forms and pops under her nose.

"Well, it's not," I say. "Dad can move out. We can stay here. Everything will be fine. Plus, he won't ever hurt you again."

At this, she cries a little because it must be hard living a lie for so long and having the person you were trying to save, save you instead. Not like I can take credit. I'm pretty sure it was ten-year-old Sarah who saved us both.

At dinner, I wear my tinfoil headpiece—seven sturdy rings intertwined with colorful additions from all the Sarahs. Twenty-three-year-old Sarah added a small rubber cupcake. Bruce used tape to secure a small pterodactyl toy. Forty-year-old Sarah went outside and found a feather from a pigeon and placed it long ways. Ten-year-old Sarah insisted on a unicorn sticker for the front. I am the queen of unicorns, cupcakes, pterodactyls, and feathers. I'm not sure over whom I rule, but I have a feeling it's me.

HELEN'S QUIET

I'm a goddamn ER night nurse. Do you know what I've seen in my life? I've seen a thousand ways to die. I've met every kind of person you can imagine. I've met murderers and child molesters and people who starve their mothers to death.

I've met men who killed their ex-wives. I've met the dead ex-wife. I've recorded her time of death on her chart. I've seen me in her.

I've met the nicest people, too. Kids and moms and dads and uncles and nephews and grandmothers who are simple and kind.

I've met Earl and a hundred more like him.

I've met Rose and a hundred more like her.

Every night there's a drunk—sometimes a big one, sometimes a small one. Sometimes they swing but I know how to duck after living with Chet for twenty-eight years. I know how to duck.

It's quiet in the house without Chet. It's a quiet I wished for a million times but never got. When he left today, I wanted to feel relief but I didn't feel it. I don't think I'll feel it until the papers are signed, the lawyers are paid, and the whole thing is over.

I will never understand why he didn't change. We could have had such a great life. We could have had some fun. Once he was gone there were no bottles hidden in the garage or the toilet cisterns. No pills or bags of smack or weed or anything. All that meanness was inside of him. Not a bottle. Not a pill. Not a needle. It was him.

Nineteen years old. At nineteen years old I knew what he was. I stayed with him anyway. Make a note: You can't change people with love. It doesn't work that way.

I'm forty-seven. I'm not going to sit here and tell you I wasted all those years because I didn't. I made a name for myself at work and helped thousands of people. I raised two excellent children. I know how to cook a decent Sunday roast. But the love I wasted on a man who couldn't love himself is lost with those years. Lost as my twenty-twenty eyesight, lost as my beach body, lost as my hair color, lost as my ability to do a cartwheel.

It's like tossing a gourmet meal into a sewer.

I'm giving my middle fingers a rest.

I'm not singing that song anymore and I'm not lying.

That's going to be the hardest part.

I never thought I'd be a liar. Not to my own kids. Not to myself. I'm a goddamn ER night nurse. I tell the truth in dark twelve-hour shifts. Harsh truth. Maybe I needed one place in my life to not be an emergency. Maybe lying to myself was the only way I could sleep.

I wanted quiet for so long.

Now I can have it.

You have no idea how much I want you to be careful. You have no idea how much I want to save you from what happened to me. Listen closely.

Thick Skin

I'm not sure what comes next. I don't know where to find my future.

I wake up in my room and ten-year-old Sarah is playing with my old Legos on my floor. Today is the day Mom meets with the lawyer. Today is the day Dad probably comes home to get his stuff.

Up until now, I wasn't nervous.

As I lie in bed, I visit scenarios I shouldn't visit. I think about Dad coming home and shooting us all. All four Sarahs, Bruce, and Mom. And probably himself. I shake the thought out of my head. I think about Dad coming home and not leaving ever again. Locking himself into his room. Barricading the door. I decide to get up and take a shower before the other Sarahs use all the hot water.

How does this work?

How do so many Sarahs exist in one place at one time?

Does the answer matter when all the answers so far have been lies and windmills and half-truths and get-on-with-its?

Thick skin is a fallacy. The skin is an *organ*. It isn't just about pimples and freckles and sunburn and wrinkles. All skin is thick skin.

I hear Mom and ten-year-old Sarah giggling and my skin absorbs the sound. The feeling. The idea of giggling. Skin lets things in and lets things out. It's a two-way system. Right now, in the shower, I let out the art club.

There are more important things in the world than the art club.

Art can't exist in the vacuum of emotion. It's why Carmen draws tornadoes. It's why Dad doesn't draw anything at all. He's the hole where the rat used to be. I guess if he wanted to change, he'd draw the rat. A million times, he'd draw the rat.

I can't figure out what I am if Dad is a rat.

I can't figure out what I am at all.

I guess that's why I'm here. Not in the shower, but in a houseful of Sarahs, in a city full of Earls, in a joust with a windmill. I can't figure out what I am at all.

Mom knocks on the bathroom door. She tells me to hurry up. She says, "We're going out for breakfast."

I try to imagine four Sarahs, a Bruce, and their mother going out to breakfast. What restaurant could handle all of us?

The only thing the waiter says is "What a beautiful family!"

And we are. We are a beautiful family.

Mom and Bruce go to the lawyer's office together. All Sarahs stay at the house and hope Dad doesn't come home. We sit at the study table.

> 10: You're all so uptight. Dad isn't gonna freak out again.
> ME: You don't know that.
> 23: She has a point. We'd just call the police again. He knows that.
> ME: It doesn't matter what he knows. He can't control himself.
> 40: His whole gig is control. He'll be fine. We'll talk to him.
> 23: He won't know what to do with us.

10: I've met him twice and he still has no idea who I am.

ME: True. She even came over for dinner.

23: You went to dinner?

10: We ate tacos.

ME: He thinks her name is Katie.

40: Katie?

10: It was the first name that came to mind.

ME: She even played "Eleanor Rigby" for him on piano.

40: God, I'd love to hear that.

Ten-year-old Sarah sits at the piano and plays her rusty version again. She tells me to play, so I do and it's a little less rusty than it was when I played for Mom last week. Twenty-three-year-old Sarah looks sad. Forty-year-old Sarah says, "I really should take up piano again."

23: Me too.

ME: The skin is the largest organ in the human body. Did you know that?

10: If you know it, then we all know it.

23: We have thick skin. I know that.

ME: I'm still mad about never finding out who stole the headpiece. I know I shouldn't be. I know I should get over it. I just want to know.

40: You find out.

23: I do?

ME: I do?

10: Who was it?

40: It's exactly who you think it is.

ME: How did you find out?

40: Carmen.

ME: You still know Carmen?

40: She's my best friend.

23: I'm so glad. She's been so hard to reach lately. I thought things were going to go bad between us.

40: You're spending too much time with your boy-friend. She thinks he's an asshole but can't tell you.

10: I don't even know how you can go with boys. They're so dumb.

ME: So it was Vicky? Or Miss Smith?

40: Trust your gut.

I know it was both. Vicky. And Miss Smith. I find my queen of the unicorns tinfoil headpiece and start working on it again. More foil. Spikes like the Statue of Liberty, but longer and more disorganized.

ME: But the whole art club knew, though, right?

40: Carmen didn't know, but then she found out. The art club still has a page on The Social.

23: That's pathetic.

ME: Do they all become famous artists?

40: What do you think?

23: I very much doubt any of them become famous artists.

10: Most famous artists only become famous after they die, anyway. Like José Guadalupe Posada.

I try on my new crown and stand up to see myself in the mirror. It needs work. The spikes aren't looking as good as I thought they would.

> 40: So, I took care of the Miss Smith thing yester-
> day. I figured you'd want to know.
> 23: Sick bitch. I read about that.
> 40: I know you wanted to let it go. I did, too, when I
> was you. But some things you just can't paint over.

Some things you just can't paint over. I think about 40 and how she doesn't seem married or in love with anyone. I think about how Tiffany ignored my question about love when she read my palm. I don't know how much control I have over my Sarahs. Are they really me or are they the me I think I'll be? I don't think I'll ever know the answer to this. Not until it happens.

> 10: Can I wear your crown?

I hand her the crown and say, "You can keep it. It looks best on you."

A car parks in front of the house and a car door slams. Ten-year-old Sarah goes to the front window and says, "It's Dad." I text Mom the way she told me to. I text Bruce, too, in case Mom is too busy to read her texts.

All Sarahs stand in the living room. 40 has her hands on her hips. 23 blocks the way to the kitchen. 10 opens the door. I sit on the stairs because I want a good view.

Dad hangs his head. I have seen this act before. He is now sorry for everything he did when he did it. He is now in control by being sorry for losing control. If his character had a name in our play, he would be called Pathetic Rat.

> PR (doesn't look up): Please don't ask me to
> leave. Let me say some things first.
> 40: Who are you talking to?

PR stops and slowly looks up. His face contorts.

> PR: Who are you?
> 40: Who are you?
> PR: Sarah, who are these people? Oh, hi—um—
> Katie. Nice to see you again . . . I don't under-
> stand what you're all doing here.
> 23: We're waiting for Mom to get back.

PR blinks and his frown is a thinking frown but an angry frown at the same time. His tail is between his legs.

> 40: We're here to help you pack.
> 23 (points to boxes in living room): I have a few
> boxes I found in the basement.
> 40: Bruce got the suitcases out of the attic this
> morning.

There is something in the room with us. It's familiar. It's a feeling I've known my whole life but never talked about. It's an invisible man or monster under the bed.

History. That's what it is. History is in the room with us. You absorb it even if it's not happening right in front of you. You absorb the feeling of it. It's there even though it's not there. It's in your skin.

> ME: You should really get started before Mom
> gets home.
> PR: I don't have to go anywhere.
> 40: Don't be a dick, Dad. You have to go and you
> know it.
> 23: It's about time.
> 10: You never fooled me, you know.

If this were a movie or a cartoon, Dad would faint. That's what it looks like and feels like. It feels like something big just happened. Like we're all inside a cloud of thick magician's smoke. Magic has happened. The truth has set him free. History finally caught up with him—the rat who never admitted he was a rat.

I think of the joust. Two riders galloping at full force toward each other. We are one rider. Dad is the other. All of us in armor meant to protect us from the storm of bullshit. As we ride, the adrenaline rises as we aim our lances. But then Dad falls off his horse before we ever get to knock him off.

40 got Dad to pack his bags. 23 helped him figure out where he could stay. She had her phone app set to one-bedroom apartments in Center City. 10 stayed with me because she was scared. I played a game of Uno with her and she beat me and left me with a handful of high-value cards. Neither of us wanted to be home when Mom came back, but we stayed because 23 and 40 told us we should.

> 40: You should watch it end. If you don't, you'll al-
> ways wonder.
> 23: Nothing bad is going to happen, I promise.
> 10: It's too sad.
> ME: We'll be safe now.

When Mom and Bruce come through the door, the Pathetic Rat hangs his head again. He starts his entrance speech from the beginning. He says, "Please don't make me leave. Let me say some things first."

Mom says, "We'll talk in the kitchen. Alone."

We all know that you can't be alone in our kitchen. We all sit down in the living room because we'll hear it from here. 10 sidles up next to Bruce on the love seat and he puts his arm around her and gives her a side-hug. I sit between 23 and 40 on the couch. 23. 16. 40. Our arms touch. Only our skin is between us. Thick skin. *We heal fast.*

23 says, "I'm sorry I was such a bitch to you at first."

"You didn't take me seriously," I say.

"Yeah. I guess."

"You made fun of my new name."

"Sorry. But—Umbrella?"

I say, "It has deeper meanings."

"I know," she says. "I'm you."

"So why choose to make fun of me? Why not just be nice?"

40 says, "Being twenty-three is hard. You'll see."

"No one takes me seriously, either," 23 says.

We hear Mom say "You never took me seriously" in the kitchen. She's forty-seven years old. Maybe we're destined to never be taken seriously.

Dad is begging in the kitchen. Mom has taken the weekend off—first full weekend since Mexico she won't be in the ER sewing people together at three o'clock in the morning. We have plans.

40 says, "It's getting late. We have to go or else we won't have enough time."

Bruce says, "She'll be done in a few minutes."

In the kitchen, Mom says, "I have to be somewhere."

"We can still talk, though, right? I'll call you over the weekend. We'll call it a trial separation," Dad says.

"Call it whatever makes you feel okay about it," Mom answers.

Bruce says, "He's staying with a friend for a week."

23 says, "We'll have to rent the apartment for him. He'll never do it himself."

"Mom took care of it," Bruce says. "The lawyer knows a guy. It's all taken care of."

It's all taken care of.

40 calls Dad a taxi on Bruce's phone. She gets up from the couch and tidies the mantel after Dad's rearrangement of the house yesterday. She says she wants a picture of all of us so she can give it to Mom.

We all pile onto the couch and put our heads together. 10 is up front, lying across our laps. Bruce holds his arm out as far as he can and takes a bunch of pictures of the five of us with his phone. A few of them are serious—we smile and look posed. Toward the end, we're laughing. I tickle 10 and then 23 tickles 40 and someone tickles me and some of the pictures on Bruce's phone are priceless, like *Three Musicians*.

I think of Earl.

This is art.

The five of us. 40, 23, 10, me, and Bruce.

The two of us. Me and Bruce.

Me.

I am art.

I have become Spain. I have become Macedonia. Life is art. Truth is art. Art doesn't steal. Art just is. You can take a break from art. You can make art for seventy-two hours straight if you want. You can breathe in and out and that is art. You can hold your breath and that is art.

Blinking is art. Snoring is art. Sneezing is art. It's not complicated. No one needs to be better than anyone else. That is not art. That is anti-art. Art is inclusive and it's the murals all over this city and it's the kids in the park and the old people you see at the corner grocery who only buy four things at a time. Art is dog shit next to a tree on Locust Street. Art is the sound of the Dumpster service behind the pizza place at four in the morning. Art is as big as Liberty Two. Art is as small as two wedding rings at the bottom of the sea.

You get the picture.

Nothing new ever really happens.

The museum closes at five and we get there just after one. We travel in a pack and don't split up even when Bruce drags us through the medieval art. Ten-year-old Sarah really wants to see the armor room, but she knows we'll get there. She holds Mom's hand, and I'm not jealous even for a second.

We get to the gallery with Salvador Dalí's *Soft Construction with Boiled Beans (Premonition of Civl War)*, and Mom stops in front of it. "Grotesque, but I like it," she says. This is a woman who reaches into people's bodies and removes foreign objects and sometimes small animals and sometimes four hundred pills.

I tell them I want to show them *Sleeping Girl*. They follow me through the maze of contemporary galleries and I get to where the Lichtenstein was, but it's not there anymore. I ask the security guard, "Where'd the Lichtenstein go?"

She answers, "They moved it last week."

Sleeping girl. On the move. Maybe she woke up. Maybe she's happier now.

40 says, "Where's the Twombly room?"

I lead us to the Twombly room. Ten-year-old Sarah gets impatient for the armor. She says, "This looks like scribbling!" I tell her to be quiet and point to the writing at the bottom of my favorite piece in the collection. It says: *Like a fire that consumes all before it.*

All of us stop here.

All of us stop at this scratched message meant just for us.

We are allowed to relax now.

Mom takes a deep breath and I hug her and Bruce hugs both of us and the Sarahs gather round and we form a family of Spain. A family of Macedonia.

This family—no matter what it looks like on any given day—we are art.

Mom says, "I'm so sorry," and her words are art.

I say, "You don't have anything to be sorry for," and my words are art.

Bruce says, "I missed you so much," and his words are art.

We are so consumed by all before it we don't see the others leave us. We are suddenly three. Three relaxed people. They didn't even say good-bye.

This is what's left.

It's everything we need.

Nobody said *There's nothing we can do about it.* We did something.

It's not like anybody died or anything.

I wonder if I'll ever see ten-year-old Sarah again. I decide that I will.

Then I see my reflection on the glass outside the Twombly room and I see her there. Ten-year-old Sarah is there. In my reflection.

I did this.

I did it my own way, just like the headpiece. No one else would understand what my skin absorbed in all those years of lying.

I will sweat out the lies.

I will sweat out the truth.

My scars will tell stories until the day I stop breathing.

Thick skin? You can't make art if you can't feel the tips of your fingers.

So I had an existential crisis. I didn't know why I was here. I couldn't draw a pear. Who cares? I saw a teacher kissing a student. I had my art project sabotaged. I lived inside a thirteen-million-peso windmill that couldn't generate electricity. Some days I carry an umbrella in case it rains bullshit.

I am a human being. I am sixteen years old.

And that is enough.

I get a text on my phone from Bruce, who is standing in the same hallway with me. It's our picture—all four Sarahs on the couch, and Bruce. I regret not taking ten-year-old Sarah to the armor room one last time, so I go there myself.

There's a detour. Strange. I have to slow down behind a guy on the steps who's carrying a ladder, then weave around to the right to get into the armor gallery from a side door. But I want to see where the guy with the ladder is going, so I follow him to a gallery room that's sealed off with plastic. There's a sign. PARDON OUR APPEARANCE. WE'RE SETTING UP A NEW EXHIBIT! The whole second floor smells like fresh paint.

He parts the plastic and walks through it and I stop because I'm afraid I'll get in trouble if I go into the room. I stand there and try to see through the plastic, but it's several sheets thick and everything is blurry like heavy rain on a bus windshield.

I open the plastic overlap a little and peek in and it's just blank walls. Whiter than white. Blanker than blank. *Just like me.* But this is a fresh start. In a week or two, this room will house something new—something I've never seen before. *Just like me.* I stand there until the security guard from the adjacent armor room taps me lightly on the shoulder. I say, "Sorry," but I don't really mean it. I've been to this museum so many times and I've never been as moved as this— by something so ordinary. A blank room. A man with a ladder. The smell of fresh paint. Construction.

The burr in my sternum melts and I can't feel its spurs anymore. I walk around a big pillar and into the armor room with my hand on my chest. I think of ten-year-old Sarah and I remember she had the burr. I never met six-year-old Sarah, but I know she had the burr, too. And now it's gone. Just like that.

I stare at the sixteenth-century Saxon armor with its chest spike. I picture this armor in action. Jousting—galloping full speed at another man on a horse, aiming a huge stick at him and thinking of nothing else but to knock him off. It's a furious pace. It's a violent game. Your heart beats out of its cage. Every time it's original because you never know what's going to happen.

As I stare at the armor, I decide to get back on my horse. I decide that tomorrow, I'm going to draw a pear. I decide originality is inborn, same as my circular fun wave. I decide something new happens every single day.

I am left with myself—I can't get away from her.

I tell her: Slow down.

I tell her: *You can't listen closely when you're galloping.*

I tell her: *Maybe if you take off all that armor, you won't feel so heavy.*

ACKNOWLEDGMENTS

Books don't find their way to readers all by themselves. I owe thanks to many people.

None of my books would have been possible without Andrew Karre, who plucked me from obscurity after fifteen years of rejection letters. But this book wouldn't be possible if not for his continuing belief in me. Thank you, AK. Also, to the fine people at Dutton, all of you—thank you. And Michael Bourret, thank you for always steering me in the right direction. You are my ambassador of Kwan and I am so grateful.

My sister Robyn, a solid-scrubs kind of ER nurse: Thank you for Mexico where this book was born and thank you for putting people together again in the middle of the night. Kathryn Gaglione Hughes, thank you so much for the bus stop—this book is proof that graduate lectures inspire. Azaan, Kate, Isabel, and Lilly from Austin TBF in fall 2014: Thank you for encouraging me to keep writing a book that was causing me pain and confusion. Your words were gold.

These friends helped me deal with a lot of crazy stuff during the writing of this novel: Kathy Snyder, C.G. Watson, e.E. Charlton-Trujillo, Beth Kephart, Zac Brewer, Sr., Kim Miller, Andrew Smith, Beth Zimmerman, and a few others not listed here because it's hard to remember everyone at one time. I can't thank you enough for your advice, listening ears, kindness. Without friends like you, nothing new would ever happen. And as always, thank you to my readers. All of you. And to the librarians, booksellers, teachers, bloggers, and anyone who digs my groove enough to pass the word along. Your support means the world to me. My gratitude is galaxy-sized.

KEEP READING FOR A GLIMPSE OF

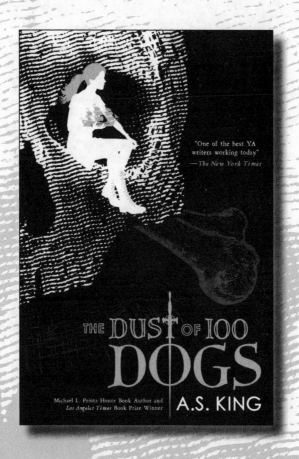

"One of the best YA writers working today"
—*The New York Times*

THE DUST OF 100 DOGS

A.S. KING

Michael L. Printz Honor Book Author and
Los Angeles Times Book Prize Winner

Prologue

With one last, almighty roar, the Frenchman fell to his knees and died. When the smoke cleared, Emer kicked him to make sure he was dead. Bent on one knee in the moonlight, holding his head with her left hand, she took a marlinspike and removed his right eyeball with relative ease. She rolled it in the sand next to his head and shoved the spike deep into his empty socket.

She placed her pistol gently into her waistband and looked toward the sea.

"I curse you!" she screamed at the dark water. "I curse you for all you gave me and for all you pilfered! I curse you for the journeys you begin and the journeys you end! I curse you until I can't hate you anymore! And I scarcely think I will ever hate you more than on this wretched day!" Her fair hair stuck to her face, wet with sorrow and surf, and her hand-embroidered cotton blouse clung to her, stained with her lover's blood.

Turning again to the two dead bodies, she retrieved the shovel from underneath Seanie—Seanie, her first and only love. She limped back to the clearing. Looking around to make sure no one was watching, she sat down on the edge of the hole and talked to herself.

"There was only one reason to stop all of this poxy business." She turned and looked at the distant dead. "What worth is a precious jewel now? Damn it! In all these years, over all this water! And I end up a fool with a lap full of precious nothing."

She dragged the two crates into the hole and began to cover them quickly, concerned that the Frenchman's reinforcements would arrive at any minute. She buried the shovel last, on top, and used her hands to fill the remaining depression, covering the sand with sticks and dead leaves.

Returning to the scene of the dead men, she lay down beside Seanie, placed her head on his chest, and sobbed.

"It's like two different lives in the same bloody day."

Through her sobs, Emer heard footsteps. A voice boomed from the darkness, making her jump. She scrambled to her feet and reloaded her pistol.

"Foul bitch!" he began, in island-accented English. "You have meddled in my life for *too many* years! I'm sure you didn't know every whore in these islands heard him scream your name a thousand times! And me, too! Now look at him! Dead!"

Emer saw the man emerging from the tree line, his hands hidden. She had seen him before, on Tortuga and on board the *Chester*. The Frenchman's first mate.

"You will *see!*" he yelled, jumping from the brush. "You will see how true love lasts! You will *see* how real love spans time and distance we know nothing of!"

He rushed forward then, shaking a small purse toward her. From it came a fine powder that covered Emer's hair and face. She reached up and wiped her eyes clear, confused.

"What are you at?" she asked, spitting dust from her lips.

He stood with his arms and face raised to the night sky. "I curse you with the power of every spirit who ever knew love!" he screamed. "I curse you to one hundred lives as the bitch you are, and hope wild dogs tear your heart into the state you've left mine!" He began chanting in a frightful foreign language.

Still brushing the dust from her hair, Emer took aim with her gun and fired.

As she watched the man fall, she felt a burning prod in her back and stumbled sideways—long enough to see that the Frenchman had miraculously not been all dead, and long enough to see that he was covered in stray pieces of the strange dust his first mate had thrown at her.

She tried to fall as near to Seanie as possible, and managed to get close enough to reach out and grab his cold hand. She took her dying breath lying halfway between her lover and her killer, covered in the dust of one hundred dogs, knowing she was the only person on the planet who knew what was buried beneath the chilly sand ten yards away.

.I.

Isn't She Sweet?

Imagine my surprise when, after three centuries of fighting with siblings over a spare furry teat and licking my water from a bowl, I was given a huge human nipple, all to myself, filled with warm mother's milk. I say it was huge because Sadie Adams, my mother, has enormous breasts, something I never inherited.

When I was born into a typical family in Hollow Ford, Pennsylvania, in 1972, my life was finally mine again. No more obeying orders from masters, no more performing silly tricks, and no more rancid scraps to eat. Within seconds of my birth, I was suckling like no other child in the local maternity ward, in order to grow strong quickly and return to a life cut short by the blade.

A puppy can walk and wander and whine from the minute they leave the amniotic sac. There is a freedom in that which I learned to appreciate during those first years as a human again. Lying on my back for hours in a crib, wearing a diaper, and drooling made me feel like an idiot. I first tried to walk again at five months old and promptly fell over onto the linoleum floor, wailing from pain and frustration.

I was the youngest of five children born to Sadie and Alfred. Being the last, there was no wonder for them in my first steps or mutterings, and only a sigh of relief when I started to use the toilet by myself.

I don't know if my parents saw it then, but they certainly noticed later that I was completely different from other children. When I first began talking, I sometimes spoke of places I'd never been, and they would look at me, confused. When I started school, my kindergarten teacher arranged a meeting with them and asked where I'd gotten so much knowledge of history and language. They shrugged and figured I was going to be the genius in the family—so I didn't let them down.

In all fairness, they needed a genius. As I grew up, I started to notice that life in the Adams household was less typical than it appeared on the outside. My father suffered horribly from the side effects of his tour in the Vietnam War and my mother had never recovered from her childhood. Their lives had been lived on the edge of poverty and emotional instability. In me and my superhuman intelligence, they saw a way out of their troubles and shame, and so they rarely questioned any of it.

But after a meeting with my first grade teacher, they had to sit me down and ask a few things.

"Saffron, how did you know so much about the second world war?"

"I guess I saw it on the TV," I answered, trying not to sound coy.

My father frowned. "You couldn't have seen it on the TV. They don't say that much on the TV."

"Must have read it in a book, then."

"Sweetie, we don't have any books like that. Did you read it somewhere else?" my mother cooed.

"I must have."

"Hmmm."

"Saffron, we know you're a very clever girl, but do you think there's a way you could stop showing off in class? Mrs. Zeiber is concerned that you're making the other children feel bad," she said.

"Then why don't they put me in a higher grade?" I didn't like Mrs. Zeiber, but now I had reason to like her even less. I pictured myself liberating her eyeball from its socket and tossing it onto the merry-go-round in the first grade recess area.

"But we thought you liked being in Mrs. Zeiber's class."

"I do, but I'm pretty bored. I'm sick of counting to a hundred," I whined.

They looked at me, and shrugged at each other. Two weeks later, after winter break, I was enrolled in the district's gifted program—the ultimate place for showing off knowledge that no other first grader could have. I blabbered about everything—the goings-on in the Truman White House, the main tenets of Hinduism, the political complications of Central Africa. My peers envied me, even the teachers envied me. I was like a miracle kid or something, and people started to talk.

The next year, I realized that life as Saffron Adams would have to be far more inconspicuous. I couldn't go around claiming to be a genius, and I couldn't go telling stories from history that I shouldn't know yet. I guess I realized that the more I said, the more chance I had of ruining everything I was working toward.

It was then, in 1980, the year I turned eight years old, that I forged my plan to return to the Caribbean Sea. Most of the other kids in my class were toying with being rock stars or President of the United States, but I had something much more appealing in mind. Finally done with my one hundred lives as a dog, I would one day reclaim my jewels and gold, hold them close to my heart, and live happily ever after.

So from that day forward, in order to seem my age when people asked me what I wanted to be when I grew up, I answered accordingly.

"I want to be a pirate," I would say. And they would smile and think, "Isn't she sweet?"

.2.

My Mother's Lament

Growing up where I did, it was kind of funny for a kid to want to be a pirate, I guess. There wasn't a spot of water for miles. Three hundred miles, to be exact, to the New Jersey shoreline. My mother liked it that way. When we took our weeklong vacation in the summer, we always went west or north or south, but never east.

"I've spent enough time near the sea for this life," she would say. But still, all my sister's friends spent their vacations walking the boardwalk eating ice cream and salt-water taffy, while we took historical outings. Sometimes, if we would whine too much about the mosquitoes or the boring Civil War battlefields of Virginia, she would scare us with lies: "Children your age go missing every summer on the boardwalk," or "I won't have you running around half naked in front of old perverts." She would turn her eye to my teenaged sister and whisper, "Especially you, Patricia."

It wasn't until I got older that I learned what she had against the sea.

Once Patricia had moved out and Darren was packed for college, my mother began to need me more. I used to talk to her on the rare nights when, feeling lonely, she would sit at the kitchen table with a bottle of Irish whiskey. On a night in 1985, she told me what happened to her family back in the 1950s. I was thirteen.

Her brother Jim had called from Ireland that night, which he often did since he'd found us six years earlier. They'd talked for about an hour and, when my mother hung up the phone, she turned off the lights in the kitchen and lit a candle. She fetched a glass from the cupboard and sat down with her bottle. (She would sip minute amounts of drink and never get tipsy, but seemed to get some sort of familiar relief from it.) Teary eyed, she made me sit down, and poured herself another short measure.

"Saffron?"

"Yeah?"

"Do you know the story of my brother Willie?" My mother spoke in a mixed Irish-English accent, the kind that sounds like a question all the time.

"Willie?" I asked, having never heard her mention him before.

"The second youngest?" She pulled her fattening fingers through her black mop of dyed hair, which seemed more like a wig than real hair. Maybe it was the stark color or the three-day-old hair-spray consistency that made it seem fake, but somehow it suited her. She pulled her bangs from her face and tried to tuck them behind her ears.

"I don't think you ever told me about him," I answered.

She got up from the table and poured me a cup of weak tea from the hot kettle. "He was some little dote, that one. I think it's time you knew."

"Is that what you were talking about with Uncle Jimmy?"

"That and the rest," she answered, sighing and sitting back down. Her eyes had sunk deep into her head recently. I noticed near-black circles hidden behind her out-of-fashion 1970s glasses. She looked a lot older than forty-one, which was how old she told us she was. Her stray bangs continued to make her face itch, and she continued to try to plaster them back somehow.

"I thought there were eight of you," I said, "but I never heard of Willie."

"There were nine of us—well, ten if you count the baby that died our first winter out of Wexford town. Four girls and five boys. Poor as this," she said, holding out her empty hand. "Willie was the most stubborn of all of us. He'd do whatever my Mum told him not to."

I nodded.

"And you know, my father was an awful man who sold every last scrap we had for the drink." She wiggled the bottle. "This shite. That's how the nuns got my sisters and me. That's how the brothers got your Uncle Jimmy and the boys. Willie never made it past the docks in Dun Laoghaire.

He was drowned there, before we all got on the mailboat to England with my mother."

I was doubting that my mother was sober at that point. She'd never spoken of her father so roughly before. "What do you mean, Willie 'was drowned'? Like someone killed him?"

She nodded her head and continued her story, looking all the while at her glass and the Formica table. "Yes. Last I saw him he was crying, calling for our mum, and a nun was giving out, telling him to shut up. He must have talked back, because she slapped him and he ran to the edge of the dock."

I stopped sipping from my cup and sat completely still, wondering what she would say next.

"When he jumped, I don't know. I saw him from the stairway to the boat—thrashing around for a few seconds and then going under. I tried to stop and go back down, but there were too many people. My mother watched from close by, but was stuck in the crowd the same as I was. I remember her yelling his name over and over. Before I knew it, I had lost all sight of my brothers and never saw them again, until your Uncle Jimmy came to see us in seventy-nine."

"Didn't anyone dive in after Willie?"

"No," she answered, still looking at the table, now firmly holding her misbehaving bangs at the sides of her temples. "No one."

"What did the other people on the dock do?"

"They just stood there. The nuns turned their back on him and told everyone to go back to what they were doing."